FALLING INTO HER

Visit us at www.boldstrokesbooks.com

FALLING INTO HER

by

Erin Zak

2017

FALLING INTO HER
© 2017 By Erin Zak. All Rights Reserved.

ISBN 13: 978-1-63555-092-4

This Trade Paperback Original Is Published By
Bold Strokes Books, Inc.
P.O. Box 249
Valley Falls, NY 12185

First Edition: December 2017

CREDITS
EDITOR: KATIA NOYES
PRODUCTION DESIGN: STACIA SEAMAN
COVER DESIGN BY MELODY POND

Acknowledgments

I want to thank Gail. You are the reason this has happened. Without you, nothing is possible. I love you so much and I cannot imagine doing any of this without you.

And Cadie, thank you for always encouraging me.

I also want to thank Bold Strokes Books and my editor, Katia. You all have been so wonderful. You've made this entire process wonderful and fun.

Last, but certainly not least, I want to thank my fans. You know who you are.

This is for my dear friend, S.
Fajitas, fizzy milk, and rolled dollar bills. Pirates until the end.

CHAPTER ONE

The cool air caused a chill to shoot through Kathryn Hawthorne's body, leaving goose bumps in its wake. She blinked and looked around her bedroom. There was a thread of hope inside her that maybe, just maybe, she was alone. She sat up slowly, glanced over her bare shoulder, and sighed. *Krystal? Kristine. No, Krista. Whatever her name is*—was still lying next to her. Auburn hair spilled over the pillow, the dark purple sheet covering most of her naked body, a tattoo of a peacock feather on the underside of her left breast sneaking out from under the material. Kathryn rolled her eyes at herself and rubbed her hands over her face. Clearly, she was a weak, *weak* woman who, at thirty-two, was way too old to be acting like she was twenty-one.

Maybe she was *slightly* taking advantage of being a celebrity in the bustling city of Chicago. She had to admit that it did have its conveniences. Kathryn didn't want to brag—and honestly, she never did—but even after her first two or three appearances on *Windy City Now!* as a movie critic, she was being spotted, recognized, and fawned over. And it was crazy! She'd never needed help getting women in the past, but now she barely had to try. Last night was no exception. She'd pulled up to her Wrigleyville brownstone in a cab, bringing with her the most attractive woman at the bar.

The only problem?

The woman hadn't left in the morning. And was obviously far from leaving.

Kathryn was absolutely not a fan of sleepovers and snuggle buddies or anything else that could lead to trusting people and relationships. Getting her heart broken into a million pieces had proven to be quite the deterrent when it came to relationships.

She looked once more at the girl in her bed and bit her lip when legit fear washed over her at the thought of waking her up. That would mean a conversation in the light of day.

Yeah, she was definitely turning into the type of person that should never let them fall asleep after having sex with them.

Kathryn slid from under the sheets and tiptoed across the wood floor to the oversized reading chair next to the floor-to-ceiling windows. In one smooth movement, she slipped into the robe that had been discarded onto the back of the chair. The morning sun crept over the top of the Chicago skyline, and if it weren't for the woman in her bed and the start of a horrendous stress (*yeah, right, it's stress and not a hangover*) headache, it would have probably shaped up to be an amazing morning.

She hurried from the bedroom, closing the door as quietly as possible and sweeping her dark hair into a loose ponytail. The smell of coffee hit her when she padded downstairs and rounded the corner into the kitchen. She was happy that in her drunken stupor she had remembered to set the timer on the coffeepot. Kathryn pulled a cup from the shelves and filled it to the brim, bringing it carefully to her lips. She let the smell of coffee fill her nose, then took a sip.

"God," she moaned and leaned against the counter. This headache was gearing up to be a real doozy. At least she didn't have anything to do—"Fuck fuck *fuck*," she said, as the calendar caught her attention. In red ink around today's date was "Virginia's Birthday Party—4:00 p.m." with a sad face scribbled in red marker. A wave of nausea washed over her. She wanted to believe it was from her hangover, but she knew it was really because she still hadn't found her mother a gift.

❖

Kathryn stared hopelessly at the wall of aromatherapy products that lined the walls of Skin, an upscale downtown Chicago boutique. The store was busy with the typical classy and stuck-up clientele, but not as crazy as normal, for which Kathryn was thankful. She couldn't even imagine dealing with a crowd in her current stressed-out and hungover state. And she was thrilled that the lighting was dim and the jazz music playing in the background was low. She was nursing her headache with ibuprofen and caffeine, and she still had absolutely no idea what gift to buy. And it was only two hours until her mother's birthday party.

Really the biggest problem with waiting until the last minute to buy Virginia Striker a gift was that she was quite possibly the most judgmental, unfriendly, uncaring woman on the face of the planet. If Kathryn couldn't find the perfect gift, she would get an earful about it eventually. She could already hear the disdain in her mother's voice. It wouldn't matter what she bought the woman; it would never be good enough.

Kathryn's stomach churned. Maybe she could just say she was ill. Technically, drinking herself into a stupor could be classified as an illness, right?

"Is there something I can help you with?"

Kathryn, irritated, turned toward the soft female voice and was immediately captivated by the woman's smile. It lit up her entire face, and there were tiny crinkles at the corners of her eyes that seemed to tell a story. Her teeth were so white and so straight, and honestly, it was the most beautiful smile Kathryn had ever seen. She had blond hair that was pulled back in a loose French braid, the end of the braid trailing over her shoulder. The woman looked as if she didn't belong in that store, like somehow someone plucked her out of a dream and plopped her into an aromatherapy store, thinking that if nothing else at least her smile would help relax people. It was unnerving how much Kathryn felt connected to someone she had never met before. But as they stood there, Kathryn frozen with nerves and the woman smiling as if she thought maybe Kathryn was deaf, it was clear Kathryn had no idea how to handle the encounter. She wanted to kick herself. She was normally much better at handling these types of situations. Maybe this woman caught her in a rare moment of hungover stupidity. Kathryn had to basically shake herself to remember how to speak.

She glanced down at the woman's gold-plated name tag and saw "Pam" neatly engraved. "Um, yeah, I think so," she stammered, running her fingers through her dark hair and searching madly for words. "I'm trying to find a birthday present."

"A gift? Well, this is your lucky day. Gifts just happen to be my specialty." Pam's eyes lit up. "Who is it for? Anyone special?"

"No judging?"

"I would never judge. Promise," Pam replied. She held three fingers in the air. "Girl Scouts' honor."

Kathryn chuckled and then said with an embarrassed tone, "My mom. Her party is in," she checked her watch, "two hours."

"Oh, so you're a procrastinator? Remind me to never expect a gift on time from you, then."

Kathryn's mouth fell open in shock. "Hey, you said no judging! And aren't you supposed to make me feel better about this? So I actually *buy* something? 'Salesperson of the Year Award' should clearly not go to you."

Pam's eyes sparkled. "A procrastinator *and* a comedian with a sharp tongue? *Amazing.*"

"Lady, you have no idea." The corner of Kathryn's mouth turned up, and she raised an eyebrow slightly. Kathryn felt the familiar feeling of butterflies springing to life in her stomach. She flashed her megawatt smile and reached over to touch Pam's arm. "Do you want to hear my awesome excuse?"

"I feel like I need to now."

Kathryn noticed Pam glance at her hand and then back up to her eyes. She wondered if she had overstepped a boundary. "I can't stand my mom, and she's a judgmental, mean-spirited bully."

"Well, in that case," Pam leaned in toward Kathryn and lowered her voice, "Bath and Body Works is just around the corner."

"I don't want her to hate me *back*, Pam." Kathryn felt the woman's name slip from her lips and into the air before she could think twice. She waited for a demeanor change or a freak-out or security to be called or something equally dramatic, but it didn't seem to faze Pam. She carried on talking, pulling soaps and body care products from the shelves.

"Lavender Vanilla and Cherry Vanilla, bath foams, sugar scrubs, and lotions. It's definitely a wonderful gift. All of these products will last her, too. A little goes a long way with the bath foams. And the sugar scrubs are incredible. Your skin feels so supple after using these products together."

"Do you use these?" Kathryn prodded. This woman was seriously the cutest thing she had ever seen, her eyes shining and her black pants clinging to all the right places. Not to mention that the buttons on Pam's white shirt were pulling and straining in ways that made Kathryn feel like a teenager again.

"Absolutely. Here." Pam reached for Kathryn's hand and pulled her toward one of the tester sinks. "Roll your sleeve up."

Kathryn did as instructed.

Pam took some of the sugar scrub and started to massage her hand. If Kathryn didn't know better, she would have bet a million dollars that this woman was interested. The signs were all there. Everything Kathryn looked for when she was on the prowl: the smiles, the eye contact, the touching of the hands and arms. But years of practice and more one-night stands than she could count should have conditioned her to know this was not something to get excited about. Not to mention the woman had a gold wedding band on her left hand. Just another straight woman with no idea that Kathryn would give anything to take her in the back and have her way with her, blond hair being pulled in all sorts of ways.

"That feels really nice," Kathryn murmured, finally breaking the silence. She could tell that she was blushing. If she had to name only one weakness, it would be her insane blushing mechanism.

Pam rinsed the scrub off. She applied a thin layer of lotion and then had Kathryn test out the difference. "See?" Pam asked, her eyes darting up to Kathryn's. "Imagine your whole body feeling that way."

Kathryn's eyes went wide and she pulled in a breath, which she promptly choked on. "Yeah," she replied through a coughing spell. "That's nice."

"Sorry about that. I say what's on my mind a lot." Pam shrugged. "It sometimes catches people off guard."

"That's not a problem at all." Kathryn licked her lips. "It's refreshing. Very refreshing."

"Good to know." Pam glanced down at the floor before she looked back at Kathryn. "I will have our package experts get this ready for you. It was really nice working with you—" Pam held out her hand and waited for Kathryn to reciprocate the handshake.

"Kathryn." Their hands met, and Kathryn felt her entire body warm up. It had been a long time since she had felt like this.

"Well, Kathryn, your hand feels amazing," said Pam as she breezed past Kathryn, winking at her when she looked over her shoulder.

Kathryn took a deep breath, her gaze following Pam as she walked away. "You gotta be kidding me," she said under her breath. *Fucking straight women.*

CHAPTER TWO

W ine at eleven thirty on a school night? Such a good plan."
      Pam looked over at her best friend, Judy, who was sprawled across the oversized armchair in Pam's living room. She swirled Chardonnay in her glass lazily as if it took all her strength. The pair always seemed to fall into the same seats when they invaded Pam's house for their late-night chats. "Yeah, well, you're the one with the kids. And I had a long day. A long, *weird* day," Pam replied. She sank farther into the dark brown couch across from Judy, propped her feet up on the coffee table, and looked around the dimly lit living room. Her golden retriever, Dorothy, was in front of the fireplace on the wood floor, sound asleep.

"I doubt it was as weird as mine." Judy raised her glass. "To weird days."

"To weird days," Pam echoed, raising her glass from her position on the couch. "What happened that made yours so weird? Have to interview another murderer on death row or...?" She secretly loved that her best friend happened to also be a top Chicago news reporter.

"Hardly," Judy replied. "I actually..." She paused, glanced at Pam and then looked away. "I kind of," another pause, a deep breath, "set you up on a date."

Pam raked her fingers through her hair and let out a small, angry sigh. "You're kidding me, right?" Her response was low, followed by a forced chuckle.

Judy instantly sat up, pulled her legs up underneath her, and leaned forward toward Pam. "Look, you *need* to get back out there."

"I am back out there, Judes. I have a job. I'm making new friends. I'm happy." Pam's irritation was starting to bleed through her wine-soaked façade. "I don't need a man to fill some void."

"Pam," Judy started, her voice calm. "That's not it. I just," she paused again, "I just don't want you to miss out."

"Oh, come on! Miss out on what?" Pam smoothed her hand over her face. "I'm fine. I'm actually better than fine."

"Pam," Judy started, but was immediately silenced by Pam raising her hand.

"Just stop. Okay? It's not worth arguing with you about something that isn't going to happen."

"You are so fucking stubborn," Judy said, followed by an exasperated groan. "All I want is for you to not be sleeping alone every single night."

Pam shook her head. "Drop it, Judes. Please?"

"Fine." Judy raised her glass to her lips, paused before taking a sip, and said, "Of course, the date I set you up on is still there if you change your mind."

"And I'm the stubborn one?"

"Yeah, actually."

A laugh bubbled from Pam's throat as she held back her anger. "You are absolutely horrible," she said through the laugh. "Horrible!"

"Well," Judy took a drink of her wine, "I mean, come on. You can't tell me it wouldn't feel nice to have sex or be intimate with someone else. Or at the very least be hit on."

"Of course it feels nice to get hit on," Pam responded with a huff.

"Oh, so you get hit on a lot, do you?"

"Occasionally. I mean, I'm not *ugly*, Judy."

"No shit," Judy replied. "You know what I meant."

"I know." Pam pulled a piece of paper from her uniform pants pocket. She hadn't changed clothes before Judy barged in the front door asking why the hell she was at work so late. "Read this," she said as she handed over the paper.

Judy stretched to get the white paper and inspected it. She turned it over and then back, reading the words carefully. *Thank you so much for all the help. And the hand massage. Text me sometime.* She glanced at Pam, who was staring straight at her. "Who is this from?" she asked, an eyebrow arched.

"Well, I was in charge of hand massages today, so whenever I could I made sure to work a complimentary massage into my sales pitch," Pam explained. "So I honestly don't know who it was."

"Pam, you have to text the number."

"Oh, my God, no. What if it's a creep? I'm not calling a creeper customer just because I'm hard up."

"Aha!" Judy gasped at Pam from her position on the chair. "So you admit that you're hard up."

Pam rolled her eyes. "Not the *point*. I am just showing you that I do get hit on. Just not always out loud, I guess."

"Who could this have been? Who all did you rub today?" Judy asked, followed by a snort. "That sounds so dirty."

"When you say it like that, you ass." Pam thought back over her day. "Well…" She took a breath, looked up at the ceiling, and tried to tally the numbers. She thought about the ten or so people she sold product to and realized only one would have hit on her. "Well, shit."

"What?"

"I didn't give any men hand massages today."

Judy's eyes almost bugged out of her head. "You were hit on by a *woman*," she hissed.

"No, I was *not*."

"If there were no men, that would mean it was probably a woman." Judy sat with her eyebrow still arched to her hairline, a look of complete victory displayed on her face.

"Kathryn," Pam whispered, her hand shooting to her mouth.

"Um, I'm sorry. Who the hell now?"

Pam's memory flooded with the woman's laughter and long,

dark hair. "There was a younger woman that came in today, all flustered because she needed a gift for her mother. She was super friendly, very outgoing, funny. I just…" Pam's voice trailed off as she stared at the piece of paper still in Judy's hand. "It can't be her, though."

"It's her," Judy confirmed, nodding as she passed the paper back to Pam. "It's gotta be."

Pam reread the note, the cursive handwriting, the phone number.

"You were totally hit on by a lesbian," Judy squealed as she threw one of the decorative pillows from the chair across the room at Pam.

Pam caught the pillow, shock still on her face as her shoulders fell. She glanced at Judy, her expression as stoic as possible, and said, "Judy, please. Giving me her phone number does not mean that she's a lesbian."

"Would you randomly give your number to a woman?" Judy asked. When she was met with silence she said, "Yep. Gay as the day is long."

Pam rolled her eyes. "Real *nice*, Judes."

"Did you notice anything else about her?"

"Like, did she have a T-shirt on that read 'I'm not gay but my girlfriend is'?"

Judy's mouth dropped open. "Did she?"

"God, no!" Pam reached up and pushed her hair away from her face. "I noticed that she seemed, I don't know. Maybe she did seem flirtatious. Or nervous. Or perhaps a bit of both."

"You made her nervous?"

"I mean, I don't think so? But maybe. It's not possible, though. I'm not intimidating at all," Pam said as she tried to convince not only Judy but also herself.

"Maybe not intimidating, but you are really beautiful."

Pam shook her head. "You're nuts. Besides, she was way too young for me to be friends with." She paused, nervous laughter spilling from her mouth. "I don't even know what I would say to her. 'Let's go to Forever 21'?"

Judy echoed the laughter. "Maybe you could talk to her about barhopping?"

"Or dorm room living!"

Judy took a gulp of her wine, then a deep breath, and looked down at her hands. "I know this is kinda crazy, Pam. I mean," she pulled her gaze back to Pam's, "this Kathryn woman could be *great* for you, Pamela."

Pam swallowed the unexplained lump in her throat. "Why would you think that?"

"I don't know." Judy shrugged. "Maybe because surrounding yourself with people who want to be around you is never a bad thing—regardless of the type of emotions they are feeling." She motioned toward Pam with her glass of wine. "Even if this girl ends up being really gay," Pam laughed and Judy continued, "that doesn't mean you have to be gay *with* her. I mean, come on, we both know you're as straight as an arrow." Another shrug of the shoulders. "I love you, Pam. You're my best friend. I want you to be happy. And I know you say you are, but come on, you're not fooling anyone, especially me."

"Judy," Pam groaned. "I just watched my husband die. Life hasn't exactly been a hayride."

"It doesn't have to be a hayride *all* the time," Judy said, "but it can be one *most* of the time."

Pam pulled her gaze from Judy's and looked across the room. "I guess it can't hurt," she said, barely above a whisper.

❖

Dorothy snored at the end of the bed, the clock ticked in the hallway, and the wind blew outside. "Dammit," Pam almost yelled as she opened her eyes. She could hear every little noise, and it was driving her nuts. She checked the clock on the night table. Midnight. "Screw it." Pam leaned over to grab her cell phone and slid her finger across the screen; the light filled the room and illuminated her face. She tapped the screen until she got to *Contacts*. Her heart thudded away as she scrolled through and found *Kathryn*.

Hi. It's Pam. From Skin.

Pam deleted the text and sighed, groaned, and then retyped the same text. Her thumb hovered over Send. She could feel her heartbeat in her eardrums. Judy's words from earlier about how Kathryn could be good for her echoed through her head. And then she pressed Send.

Instantly her hands became clammy. Her mouth turned dry. Her stomach filled with butterflies when her phone screen lit up and *New Message from Kathryn* appeared on the screen. She closed her eyes, counted to three, opened her eyes, and clicked on the message.

Hey there. I'm surprised to hear from you.

Not as surprised as I am to actually be doing this.

Not the adventurous type?

Pam shook her head, typed, *Not typically*, and hit Send.

Me either.

Somehow, I don't believe that. You did just give me your phone number, Kathryn.

And you texted me. I'd say you're more adventurous than you think.

Maybe you're right.

I'm rarely wrong.

Pam rolled her eyes. *Oh, really?* she texted, pressed Send, and then typed out, *Why did you give me your number?*

I want to get to know you.

Pam's breath caught in her throat upon reading that text. *Why?*

The same reason you want to get to know me.

And why is that?

Because I'm interesting. And nice. And because you only live once.

It was weird to see it said so plainly. *Fine,* Pam typed and pressed Send. *Coffee tomorrow?*

10 a.m.?

Yes. Starbucks on Michigan Ave.

I'll see you there.

Okay. Sleep well.

You too.

Pam finally released the breath she didn't even realize she had been holding. She rested her phone on the nightstand and closed her eyes. "Now go to sleep," she said to herself, even though she knew damn well she wouldn't.

CHAPTER THREE

It's nothing big," Kathryn said into her phone as she headed out of the television recording studio. The air was cold and damp, and winter had arrived with full force, but that didn't stop the constant crowds on the streets.

"Who are you meeting, then? Is it someone you're interviewing?"

"No, Sydney," Kathryn replied, calmly, even though she was getting irritated with the questions. "If I was interviewing anyone it'd be a celebrity, and I doubt I'd be nervous."

"Wait, why are you nervous? It's not for work? What is it for, then?"

"Y'know, for a best friend you sure are annoying."

Sydney's laugh was so loud and sharp that it sounded like a bark. "You love me and you know it! Now, who are you meeting?"

"No one. Don't worry about it." Kathryn rounded the corner of Illinois Street and took a right onto Michigan Avenue, maneuvering through the throngs of tourists with ease. "Just a friend," she added.

"Whatever, I know every single one of your friends, so it's obviously not a friend," Sydney said. "Text me if you need saving so I can call you. And then I can come over tonight to discuss over beer and popcorn."

"It's not a blind date. I don't think I need the fake emergency phone call."

"You're gonna tell me about this later. I hope you know that."

"God, Syd," Kathryn huffed and gripped her phone tighter.

"It's this woman I met at that boutique. I'm meeting her for coffee. She's straight. It's not a big deal."

"Oh, for fuck's sake," came Sydney's exasperated voice. "*Another* fucking straight woman?"

"Stop. It's not like that. I literally just want to be friends with her. I swear."

"Yeah, well, I don't believe you. So good luck with that." Sydney scoffed, her irritation coming through loud and clear. "You realize I'll be there picking up the pieces when this goes badly."

"Always," Kathryn said. "I'm at the coffee shop. I'll talk to you later. Love you."

"Love you, too, you whore."

Kathryn disconnected the call and slid her cell phone into the pocket of her navy-blue peacoat. There had been several moments since the prior night when she wanted to come up with an excuse to stand Pam up. But she didn't. And when Kathryn finally walked into the coffee shop, her mind was racing, stumbling over itself asking a million questions. Were things going to feel uncomfortable? Were they going to sit in complete silence? Were they destined to only have a salesperson-and-customer relationship? Which sounded so stupid in Kathryn's mind, but dammit, it was a real fear! Was Pam going to be one of those straight women that only wanted to experiment? She rolled her eyes and took a deep breath. *Settle the fuck down, Kathryn.* She knew she'd have to wait to get the answers, but it didn't mean she wasn't going to torture herself trying to figure them out.

Kathryn looked around and noticed that the coffee shop was packed with people. College kids were hunched over their laptops, sitting at long, reclaimed barn wood tables. Old retired men read copies of the *Wall Street Journal* and the *Chicago Tribune* along the bar tops at the windows. Soccer moms dressed in yoga gear were perched in overstuffed armchairs, bobbing their crossed legs, downing lattes. The workers shouted names and orders over the bustle, making Kathryn feel slightly more at ease. Maybe all of this was exactly what she needed to be able to focus and not freak out. *The busier the better.*

She noticed Pam toward the farthest corner of the coffee shop, a dark green mug in front of her at a small circular table. She had her head down and her legs crossed, and her fingers were drumming lightly on the table. The sunlight streamed through the window across Pam's long, blond hair and Kathryn watched from her vantage point as she moved her hair away from her face. Kathryn's heart leapt into her throat when Pam's blue eyes looked up and found hers. A small smile spread across Pam's lips, and Kathryn froze. She really needed to start knowing how to handle that incredible smile if she was going to try and just be friends with this woman. *C'mon, Kathryn, walk. One foot in front of the other.*

"Hi," Pam said casually when Kathryn approached the table.

Kathryn shrugged her coat off her shoulders and draped it over the back of the chair opposite Pam's. "Hi there," she responded, sitting and crossing her legs in one fluid motion. "Chai tea latte, please," she said to the waitress, wondering if it was obvious that she felt nauseous.

"Did your mother like her gift?"

Kathryn tilted her head, impressed that Pam remembered. "Yes, she did, actually. I got her a sweater from Burberry, too. She would have died had I showed up with only aromatherapy stuff."

"Ahhh, I see," Pam said.

Instantly Kathryn was filled with regret. Why the heck did she put her phone number on that tip card? All she wanted to do was take her drink to go.

"So, Kathryn—"

"Look," Kathryn cut Pam off. "I'm sorry about giving you my number." She stretched her fingers and realized once again the effect this woman had on her. No one she had ever met made her hands literally tremble, and she had met all sorts of people. And she had slept with a lot of women, even some men, and never had this happened. "I don't know why I did it. But I could tell from our text conversation that it probably wasn't the best thing to do."

Pam's sharp intake of breath said it all. "Oh, my goodness, don't be sorry." She looked down at her lap before finishing with, "This has just never happened to me before."

"I find that hard to believe," Kathryn said slyly, glancing up through the small curtain of her hair that had snuck from behind her ear. The long-sleeved dark-green shirt Pam was wearing was tight across the chest, and Kathryn was trying her hardest to not be inappropriate.

"Well, I mean," Pam started, raising her gaze to meet Kathryn's, "I've received quite a few phone numbers from *men* since I began working at Skin."

"Quite a few, eh?"

"No, I mean, not like *that*," Pam said, stumbling over her words. "I meant, because I was married for twenty-one years. The wedding ring sort of gave off a bad vibe for potential romances. It's kind of why I still have it on."

Kathryn hid her anxiety as she looked fully at Pam. "You think this is a potential romance?"

"Well, I don't, I mean, you know," Pam stuttered and leaned forward a little over the table. "You are gay, aren't you?"

"Wow," Kathryn exclaimed. She was in shock from the way that question just came out of Pam, but at the same time Pam's abrasiveness intrigued her.

Pam's face instantly fell. "God, I am so rude."

"Rude? No," Kathryn said as she put her game face on. "Maybe lacking tact, yes."

"I never said I had tact."

"True," Kathryn replied. "So." She paused and leaned back in the chair. "You think I'm gay, hmm?"

"Um," Pam furrowed her brow, pursed her lips, "I'm not sure now," she finished.

"Well, your gaydar is spot-on, considering that most straight women don't come equipped with such tools. I *am* a lesbian." Kathryn smoothed a wrinkle in her navy-blue fitted slacks. "But I just wanted a friendship. We seemed like we had a nice connection. You made me laugh. Making friends as an adult seems hard most of the time, but with you, I don't know. It was easy to talk to you. I'm really sorry, though. I read everything wrong, which is so unlike me." She wondered if her explanation was believable seeing as how she couldn't believe it herself. She didn't just want a friendship. She wanted more. Kathryn always wanted more, especially when the woman was as unattainable as Pam certainly seemed.

Pam's laugh was coated with embarrassment. "Oh, my God," she said as she covered her face with her hands. "I am so embarrassed!"

"It's really okay."

"No, it's not!" Pam leaned forward, "My best friend, who, by the way, is a complete spastic lunatic and has no real basis for anything she ever says, basically called my attention to the possibility that you're gay, and from there I just assumed. Goodness, can you tell that I ramble when I'm nervous?" She took a deep breath. "I'm so sorry."

Kathryn leaned forward a bit, her hair falling over her shoulder. "If I wanted to ask you out," she said, her voice low, almost seductive, "I would have just asked you out. And besides, I knew you weren't interested."

"It's not that I'm not interested." Pam corrected her. "I'm just—"

"Straight," Kathryn finished the sentence for Pam. "I know. I promise. I got it."

"I really am sorry," Pam assured her.

"Don't be. I swear that it's okay. I'm sort of shocked that you could tell that I was gay just by giving you my phone number, though. That is one hell of a way to be outed."

"Maybe it was the hundred-dollar-bill tip?" Pam asked, a shrug following her question.

"Maybe." Kathryn smiled and shrugged. "Lesson learned, I guess."

Pam took a sip of her coffee and set it on the table, both hands encircling the warm mug. "So…"

Kathryn cleared her throat, leaned back, and crossed her legs. "I guess we should settle up here and go our separate ways."

"Yeah, I guess so. I'm sorry for, you know, not knowing how to handle any of this. It's just been so long since…" She looked down at her hands. "I just don't know how to manage this."

Kathryn could see Pam's hands shaking, and it made her sad that nothing about this first meeting was going the way she wanted it to go. "Y'know," she said as she decided to take one last chance, "you realize that you could just try to relax and be my friend, right?"

Pam's eyes snapped up to Kathryn's. "What do you mean? I'm *fine*. I can be your friend."

Kathryn huffed before saying, "*Okay*," with such an air of sarcasm it dripped from the word.

"I can!" Pam protested as she pushed the sleeves of her shirt to her elbows. "You have no idea what I'm capable of."

Kathryn arched her eyebrow, questioning Pam's words without even opening her mouth. "Fine," she said, trying not to laugh. "Then let's actually try to be friends."

"Fine!" Pam exclaimed. She crossed her arms. "Ask me a question, then. Something you'd ask a friend."

"Oh, my God," Kathryn pushed out. She tried to sound aggravated, but she was secretly very pleased with her reverse psychology method. "Let's see." She tapped her fingers on the table and tilted her head. "You kept using the past tense when you were referring to your marriage. What does that mean?"

"Oh." Pam's face fell. "That's pretty deep for such a new friendship."

"Whoa, I'm sorry." The instant guilt Kathryn felt for asking the question when she saw how Pam's demeanor instantly changed was almost palpable. "We seriously do not have to talk about that. I am being an ass."

"No, really, it's okay." Pam composed herself. "He, uh, he passed three months ago. Pancreatic cancer."

Kathryn, without thinking, leaned forward and gently placed her hand over Pam's as she fidgeted with a napkin. "Oh, shit," she whispered.

Pam's eyes became wet.

"Are you okay?"

Pam nodded, somewhat unconvincingly. Kathryn squeezed Pam's hand lightly and felt her breath catch in her throat when Pam squeezed back.

"Yeah, I'm okay." Pam looked up from her lap. "It was hard. I mean, twenty-one years of marriage? Of course it was hard. We had been together since high school, so I was pretty used to him always being around. Always being there, and then for him to not be? It's just *hard*. There's no other way to say it."

"It's not easy losing your lover and your best friend."

"Yeah. Actually, he was an asshole most of the time." She shook her head as if trying not to laugh. "In high school, he always thought that if he was persistent enough, I'd eventually go out with him."

"Persistence pays off then, eh?" Kathryn responded with a gentle squeeze of Pam's hand before she finally pulled away. "Here, I have a much easier question. Do you have a favorite movie?"

"That really isn't an easier question," Pam replied, bringing her mug to her lips. "But if I had to pick, it'd be *The Big Chill*."

"That might be the most perfect answer ever," Kathryn said with an ease and confidence she hadn't meant to show.

"What's yours?" Pam asked. "And don't say it's the same movie as mine."

"Never!" Kathryn bit her bottom lip. "Honestly? I am totally old school. I love Star Wars. All of them." She launched into a tirade about the new trilogy versus the old trilogy, hardly stopping to take a breath. When she finally finished, Pam's wide-eyed stare was enough to remind Kathryn just how much of a Star Wars nerd she really was. "Clearly more than you were wanting. I'm such a geek."

"I am seriously very okay with you being a geek," Pam responded.

Kathryn pulled out her signature lopsided smirk and said, "This is the start of a very beautiful friendship."

"We'll see how well you do in the next round," Pam answered with her own smirk, holding up her mug to signify a toast. "May the Force be with you."

Kathryn leaned forward and raised her own mug to clink it with Pam's. "And also with you." She watched over the rim of her mug as Pam took a sip of her coffee. Every time she looked at Pam, she found it harder and harder to not get lost in the sea of her blue eyes.

They were calming in a way Kathryn hadn't experienced in quite some time, but they also terrified her—in the way a wave can when it comes crashing down on you. Unexpectedly.

Yep, Kathryn was already in over her head. And for some reason, she wasn't even upset about it.

CHAPTER FOUR

I'll take an Old Style."

"Really, Dad? An *Old Style?*"

Bill Hawthorne studied Kathryn, his eyebrows raised to his receding hairline. "A tiger never changes his stripes, kiddo."

"True that." Kathryn and her father were seated at the bar of the Old Town Ale House, a Chicago staple that had more history than most bars even hope to have. The walls were littered with hand-drawn pictures of naked celebrities and politicians, each with a price tag if someone really felt the need to own a piece of history. It still reeked of cigarettes and old beer that had been spilled by one too many Second City alums like Jim Belushi and Chris Farley. Kathryn glanced over at the bartender Joe, who had worked at the establishment for what seemed like forever. "I'll take Grey Goose on the rocks with a lime."

"No beer for you?"

"No, I need something a little stronger today, Dad." Kathryn rubbed her temples and fought back the urge to spill her guts about the recent events. She generally told her father everything, but lately, when it came to her love life, she felt as if that was a little too much sharing. And it was a bit too early to start crying into her drink, although the rest of the bar patrons probably wouldn't have judged her.

Bill chuckled. "Lady problems." It wasn't a question. It was clearly a statement. He knew his daughter entirely too well.

"Psh, problems? Never." Kathryn watched the snow starting to fall outside through the grimy windows of the pub. It was too early for snow, but for some strange reason, she wasn't as annoyed as she typically was with the weather.

"Don't lie to your father, KB. It's not a good habit to get into."

A puff of air escaped from Kathryn's throat as she brought her freshly delivered drink up to her lips. He had never stopped calling her KB. Kathryn Barbara, named after her grandmother. "You know me way too well. You know that, right?" She moved her gaze over to her father before taking a drink. He looked adorable in his Cubs hat and sweatshirt, his golfing tan finally fading due to the temperature change and the colder months. The retired life was treating him well.

"I know, honey. What's going on, though? You know you can't talk to your mother about these things."

"Don't I know it." Kathryn's knee bobbed up and down on the rung of the old bar stool, a nervous habit that came out whenever she was stressed. Maybe she did need to talk about it. "I met a woman that I really like."

"That's good, KB!"

"No, it's not." Kathryn looked down at her hands. "She's straight. Like, just buried her dead husband, was married for years, still wears her wedding band straight."

Bill nudged her arm with his elbow and waggled his bushy gray eyebrows at her, "You get that from me, don't you? Always on the prowl and always after something you can't have."

Kathryn started to laugh. "Dad, seriously?"

"Well, you know the ladies always loved ol' Bill Hawthorne. When you got it, you got it!"

"Oh, my God, Dad. You are relentless!"

He let out a boisterous laugh eerily similar to his daughter's and put his hand on his belly. "I think this scares them away these days. Not as slim and trim as I used to be."

"Still as handsome as ever, though." Kathryn slugged him lightly on the arm.

"KB, honey, you know these things pass with time. You'll get past it. This whole straight woman thing has happened before."

"I know, Dad, and I'm still not over it." Kathryn sighed as she remembered her last relationship and the heartbreak and trying to pick up the pieces and never actually succeeding.

"Well, that last one was a good catch. Married, but good." He nodded at Kathryn. "Did you say her husband is dead?"

"Yeah."

"Hell, KB, how old is she? Sixty-five? That's more *my* type!"

Kathryn laughed heartily, the sound echoing in the unusually quiet bar. "Dad! No! I think she's in her early forties or something. I don't even know how old she is yet—that's how new this whole predicament is."

"Well, he's dead, right?"

"Dad!"

"Well? He is, *right*?"

Kathryn studied her father's facial expression. He was serious. "Yes, he's dead."

"And just because she still has her wedding ring on doesn't mean a goddamned thing," he said with a solemn expression.

Kathryn's view shifted to his left hand. To the ring he never took off. Even though her mom and dad had been divorced for years. "Dad," Kathryn whispered.

"No, honey, look. I don't love your mother anymore. I haven't in a long time. A looooong time. Long, long, loooong time." His face softened when his daughter chuckled. "But I feel lost without this ring on. I don't know why. Believe me, I've tried, and I just feel better when I leave it on. I'm not saying this woman won't take that ring off one day. I'm just saying perhaps it's easier right now for her to leave it on. No questions, no comments, no concerns. Sometimes it's just *easier.* That's all."

"So, you're saying that it might mean nothing that she has that ring still on."

"That's exactly what I'm saying." Bill swiveled his bar stool to face his daughter. "Look, KB, you're a beautiful young woman.

You have so much going for you. You're smart, you're funny, you were on the radio and now you're on TV, in the greatest city in these United States. That's pretty impressive." He took a long drink of his beer. "Oh, *and* you have a great house—thanks to that devil of a mother and her little pony boy. Not a lot of thirty-two-year-olds can say that. You are the whole package."

"Dad, none of that is really that big a deal." She knew it was a big deal, though. It was starting to become more and more apparent that her accolades were not just well deserved but also really amazing considering her age. Kathryn continued to not let it go to her head, but really, why shouldn't she let her accomplishments speak for themselves?

"KB, come on now. Stop acting like you're not allowed to be *okay*. Accept the friggin' compliment."

Kathryn raised her glass. "Fine. I'm awesome," she said with a low drawl that was laced with sarcasm.

"Don't get carried away. I'm not saying she's going to fall in love with you." Bill looked over the top of his glasses. "I'm saying how could she not?"

Kathryn's heart felt like it was going to explode. Instantly she felt tears spring to her eyes. She wanted to crawl under the bar.

"Oh, for Christ's sake, don't you dare start crying. We're at my stomping grounds!" he hissed. "You're gonna give me a bad name." He swiveled his stool back around to face the bar, glancing at Kathryn's reflection in the mirror behind the bar and locking eyes with her. He held his beer up and they exchanged a silent toast as Kathryn composed herself.

Kathryn was so happy that she kept her tears at bay. She loved her dad more than anything in the world, and sometimes his harsh abrasiveness was exactly what she needed. It seemed every time she'd turned around since what she lovingly referred to as "the heartbreak of the century," she was always tearing up or blubbering like a fool, and it was unacceptable. It was why she kept every single woman at arm's length. She pulled a deep breath into her lungs. Things were going to be different now. They had to be. "So, the Bears. What in the world is going on with them this season?" Kathryn asked while glancing at her dad, who was moving on to his next beer.

Bill cleared his throat. "I smell a Super Bowl victory on the horizon!"

CHAPTER FIVE

Pam saw Kathryn walk into the same crowded coffee shop and pull her cream knit cap from her head, shaking the snow from it. When their eyes met, Pam waved, followed by two deep, deep breaths. It was all Pam could do to not think about their coffee date yesterday. The laughter, the touches, the accusations, the assumptions, the smiles. God, the *smiles*. She really didn't know what she was doing now. Sure, she was starting a new friendship, but it had never felt like this before. It made no sense. After a two-hour conversation with Judy, two bottles of white wine, and a long soak in the bathtub, she had decided to text Kathryn. You know, just to see if she wanted to do coffee again. Truth be told, she was actually really shocked when *sure, what time?* came across her cell phone screen.

And now here she was. Twisting, twisting, twisting her hands, trying not to hyperventilate, and wishing she had worn something cuter than a black sweater and jeans.

"Well, fancy meeting you here," Pam said with a grin when Kathryn approached the table, her cheeks pink from the cold Chicago air.

"I know, what are the odds?"

"Fairly slim." Pam watched as Kathryn took off her coat and draped it over the chair. All of her body movements were so like the day before that Pam was almost positive that she was in the middle of a five-minute déjà-vu. Except today, the jeans Kathryn had on, and the plaid button-down with a gray Columbia College T-shirt underneath, were very different. Different in a way that made Pam really happy for reasons she was sure she'd never figure out.

"Fate," Kathryn said right before she ordered the same drink as yesterday. "More cinnamon this time," she instructed kindly.

"Hmm?" Pam asked.

"I said 'fate.' Y'know, it was fate that we should meet here again." Kathryn shrugged. "It'd be much better if we hadn't actually planned it, but what the hell."

Pam chuckled. "Yes, true. I like planning it better."

"But think of how cool it'd be if we were to happen upon each other."

"Sort of like at Skin that day?" Pam asked, moving her head so her hair would fall away from her face.

"What would I have done without you?"

"You would have given your mother a horrible gift!"

"Oh, God. I would never have lived to tell the tale."

"I'm assuming things are…" Pam paused, observed Kathryn as she fidgeted with her latte that had just been delivered and waited for her to look up. She raised an eyebrow when Kathryn finally lifted her gaze and finished her question. "They are a little difficult between you and your mother?"

Kathryn closed her eyes and then slowly slid them open. "Um, yeah. I guess you could say that."

"Any particular reason?"

A nervous laugh bubbled from Kathryn's lips. "Yes, actually, because I'm a lesbian."

"Ohhh," Pam replied, immediately regretting this conversation.

"No, it's okay." Kathryn nonchalantly waved her hand through the air and shook her head. "Virginia is kind of high maintenance, I guess? And, well, she's a giant bitch. But what can I do? She's my mom." She finally looked back at Pam. "Honestly? I have always been closer to my dad, so I'm kind of over the whole 'you're not good enough because you like women' argument." She sat her cup on the table. "Enough about my picture-perfect childhood. How about your parents?"

"Oh, Lord," Pam said. "Let's see. Well, I didn't disappoint

them by being a lesbian, so that's good, right?" She locked eyes onto Kathryn's and tilted her head slightly. "Of course, I married the one person they didn't want me to, so I think you and I are even."

"Hardly," Kathryn replied, a smirk on her lips.

"You'd be surprised," Pam said, her eyes softer now. "He wasn't necessarily the most amazing husband ever." Her breath caught a little in her throat as she looked down at the table. "I shouldn't say that. He's not even here to defend himself, for Christ's sake. But he really *wasn't*. I didn't want to marry him. I never wanted the things he wanted. I was…" Pam paused, brought her eyes up and looked out the window of the coffee shop. She sighed, deeply, before finishing with, "I was so smart, yet so stupid at the same time."

"Wow," Kathryn said. She cocked an eyebrow. "Would they hate that you have a friend that's a lesbian?"

Pam grinned. "Y'know, I'm not sure."

"Parents typically love me," Kathryn said with an air of confidence Pam found insanely endearing.

"City parents probably love you. Ever met a couple of country bumpkins that have goats and bunnies and chickens?" Pam laughed when Kathryn's mouth fell open slightly. "I grew up in Michigan on a farm. My dad owned the local hardware store in New Buffalo. Believe me, they aren't your typical parents."

"Oh, *awesome*. Please tell me they are Bible-beaters, too."

Pam bit her bottom lip and nodded. "Of *course*, Kathryn. Don't you know you can't live in the country if you don't have God on your side?"

"Oh, how silly of me! I forgot!" Kathryn crossed her arms and leaned on the table. "They'd hate me."

"Probably," Pam replied, mimicking Kathryn's seated position. She leaned in a little closer and said, "My sister would probably hate you, too."

"Oh! There's more of you?"

"Yeah, definitely. Except we look and act nothing at all alike. She has dark hair, is married with kids, and lives in Colorado. Meanwhile, there's me. Widowed, no children, having coffee with a *lesbian*. The scandal of it all."

Kathryn looked into Pam's eyes. "As long as we never sleep together, I think you'll be fine."

The silence that followed those words was almost deafening.

"Pam," Kathryn said. "It's just a joke."

"I know," Pam finally replied, her eyes never leaving Kathryn's.

"So." Kathryn glanced away. She fidgeted with the napkin on the table and then looked back at Pam before asking, "Do you like to bowl?"

❖

"I can't believe I let you talk me into this."

"I can't believe you haven't been bowling since you were sixteen."

"Kathryn, I was married to a *lawyer*. He barely had time for me, let alone bowling." Pam looked around the old-school Chicago bowling alley. The lights were low, only a few lanes completely lit. A few of the lanes had the bumpers up for small children and were lit with black lights. Only about five other people were bowling, but the music was loud and the bar was hopping, and the drinks were flowing. The bartender, who doubled as the cashier, set them up on their lane. After a strange look and exchange of glances between him and Kathryn, he gave them half off their first pitcher of beer.

"I don't care if you were married to the Prince of Wales. You still need to go bowling every now and then. It's fun and it reminds you that you can only control the little things, which is clearly something we both need to work on." Kathryn sat and started to lace up the green-and-red bowling shoes. "And the shoes are fucking killer cool."

"Oh, my God. Those shoes," Pam started.

"What?!"

"Those are the ugliest bowling shoes I've ever seen." She glanced at Kathryn's legs in her skinny jeans and the shoes and laughed.

Kathryn reached over and grabbed Pam's hand, pulling Pam down next to her so she could start removing Pam's boots. "Just shut up. You're going to look great." She quickly unzipped the black leather boots and slipped them off. Kathryn methodically put on each shoe and tied the laces just right.

In all her years of marriage, Pam had never done anything fun and spontaneous with Harold. The reality of that hit Pam hard. And now here she was, with a girl she just met—strike that; a *lesbian* she just met—going bowling in the middle of the day, on a weekday no less! It was crazy and not like her, and it felt *amazing*. As she thought about how happy she was in that moment, the tears started to well up, and all she wanted to do was curse herself for crying in front of this girl.

"There," Kathryn said as she looked down at Pam's feet with an air of victory. "Stand up." She glanced over at Pam and did a double take. "What in the world? Are you okay?"

Pam couldn't find her voice. She took a deep breath. "I just, um, no one ever..."

"The shoes aren't *that* ugly that you need to cry about it, Pam." Kathryn placed her hand on Pam's knee and squeezed, a knowing smile displayed. "Now, stand up."

A shot of electricity seemed to course through Pam's body after Kathryn's gentle touch. Her heartbeat quickened; her mouth went dry. She blinked, tried to pull herself together, and stood. She swallowed as she spun around, hoping her expression didn't betray the nerves she was feeling.

"Fantastic," Kathryn said and then whistled while clapping her hands together.

A smile spread across Pam's lips as she playfully clicked her heels together. "They're actually *really* comfortable."

"That's because nine thousand other feet have been in them," Kathryn replied as she stood and grabbed a bowling ball.

Pam chuckled as she moved a couple steps closer to Kathryn, watching as Kathryn picked up a bowling ball and turned it over and over in her hands to inspect it before committing to her choice. "Kathryn, thank you."

Kathryn turned around, her head tilting to the side. "For what?"

"For this." Pam motioned around the bowling alley with her

hands. "For, I don't know? Showing me that I'm not too old to have fun."

"Never too old for fun!" Kathryn nudged Pam's side and then asked, her voice low, "How old are you, by the way?"

Pam shook her head. "No way. I'm not telling you."

"I'll guess, then."

"No, you won't, because you'll say something like, 'oh, you don't look a day over thirty-five' and I'll know you're lying and just trying to butter me up." Pam crossed her arms over her chest and stood there, defiance all over her face.

Kathryn gasped, threw a hand to her chest in mock dismay, and protested, "No, I won't. I'll be truthful. I promise. So, let's see—" She took a step back, stroked her chin while eyeing Pam from head to toe. She clapped her hands together. "I'm going to go with forty."

"That's not fair," Pam huffed. "How did you even know that?"

Kathryn laughed and shrugged. "How old do you think I am?"

Pam smirked. "Twelve?"

"Very funny. *Wow*. I didn't realize you were a comedienne."

Pam furrowed her brow and then stepped back, eyeing Kathryn from her head to her toes. "Twenty-three?"

"You're joking, right?"

"Absolutely not! And that's stretching my guess, because at first glance I thought you were twenty-one."

"Oh, for Pete's sake." Kathryn gasped at Pam. "I just turned thirty-two."

"No way!"

"Um, yeah. I can't believe you thought I was still in my twenties." Kathryn shook her head in mock disgust. "Twenty-one? *Only* twenty-one. I mean, don't I *act* older than that?"

Pam reached over and took a drink from her plastic cup of draft beer that Kathryn had insisted upon. "You clearly act like a twenty-one-year-old. Getting me to drink draft beer!" she exclaimed over the loud music streaming from the old-school jukebox.

"Oh, please, draft beer is awesome! Your head will thank you for it in the morning." Kathryn poured more beer in both of their plastic cups before grabbing a bowling ball. "Now, hold out both hands."

Pam listened to what she was told.

"Hold this." Kathryn sat a bright pink bowling ball in Pam's hands.

"Okay, I don't remember the balls ever being this light."

Kathryn raised an eyebrow. "Haven't been around balls much, eh?"

"It's not like you have." Pam shouted her comeback, and Kathryn descended into laughter.

"Nice one," she said while rolling her eyes. Pam joined in the laughter, so Kathryn finished her thought. "It's a kid's ball. I figured that you're allowed to use a kid's ball since you haven't been bowling in forty-forevers."

"Oh, well, thank you!"

"I'll still win, though."

"Don't bet on it," Pam said cockily.

Pam sat in the passenger seat of Kathryn's Jeep Wrangler. She cautiously looked over at Kathryn. "I really am sorry."

"When you said that you hadn't been bowling in forever I thought you meant just that. Not that you hadn't been bowling since you were on the bowling team in high school!"

"Yeah, I guess I sort of forgot to mention that."

"And then I gave you a lighter ball!"

Pam grinned. "Uh-huh."

"And then I kept trying to help you!"

"Yep, you sure did."

Kathryn looked over at Pam. There was a long moment of silence before Kathryn opened her mouth and said, "You're so beautiful."

And everything in the Jeep came to a screeching halt.

The air seemed to hang around them, the words trapped in an

almost cartoon-like bubble. Pam didn't know what to say. Should she act like she didn't hear Kathryn? "Um, wow."

"Oh, Jesus," Kathryn pushed out, her breath forming a cloud of frozen condensation in the air. "I really didn't mean to say that out loud."

Pam's heart had lodged itself in her throat. She tried to swallow twice before the lump seemed to dislodge itself. "It's okay, Kathryn."

"No, it's not okay. I don't want to freak you out. It's the beer and the bowling and the pizza and the loud music from the bowling alley. Apparently, that all adds up to make me say stupid shit that I just shouldn't say. Like, *ever*. I am so sorry." She leaned her head forward into her hands.

"Kath, sweetie," Pam said as she sat stock still in the passenger seat. She wasn't freaking out, which, shouldn't she be? Instead of freaking out, all she wanted to do was reach out and touch Kathryn. She wanted to hug her to get her to stop talking. She wanted to turn Kathryn's face toward hers and...*God*. She wanted, wanted, *wanted*, but couldn't. She breathed in very deep and pushed it out before finally saying, "You need to quit worrying about that. If I was freaked out, I'd be running toward the house screaming. There's nothing to worry about."

Kathryn turned her head and looked into Pam's eyes. "You're sure?"

"I'm positive," Pam reassured her. "But I really do have to go now. I have to open the store tomorrow. I had such a great time tonight. Thank you, Kathryn. I *really* needed that."

"You're more than welcome."

Kathryn's voice still sounded so unsure. Maybe it was the bowling and beer, just like Kathryn said. Whatever it was, Pam leaned in and pressed her lips to Kathryn's cheek. She heard Kathryn's sharp intake of breath, and for some reason, it made Pam feel amazing inside. "You're a really great friend," she said against the soft skin of Kathryn's cheek. The smell of Kathryn's perfume overwhelmed her senses, and her lips instantly warmed from the contact. "I'll text you."

"Great," Kathryn replied.

Pam walked inside and closed the door behind her. "Holy shit," she said. *What a night!*

❖

Kathryn looked at her iPhone sitting next to her on the couch as it dinged, indicating an incoming text. She picked it up, almost afraid to look at the screen. After a deep breath, she flipped the phone over, and *dammit.* "Fucking Sydney." She tossed the phone back down and continued to watch a *Saturday Night Live* rerun.

She was trying her hardest to not think about the moment in the Jeep.

It wasn't working.

Kathryn kept replaying it over and over in her head. Every time, she wanted to die at the end of the memory. The only benefit? She got to leave and hopefully not have to face the embarrassment anymore.

Her phone dinged again. "Sydney," she groaned and picked her phone up. Pam's name was on her phone screen. Her heart leapt into her throat. "Oh, God, here we go. The 'I don't think we should hang out anymore' text." Kathryn slid her finger across the glass and took a deep breath.

I'm not freaking out.

Kathryn pushed out a shaky breath, followed by an ill attempt at laughter. "How in the fuck did she know that?" She typed out *I'm not thinking that you are* and hit Send.

Seconds later, Pam's response came in: *Don't you think I should be freaking out, though?*

"Whoa," Kathryn whispered. She looked around her empty living room and then back at the phone. *You certainly handled yourself well.*

I had an amazing time with you tonight.

Kathryn's hands started to ache when she read that text. And then—

And today.

And seconds later—

And yesterday.

What was Kathryn supposed to say back? Her entire body was frozen. She looked away from her phone again and took a deep breath.

Now it's my turn to freak you out, hmm?

Kathryn laughed when she read the text. *I'm not freaked out. It'd take a lot more than that to freak me out.*

I'm just really happy right now. Smiling and everything.

That's good. You should smile every day...Every single day.

I'm hoping you can help with that.

I'll do whatever I can to help.

You already are.

Kathryn wasn't sure how to respond. She sat there, staring at her phone screen, wondering what the hell was happening.

Seconds later she received another text: *Can I call you tomorrow?*

What the hell? Kathryn could feel that she was starting to crack. She could feel it bubbling inside her. Hope.

Of course, she responded. *I'll be around.*

Good. Talk to you then. :)

Yep. Hope. And hope was never a good thing when it came to straight women.

CHAPTER SIX

Pam leaned against the headboard of her bed and started to laugh, her phone pressed between her shoulder and ear. "No, I don't want to go there," she commented while she ran her hand back and forth over her navy-blue duvet cover.

"But Chuck E. Cheese's is so fun."

"Judy, *seriously*." It had been three days since Pam and Kathryn's evening of beer and bowling and the perfectly timed kiss on the cheek, which Pam had been neurotically obsessing about ever since. She wanted to make sure whatever she chose for their dinner together was perfect. And Judy was a complete idiot when it came to suggestions. So far, she had picked McDonald's, Chili's, and now Chuck E. Cheese's. It was all Pam could do not to reach through the phone and throttle her. "Get your shit together, Judes. I need a real suggestion."

"Can you please tell me what the big deal is? I mean, really? Are you trying to impress her? If you need to impress this little shit, then you clearly don't need her as a friend."

"Spiteful, party of one," Pam deadpanned. Judy's irritation with Kathryn's newfound spot in Pam's life was becoming more and more apparent, which was frustrating but also completely understandable. Judy hadn't needed to share Pam in years, so the idea of someone new stealing away Pam's time was clearly making her mad. But the anger wasn't needed. Judy had to know that she would always be Pam's number one, right? Well, at least that's what Pam thought. Of course, maybe Judy was jealous because it was also becoming more and more apparent that whatever was happening between Kathryn and Pam was more than just a friendship.

A huff came from the other end of the phone. "I am *not* spiteful," Judy protested.

"Then what the hell?"

"I was only asking."

"Well, I'm not trying to impress her, okay? I just," Pam paused, looked down at her hands, and tried to find the right words, "I just don't want it to seem—"

"Like a date?"

"Yeah," Pam said with a sigh. "It's not a date. It's just…I really like hanging out with her. She is so much fun. And it's easy with her. As worried as I was the other day, and as much as I regretted even agreeing to coffee, which makes no sense because it was just coffee, I was so happy afterward. She just, I don't know."

"She gets you?" Judy asked, completing Pam's thoughts for her, with a voice that sounded way too forlorn and way too jealous.

"Judes, not like *you* get me," Pam hurriedly corrected her. "You're my other half. You're my late-night-eat-a-half-gallon-of-ice-cream-and-roll-of-cookie-dough best friend." She listened for Judy's response but was met with silence from the other end. "Judes, *please* don't do this."

"Okay," Judy said, "why not go to Quartino?"

"Really?"

"Well, Pam, it's great food. A great atmosphere. It would be perfect."

"The last time I went there I was with Harold."

"Oh, I know," Judy commented, again with so much jealousy the words were practically green.

"Seriously? You're jealous about that? Judy, he's dead!"

"Shit, Pam, I know. I'm sorry. I'm not jealous. I promise." Judy cleared her throat and said, "Just go there. Don't think about Harold. Or me. Go. Have fun!"

"Not thinking about Harold is really hard sometimes, though," Pam replied, her voice cracking with emotion.

"Then don't think about him, Pam. It's not that difficult. You've been doing it quite superbly since you buried him."

"Wow. What the hell is wrong with you?" Pam asked, her voice an octave lower than normal.

"Nothing," Judy shouted. "I'm fine."

"Then why are you being like this? You're certainly acting like something is wrong. I don't need you trying to make me feel bad for moving on, Judy. You never acted like this when I started getting closer and going out for drinks and dinner with my coworkers."

"Look, Pam," Judy's voice cracked, "I am fine. I'm sorry. I worry, though. You know me."

"What are you worrying about? That I might replace you or something?" Pam's question was again met with silence. "You're kidding me, right? You and I are way stronger than that, aren't we?"

"I hope so," Judy said. "I hope so."

"Please don't be like this. I need you to be supportive. I don't need you pointing out to me that I'm a horrible widow. Or an even worse best friend," Pam pleaded.

"You are not a bad best friend! And you're right. I shouldn't say things like that about Harold," Judy replied. "He would be happy that you're happy."

Pam stared at herself in the mirror on the dresser that was across from her bed. There were moments when she did feel like a horrible person for not grieving the loss of her husband every second of every day. And being with Kathryn was so different than hanging out with Judy that it was easy to just let go of everything. Maybe she *was* being a bad best friend. "You're sure it's okay?"

"Yes, I swear, it's okay. Go to Quartino. Dress up. Look beautiful."

"I guess it would be nice to get a little dressed up."

"See?" Judy laughed an obviously forced laugh, but a laugh nonetheless. "Hang up with me and call Kathryn."

"Judy?"

"Hmm?"

"Thank you," Pam said. "For everything."

"Stop," Judy protested. "But before you hang up, I do have one more thing to say."

"Ugh, now what?"

"I still need to meet this little shit."

"Woman," Pam corrected her.

"Little shit."

Pam let out a groan. "Judy, she's thirty-two. She's a woman."

"Ohhh, is that the deciding factor? Her age?"

"I'm hanging up."

Judy sighed. "So am I."

As Kathryn walked into Quartino Ristorante she wondered, for about the millionth time, why she agreed to this restaurant. She had replayed the bowling outing in her head over and over and over again. And that fucking cheek kiss countless times more. And the texting conversation afterward? *Please.* She had it memorized. This whole thing was escalating to out of control really quickly. She confided in her group of friends, of course, and each one of them said that Pam was giving her mixed signals. And her best friend Sydney, in her overprotective mode, told Kathryn that this woman was only out to experiment with her. *Remember straight women?* Sydney had shouted. *They just want to break hearts, Kathryn. Run away!* And now, as she stood in the doorway, visibly uncomfortable, she wished she had listened.

This was a date restaurant.

This fucking place was going to kill her. And this woman... Kathryn closed her eyes and took a deep breath. *This fucking woman.*

"May I help you?" the maître d' asked as Kathryn approached the podium.

"Yes. I'm meeting someone."

"Oh yes, you must be Kathryn. Miss Pam told us that you would be coming. Follow me."

Miss Pam? What the hell? Kathryn followed the slender man through the dimly lit restaurant and over to a line of small tables along the windows that faced State Street. The place was packed, of course, and everything smelled delicious. Kathryn spotted a server carrying a loaf of Italian bread and a bowl of dipping oil and felt her stomach start to growl. Maybe she could settle the hell down for Italian food. *Maybe.* Of course, when she started noticing all the couples scattered throughout the dining room with their lovestruck looks on their faces, she started to regret letting her stomach control her heart.

Kathryn's eyes were glued to the maître d's back. She pulled in a deep breath as he slowed, moved to the side, and started to pull a chair out from a table. "Oh wow," Kathryn said under her breath when she finally saw Pam, her legs crossed, her shirt so far unbuttoned that her cleavage was showing beneath the black camisole under her sheer black shirt. Pam's left hand was on the table, fingers lightly tracing the base of a wineglass, and Kathryn immediately noticed that the wedding band that normally resided on her ring finger was nowhere to be found. Her throat almost closed upon that realization. *It's a mistake to be here.* She sat in the chair, smiling up at the maître d'.

"Thank you," she said as he handed her the menu.

"Your server will be with you shortly."

Kathryn cleared her throat and tried to find words. "Sorry that I'm running late. I, uh..." She paused, bit down on her bottom lip. Should she lie? Come up with an awesome excuse? Or just tell the truth, that she was late because she was going to bail? "I don't have an excuse," she finished with an exasperated laugh. "I'm just late."

"Don't worry about it." Pam smiled. "You're not super late. I'm just always early, as I'm sure you kind of figured out by now." Pam licked her lips and leaned forward. "I don't think I've ever seen you look so—"

"Overdressed? Out of my element? Stupid?" Kathryn offered, an eyebrow slightly arched.

"No, no, no," Pam exclaimed. "You look amazing. You look really, really amazing."

"You're clearly blind. When was your last eye exam?" Kathryn remarked with a smirk and took in Pam's adorable eye roll. "You

look really beaut—" Kathryn caught herself. "Nice. You look nice."
She cursed silently. "How long have you been here?" she asked,
skillfully changing the subject. She did a quick once-over of the
room where they were seated and felt even more that it looked like
they were on a date. The table was tucked into a corner, and the
lighting was so romantic, and dammit, there was even a lit candle
on the tabletop. Kathryn almost wanted to blow it out, act like she
sneezed or something.

"About ten minutes." Pam leaned forward. "I have a question,
though."

"Oh, no, what?"

"So," Pam started, pausing while Kathryn ordered a drink with
the server and then, almost whispering, said, "That couple over
there is looking at us. Why?"

Kathryn looked up and noticed a man and a woman smiling at
her. She picked her hand up and waved and the couple laughed and
waved back, then descended into giggles with each other.

"What the hell was that?" Pam hissed.

"Well, if you had ever asked me what I do for a living, you'd
know. But every conversation is always about you, you, *you*,"
Kathryn replied while trying to not laugh.

"Holy shit, I haven't ever asked you, have I?" Pam slapped her
hand over her mouth and then mumbled, "I am so sorry."

Kathryn tilted her head while picking up her glass of water and
assured Pam it was okay.

"So?"

"What?"

"Are you going to tell me what you do?"

"Oh! I didn't know that you wanted to know," Kathryn
responded, feigning a shocked expression. "I'm on *Windy City
Now!* I'm a movie critic." Pam's eyes almost fell out of her head
and Kathryn just smiled again. "I take it you never watch?"

"Uh, no! Clearly! Kathryn, I am so sorry!"

"Pam," Kathryn soothed as she placed her hand over Pam's.
She squeezed lightly and then said, "It's honestly okay. I've only
been on for about half a year."

"I still feel horrible. What kind of person monopolizes a conversation like that?"

"I swear I'm fine," Kathryn reassured her and moved her hand back, realizing then that her hands were clammy, and it made her want to descend into a ball onto the floor. How embarrassing! "Besides, I was the one asking you all those questions."

"I promise," Pam started as she tossed her blond hair over her shoulder, "to watch your show tomorrow. I promise."

"I won't be on tomorrow." Kathryn cracked up when Pam's face fell.

Pam leaned her head back and let out a groan. *"Dammit."*

"Monday through Thursday."

"Okay, okay. Monday! I will watch it Monday!" She took a drink of her wine and then stopped mid-drink. "Oh, now I get it! That's why you asked the movie question the other day!"

Kathryn raised both eyebrows and licked her lips. "Can't get anything by you," she teased. She took a sip of her freshly delivered Bellini, even though she wanted to down the whole thing.

Pam cleared her throat and shifted in her seat. "So, a movie critic. How'd that happen?"

"Ahh, now you want me to talk about me? I don't know if I like this," Kathryn said while twirling her drink in the martini glass. "Honestly? I don't know. I love movies. I love writing. I kind of like being the center of attention, so being on TV doesn't really make me nervous. I started as a news reporter and then just moved on from there. Selfishly, it's more fun to me than reporting the latest shooting victim or burning building. I know that probably sounds shitty, but I just love the whole idea of hobnobbing with famous people. Kinda stupid, eh?"

"Not at all," Pam responded. "I totally understand what you mean. Who doesn't love a good movie, right? And who doesn't have a crush on at least one movie star?"

"True."

"And yours is?" Pam asked.

"Tina Fey. And yours?"

Pam leaned forward and propped her elbows on the table. "I

love Sandra Bullock. I literally will watch any movie she's in. Any movie. My best friend—"

"The spastic lunatic?"

"Yes, that one," Pam answered, pointing her finger at Kathryn. "She always says that I should like a male actor because it makes me sound, y'know, *gay*, or whatever." Pam's eyes flitted up to Kathryn's.

"You don't have a male actor to go with your Sandy B crush, then, eh?"

"I've always been a one-crush kind of person."

"Have you had a lot of crushes?" Kathryn asked, her voice low as she leaned back in her chair. She could feel herself flirting, and it was sickening and exhilarating all at once.

"Not really." Pam pulled her eyes from Kathryn's. "Not in a long time, at least."

"Being married probably got in the way of those kinds of things," Kathryn offered.

Pam glanced at her wine and then up at Kathryn. "It got in the way of a lot."

And there went Kathryn's stomach all the way down to her feet. One minute she was smooth as silk, and the next she felt like a fish out of water. She pulled a breath into her lungs, her eyes glued to Pam's. It wasn't until Pam broke the eye contact that Kathryn released the breath. "So, why Skin?"

"You want the truth? Or do you want what I tell everyone?"

"What do you think?"

"I think you probably always want the truth from me," Pam began, her voice catching slightly before she looked around the restaurant, then out the window, and then over Kathryn's shoulder. "Harold wouldn't let me work. Strictly forbade it. So when he passed, I got a job, because for the first time in over twenty-one years I was *free*."

Kathryn watched as Pam visibly filled with anxiety. "Pam, I didn't mean to make you uncomfortable."

"No." Pam held her hand up. "It's not that. I don't tell many people that part. Seems like I'm begging for attention." Pam shrugged a shoulder. "You know that the week after his funeral I made it my mission to find a job? I mean, don't most widows grieve?"

"You have to grieve in your own way," Kathryn explained.

"Yeah, well, all I wanted to do was find a sense of meaning, find myself. No one would understand. No one. And it's—" Pam's hand moved to her face. She tugged on her upper lip before she said, "It's not easy to admit that I was what I hated. I was *his* wife. I wasn't a *person*. I wasn't *me*."

"Pam?"

"What?"

"Look at me," Kathryn prompted, her voice low. She waited for Pam to finally turn to face her. Her eyes were sad; her cheeks flushed. "I will never judge you."

Pam let out a half-hearted laugh. "Why?"

"Because you don't have to worry about that shit with me."

Pam tilted her head to the side before she clarified, "I meant why are you so amazing?"

It was Kathryn's turn to fumble a bit, her face instantly heating up. "Well, I do what I can," she said with a laugh, trying her hardest to not let Pam know she was insanely tempted to reach across the table and take her pain and heartache away.

❖

Their waiter poured the coffee, proficiently switching cups while the hot liquid was still pouring. "Is there anything else I can get you two ladies?"

"No, I think we're fine for now," Pam answered, making eye contact with Kathryn.

"Okay, I'll be around shortly."

Pam thanked the waiter while continuing to take in all of Kathryn's features, her jawline, her dark eyes, the way her hair was pulled into a mass of curls on top of her head. She looked so beautiful. Her black fitted dress wonderfully accentuated all the right areas. Well, all the areas Pam never thought she'd think twice about looking at until now. She was out of her element for sure.

Everything about Kathryn was intriguing to Pam, from the way she seemed to be guarding herself to the way she seemed to want nothing but the best for Pam. She was finding it hard to remember what her life was like before Kathryn waltzed onto the scene. And honestly, Pam didn't want to think about a life without Kathryn, which was frightening and exciting at the same time.

"This has been really fun," she said, breaking the silence that had fallen between the pair.

"Yes, it has." Kathryn crossed her arms and propped them on the table as she leaned forward a bit. "Can I ask you a question?"

Pam's eyes traveled down the line of Kathryn's neck to her chest. Her eyes instantly shot back up to Kathryn's. "Of course."

"Why didn't you have children?"

Pam shook her head slowly and adjusted her gaze downward. She stared at her cup of coffee as she remembered the miscarriage and the aftermath of losing a child. And then the months and months of taking fertility drugs years later and then hoping to God that something, *anything*, would happen. "We got married because I was pregnant."

Kathryn cocked an eyebrow. "Totally wasn't expecting that."

"Yeah," Pam replied with a laugh. "No one was. I broke up with Harold right before he went to college. I figured it'd be easier on both of us, considering that I was not in love with him." Pam looked out the window of the restaurant. "God, I remember it like it was yesterday. His parents' station wagon and the moonlight, how it was streaming in the back of the car. And the car smelled like his dad's cigars."

"It's weird how our brains remember things like that," Kathryn offered before sipping on her coffee. "I'll never forget the smell of my friend Elizabeth's carpet, as weird as that sounds."

Pam cocked her head to the side. "I'm assuming there's a story there?"

Kathryn tore her eyes away from Pam and looked around the restaurant. She took a deep breath and then let it slowly out. "You could say that."

The apparent shift in Kathryn's mood and tone made Pam

slightly uncomfortable. She cleared her throat. "So, anyway, I missed my period shortly after that night." She watched as Kathryn visibly relaxed, which made her want to know the story behind those sad, dark eyes even more. "I was so worried," she continued. "I can't even begin to tell you how scared I was. It was such a surprise. I mean, we were always safe." Pam shrugged. "I told Harold over the phone. He came home that weekend and asked me to marry him. To this day, I have no idea why I said yes. How fucked up is that?" Pam asked, not really wanting an answer. She looked down at her hands. "But who does something like that? Who marries someone they don't want to? Who commits herself to someone when she doesn't even love that person? I wonder what my life would be like had I waited and found the right person." She let out a strangled laugh. "I don't even like how 'Pamela Phillips' sounds."

"I mean," Kathryn said, leaning forward with a smile on her lips, "it doesn't sound awful."

Pam's eyes caught Kathryn's, and the temperature in the restaurant seemed to shoot up ten degrees.

Kathryn looked away first and let out a shaky breath. "How did your ultra-religious parents take all of this?" she asked, her eyes locked onto her coffee cup.

"My mom was furious, of course. Big shocker. She used to say things like, 'He doesn't love you, Pamela. He only wanted sex.'"

"And your dad?"

"He didn't talk to me for months. He eventually came around, but he never really liked Harold. I guess for good reason."

Kathryn glanced back up at Pam. "Then what happened?"

"Well, we moved in together, and I enrolled in college with him. And about three months later, I started cramping and bleeding and..."

"Pam," Kathryn sighed. "I'm so sorry."

Pam's eyes welled with tears and she tried to shake it off. She did not need or want to cry about this—especially at a restaurant. "I'm okay," she said. "I got over it." She looked out at the people on State Street, walking briskly with their coat collars pulled up over their ears. She wondered if she should just stop talking, because it was making her way too emotional. Why was she opening up like this to Kathryn? As much as Pam liked her, she didn't need to tell Kathryn her life story. There was no reason to get close to this woman. *Ever.* She was just a friend. A friend that had the most intense brown eyes Pam had ever seen. A friend that felt like a breath of fresh air. A friend that made Pam's insides ache. A friend she was starting to have feelings for. *Shit.* Her eyes drifted downward.

"Why are you so easy to talk to?" Pam heard herself ask before looking up into those dark eyes she couldn't stop thinking about. "I love talking to you," she admitted, a sharp intake of breath following the admission. "God. I'm sorry."

Kathryn narrowed her eyes. "Why are you sorry?"

"I shouldn't say things like that."

"Yes, you should. I never want you to feel like you can't say what you're thinking or feeling," Kathryn explained, her voice completely sincere.

"I…" Pam searched for her courage amidst all the confusion in her brain. "Have dinner with me again tomorrow." She leaned forward slowly. "Please?"

"Okay."

"My house."

"Okay."

Pam kept her eyes on Kathryn's. "Good," she replied. What was she getting herself into?

CHAPTER SEVEN

It's not a date." Pam poured a glass of wine for herself and motioned toward Judy as she continued to wash potatoes in the sink. Judy, of course, accepted the wine, because apparently as she was on her way over to Pam's, one of her kids decided to throw a horrific fit. When she rushed into Pam's house to help Pam cook dinner for her "not a date" with Kathryn, she was a hot mess, covered in snow, looking like she was ready to commit murder. And so far, all Judy had done was ask way too many questions and act way too jealous for Pam's liking.

"Just like last night wasn't a date?"

"Judy."

Judy walked over and stirred the green beans. "Okay. I believe you."

"Well, seriously, it's not. I invited her over for dinner, just like I invite you over for dinner sometimes."

"Yes, but I come complete with three kids and a husband." Judy turned her head to look at Pam. "This little shit—"

"Judy," Pam sighed.

"I'm sorry, 'woman,' comes waltzing into your life with nothing more than an amazing gift of reading you like a book."

Pam walked over to the refrigerator and pulled out a tangerine. "Remember what you said to me?"

"No," Judy said firmly.

"You said that this Kathryn woman could be good for me."

"I have no idea what you're talking about."

Pam threw a piece of the tangerine rind at Judy. It hit her in the middle of the back. "Come on! You told me to go for it, whatever *it* is. A friendship. Whatever. And I am going for it. And so far, I really like what I've found. Why is that a bad thing?"

Judy bent down and picked up the rind. "Okay, okay. I'm sorry that I'm having doubts about this whole thing."

"Why are you having doubts, though? It doesn't make sense," Pam said. "I don't get it. Are you jealous?"

"No!" Judy huffed. She took a long drink of her wine. "Why would you think that? Just because I'm a little nervous that I'm going to lose you does not mean that I'm jealous."

"Whoa, whoa, *whoa.*" Pam stopped chopping the tomatoes. "Judith, you are not going to lose me."

"Yeah, you say that now."

"Oh, my God. You cannot be serious."

"Pam, I'm allowed to be worried."

"No, you aren't. Because it won't happen. You are my best friend. Period."

Judy sighed and glanced at Pam over her shoulder. "I feel like I'm already losing you."

"Judes," Pam lowered her hands and rested them on the chopping block in front of her, "you have absolutely nothing to worry about. Why would you think you could ever be replaced?" She watched Judy's back, her head bent down, her shoulders slumped. "You can't keep being like that when you're the one that told me to do this."

"The adult inside me knows that, but the spoiled child inside me can't quite be okay with it." Judy let out a small chuckle. "I've never been jealous before. What the hell is wrong with me?"

"Well, I'm pretty amazing." Pam smirked.

"Oh, I know," Judy sighed.

"And you don't need to doubt her so much. I very rarely trust people, Judy. You know this."

"I know, Pam. I know." Judy turned and watched Pam squeeze the tangerine lightly and then drop the pieces into the salad. "Be careful."

"She's not a predator," Pam said, knowing exactly what Judy was talking about.

Judy looked over at Pam. "You're sure about all of this?"

Pam tossed the salad with a pair of tongs. "Yeah, I am. Surrounding myself with people that like me isn't a bad thing, remember?"

"Yes, I remember." Judy bent down and took the potatoes out of the oven. "Double baked, right?"

Pam laughed. "Yes." She watched as Judy cut open the potatoes and scooped out the insides into a bowl. A flood of emotion came over Pam as she stood there. "What would I do without you, Judy?"

Judy looked back at Pam, displaying a giant grin. "You'd be talking to your dog even more than you already do." Judy chuckled when Pam stuck her tongue out at her. "And besides, it's me that would be lost without you. Who would I complain to about Tom?"

Pam started to laugh. "So true. You'd have gone stark raving mad."

"Exactly." Judy looked over at the clock. "You need to go get ready."

"Oh God," Pam said. "You're right."

"I've got this covered."

"Thank you so much, Judes. I'll be down in a flash."

❖

Kathryn looked down at the GPS on her phone as she pulled into the driveway of Pam's large suburban home. She was so nervous, and she honestly shouldn't have been. It wasn't like she hadn't seen Pam at all outside the store. Not only had they gone to lunch a number of times, but Kathryn had made a couple impromptu stops into Skin to see Pam. And every time, Pam was so excited to see her that it made Kathryn feel like a million dollars. So being stressed out with shaking hands and weak knees should not have been happening.

Yet there she was.

She knew what was happening. She could feel it in her head

and her heart. Kathryn was falling for this woman. She was falling, and falling hard, and nothing was stopping her. Except, of course, the fact that Pam was straight. And had just buried her husband. And a litany of other reasons that were like red flags warning Kathryn to tread carefully. Or better yet, run. Either way, there was nothing telling her to head over for a lovely dinner between the two of them with no one else in the vicinity.

Kathryn leaned her head back. "Calm down. Calm the fuck down, Kath," she said, her words deafening inside her quiet Jeep. "You can do this. You can be this woman's friend. You can do this." She reached over and grabbed the bottle of Riesling she had brought with her. When she got to the front door, she noticed that Pam must have a dog, because there were prints all over the yard in the freshly fallen snow.

She rang the doorbell and immediately heard a dog bark. When the door swung open and she got a good look at Pam, Kathryn's stomach fell to the floor. She forgot how to speak. Pam was standing there in her dark blue jeans and cream turtleneck sweater with a smile on her soft, pink lips. Kathryn was sure she had never seen someone look so beautiful. The way her hair framed her face and the way her eyes sparkled made Kathryn think that maybe it wasn't such a bad thing that she was falling for this woman, even if it was going to be disastrous in the end.

"Hi," Kathryn finally said as she shook herself out of the trance.

"Well, hello there," Pam said with a laugh. "You look like you've seen a ghost. Are you okay?"

"Who? Me? Oh, I'm fine," Kathryn stammered, tripping over her false protest, and quickly changed the subject. "I brought wine." She held out the bottle and looked down at it, trying to control her breathing. "I hope you like Riesling," she said when she looked back up at Pam.

"I do." Pam reached forward and took the bottle, her fingers brushing Kathryn's. "You're getting all covered in snow! Get in here before you freeze to death."

Kathryn stepped into the house and was immediately hit in the face with the smell of a home-cooked meal. If she wasn't hungry before, she certainly was now. After she bent to remove her boots, she stood and looked around the entryway with the large staircase before her. Pam's house was beautiful. The open concept of the foyer and the kitchen was amazing. Kathryn instantly fell in love with the decorations, which were rustic and trendy in a way that made Kathryn feel a little more at ease. It was as if she had been teleported into the pages of a home decorating magazine. As she stepped farther inside, she was suddenly attacked by dog kisses on her hand.

"Who is this?" Kathryn asked, a giggle spilling from her throat as she squatted down to pet the golden retriever, who was graying around the eyes and mouth as if she were an older addition to Pam's life.

"That's Dorothy." Pam smiled. "She's my baby."

"She's adorable," Kathryn said while petting Dorothy. The dog was in heaven, looking up at Kathryn like she was a savior.

"Give me your coat," Pam instructed.

"I'm sorry that I didn't dress up," Kathryn said, motioning to her Star Wars T-shirt, navy cardigan, and jeans. She handed over her long, black winter parka and watched as Pam hung it on a hook next to the door. Kathryn's eyes wandered over Pam's backside, and she hid the smile that crept to her lips before Pam turned around to face her.

"Seriously? Being comfortable is way more important. And you look adorable."

Kathryn didn't react to that comment as she continued to pet Dorothy, who was now lying on her back, all four paws in the air, soaking up the attention Kathryn was lavishing on her.

Pam chuckled as she walked over and sat on the second to last stair. "She's an attention whore. She won't leave you alone now that you've shown her that you like her."

"Hmm," Kathryn started as she glanced up at Pam. "I wonder who that sounds like?" *Ugh.* She was flirting. And it was unacceptable. But dammit, it was also so much fun.

Pam leaned forward and propped her elbows on her knees. "It is kind of hard to not want to be around you," she answered.

Kathryn tried to not let that comment fill her with butterflies, but resistance was futile. She swallowed the lump that had formed in her throat and forced a smile. "I guess I do have that effect on people," she said, her voice shaking ever so slightly.

Pam cleared her throat, made a gesture with her hand as if to wave off the uncomfortable feeling this entire conversation was causing, and stood. "Come with me into the kitchen," she said as she walked through an arched entryway.

Kathryn stood and followed Pam, Dorothy hot on her trail. "You weren't lying." She walked over to the sink and washed her hands, listening to the eighties music that played softly in the background.

"Oh, yeah. She won't leave your side now." Pam pulled out the chicken and potatoes from the oven. "Dinner is actually ready if you're hungry."

"I am seriously starved."

"Let's eat, then. Grab that wine and wine key."

Kathryn followed Pam to the table that was toward the back of the kitchen. She opened the wine, expertly poured two glasses, and then set the bottle on the table. When she sat she picked up a glass and handed it over to Pam. "Your wine, madam."

"A toast," Pam said, a smile spreading across her face as she lifted her glass.

"To what? Friendship?"

"How about to the beginning of something great."

"I'll toast to that." Kathryn clinked her glass against Pam's and then took a long drink.

❖

Dinner was a complete success. The chicken tasted wonderful. Judy had made perfect double baked potatoes. And Kathryn commented on how amazing the salad was more times than Pam could count. The soft jazz and the lighting were both the right touches, as well. Pam was so happy with how everything turned out.

Their conversation over dinner was relaxed, too, which Pam still found hard to believe. She vividly remembered squirming in her chair during many dinners with Harold, so anxious to get up from her seat that she felt as if she was in high school again, being forced to eat with the family.

Pam picked up her wineglass and eyed Kathryn over the rim. They were on their second bottle of wine, and it was starting to affect Pam in all the right ways. She watched as Kathryn pushed her long, dark hair behind her ear as she ate. A grin came to Pam's lips when she saw Kathryn pick up a green bean that had fallen off her plate and slyly reach down and feed it to Dorothy.

"She does enjoy her vegetables," Pam commented before drinking the last of the wine in her glass.

Kathryn's head shot up and she instantly started laughing. "You weren't supposed to see that."

"Mmm-hmm." Pam laughed and then leaned forward, pushing her plate away and propping her elbows on the table. "She loves you if she eats from your hand like that."

"Well, I have been told that I'm very lovable."

"I would agree with that," Pam said quietly, her voice an octave lower than normal. "And I think I might be a little tipsy."

Kathryn chuckled and shook her head back and forth. "*You* are a lightweight," she replied, her finger lightly touching the stem of the wineglass.

"This is true." Pam placed her palm under her chin and leaned her head to the side slightly. "How did you know that you were a lesbian or whatever?" Pam winced at herself. The wine was making her far braver than anticipated.

"Why does everyone ask me that?"

"Probably because it's obvious how sure you are of yourself."

"Irony at its finest," Kathryn said as she swirled her wine in its glass.

"What do you mean?"

A blush flooded Kathryn's cheeks. "I never feel sure of myself."

"I find that so hard to believe," Pam commented, her eyes never leaving Kathryn's.

Kathryn leaned back in her chair, pushed her hair behind her ears, and studied Pam. "I certainly have the assertiveness needed when I'm at work. And in certain situations, I am *very* sure. But then in other situations, I feel like I'm a ball of nerves."

Pam was intrigued and confused. If anyone was unsure about anything, it was *her*. It was strange for her to have these feelings of excitement and desire happening all at the same time. The last time she had looked forward to an evening spent with someone on an *almost* romantic level was during her junior year of high school when she went to the prom with Harold for the first time. And here she was, feeling the butterflies and the clammy hands all over again. But this time, the feelings seemed stronger, determined, *real*. It frightened her. She had no idea how to handle feelings like this, especially when they were for another woman. So if anyone was unsure, it was Pam.

Kathryn cleared her throat. "Anyway, what was the question again?"

"How did you know?"

"Oh, yes, how did I know that I like ladies?" Kathryn leaned back in her chair and sighed. "Well, I remember having a crush on my fifth-grade science teacher."

Pam listened intently as Kathryn spoke about her many crushes. Her keyboarding teacher and drama coach, and this woman that lived behind her when she was in high school. Kathryn talked about how she never really understood any of it, how she thought something was wrong with her, how it didn't make sense that she didn't like boys that much, especially since all her friends did. Pam leaned in closer when Kathryn started to speak about a friend of hers from junior year of high school that was a year younger than her. They would hang out, laugh, and have fun, and then she found herself wanting to *kiss* her friend, which completely freaked Kathryn out.

And at that moment, Pam's mind stopped dead in its tracks. Everything that Kathryn was talking about was everything Pam had been feeling since the moment she sat at the coffee shop with

Kathryn. And hearing about a kiss and it being with two girls and one of those girls being Kathryn was almost too much for Pam to handle. Hearing about it with so much emotional detail was making her insides shake.

Pam watched as Kathryn explained how she knew she had to figure it out, so she made her best guy friend have sex with her. "And that's how you knew?" Pam asked, hoping that it really wasn't as similar as her situation.

"Yeah," Kathryn answered with a smile. "Best part of that whole story is that we are both gay now."

Pam bit her bottom lip lightly. "Begs the question if you were both that bad or...?"

Kathryn leaned her head back and a roar of laughter spilled from her mouth. Pam couldn't help but join in. She was loving every minute of getting to know this side of Kathryn. And watching her laugh? That was quickly becoming one of Pam's favorite things.

"Yeah, I guess you could be right. Maybe I really am straight!"

Pam raised her eyebrows and shrugged. "Maybe?"

Another laugh burst out of Kathryn's mouth. "Um, no. I'm one hundred percent positive that I'm gay."

"It must have been nice to finally *know*, though," Pam whispered, then cleared her throat, wishing desperately for more wine.

Kathryn's eyes locked onto Pam's. "It is," she agreed. "It's really nice."

"What if I told you I feel a lot of what—"

"Pam," Kathryn interrupted, her voice soothing.

The pressure in Pam's chest was palpable. She so badly wanted to finish her sentence, but the look in Kathryn's eyes was begging her not to continue, which made no sense. Pam had no idea what she was doing. All she knew was that she wanted more. She wanted more stories, more feelings, more Kathryn. "Tell me more," Pam pleaded.

Kathryn leaned forward and started with, "My first relationship was with my fencing coach in college." Kathryn blushed a deep red. "She was tall and blond and just ridiculously amazing. She was smart, well read. She would stand behind me and slide her hands up my torso, tell me to keep my abdominal muscles tight. We had a lot of late-night practices that eventually turned into drinks at this smoky blues bar downtown, and then those nights turned into drinks back at her place. The first time we did anything I was drunk, so I thought it was just me being a drunk college student. And then the next time, I wasn't drunk and neither was she, and," Kathryn paused as she brought her fingertips to her lips, a faraway look in her eyes, "it was really amazing."

Something inside Pam's core tightened at the thought of a young Kathryn figuring herself out with another woman. She couldn't figure it out, though. Was the feeling jealousy? Or was she turned on? Either way, Pam was so intrigued she could barely breathe.

"It was so incredibly hot and against the rules, but we did it anyway."

"Was it fun?"

"Oh yeah," Kathryn said with a laugh. "It was really mind boggling."

"Why?" Pam was literally on the edge of her seat.

"It was just amazing to be in this relationship where I was actually *wanted*. And I wanted her more than I had ever wanted someone before. When we were together in a room full of people, it would take everything in us to not sneak off to the bathroom and make love in one of the stalls. And well, the sex was—" Kathryn stopped. "It was wonderful."

"I bet it was," Pam whispered. She felt her heart thudding away beneath her chest, her mouth dry, other parts of her not so much. She was scared and excited, and hearing everything that Kathryn had been saying was just too much. She needed to watch herself, to figure this all out. Clearly something was being awoken inside Pam that had been dormant for years. And the idea of it all coming to fruition with Kathryn was not only scary but insanely exhilarating. And Pam had no idea how to handle it all. Why wasn't it making her uncomfortable? Why was it making her want to see where this all went with Kathryn, how fast it happened, how wonderful Kathryn's lips probably tasted? Dammit, she was handling this so wrong. So, so, so wrong. But everything about Kathryn was so, so, so *right*. And how was she supposed to handle a situation like this that involved someone that she should never have been attracted to? Or maybe the real question was why did she feel like this was everything she ever wanted, even though the idea of it frightened the hell out of her?

"Are you okay?" Kathryn asked, her voice breaking through Pam's thoughts.

Pam didn't know what to say. She wasn't okay, but at the same time she really was. "Yeah," she answered, her voice cracking. "I think so."

"What's going on in that head of yours?"

Pam looked into Kathryn's eyes. She felt her heart leap into her throat. *God.* "I'm just thinking."

"About what?"

"About you," Pam answered so matter-of-factly that it even shocked herself. "About what is happening."

Kathryn leaned back in her chair. "What do you mean? We're having dinner."

"I know that," Pam said calmly. "I mean, between us."

"We're forming a friendship." Kathryn put her hands in her lap.

"I've never had a friendship like this before, Kathryn."

The smile that came to Kathryn's lips was breathtaking. "What do you mean?" she asked, her eyes sparkling.

"I mean my clammy hands, my uneven breathing, my heart beating nine thousand times faster than normal."

"Well," Kathryn started as she raised her eyebrows.

The only word to describe Kathryn raising her eyebrows like that was "seductive," and Pam wanted to scream.

"Maybe you're realizing something you didn't know about yourself," Kathryn finished before she ran her fingers through her dark hair.

Pam sighed as she leaned back in her chair and looked up at the ceiling. A deep breath filled her lungs and she let it out slowly.

Okay, just drop it. "Let me just get these dishes in the dishwasher, and we'll have dessert."

Kathryn stood and followed with her plate. "I'll help you."

❖

Pam leaned against the doorway that led into the living room. She slowly lifted the tumbler of scotch to her lips and took a small sip of the strong liquor. She had calmed down a considerable amount since her question-and-answer session during dinner. Her mind had been racing. One minute she knew exactly what she wanted from Kathryn: friendship. Nothing more. And then the next minute she couldn't stop herself from imagining Kathryn's lips and her hands. Pam didn't want to ruin whatever was going on between them, though. And she also didn't want to hurt Kathryn. What if it wasn't what Pam really wanted? What if she was just bored? And lonely? And she ended up breaking Kathryn's heart? She couldn't handle the thought of that.

Pam stood and watched Kathryn as she examined her surroundings. Pam wasn't sure if she should smile and acknowledge the fact that she was watching her or keep on disguising it by slyly observing over the top of her glass.

"You're not being that discreet," Kathryn commented as she kept her back to Pam.

"I didn't want to interrupt." Pam quickly covered her tracks. She took another sip of her scotch. She decided as the strong liquor burned her throat that she would let the liquid enhance her inability to function instead of trying to constantly cover up her desire.

"These pictures are beautiful, Pam," Kathryn said as she pushed her hair away from her face.

"You like them?"

"Yes, a lot. Who was the photographer?" Kathryn asked, motioning to the picture of a pair of hands folded on a lap, a picture of a pair of glasses on a dark-haired woman's face, a close-up picture of full, red lips.

"An unknown artist," Pam answered.

"Who? Maybe I've heard of him."

"*Her*," Pam corrected her as she ducked her head. "I took them."

Kathryn looked back at Pam. "Really?"

"I'm much more than a pretty face."

"I'm starting to figure that out." Kathryn threw out the comment as she turned her head back toward the pictures. "So, when did this artistic streak come out?"

"College. After college. I guess I've always had it but kind of kept it hidden." Pam looked at the pictures, breathed in through her nose, and then sighed before saying, "Kind of makes me nervous to talk about, to be honest."

"Why?"

"It's like showing you a piece of myself I rarely show anyone." Pam took the remaining steps into the living room area and over toward Kathryn. "Harold hated them. I love them, though. I hung them after he passed." Pam tilted her head and studied the picture of the pair of lips. "The pictures just mean a lot to me. They're, you know, they're *real*."

"Who is this one of?" Kathryn asked, pointing to a picture of two pairs of legs intertwined.

"It's actually my best friend and me. Taken about seven years ago with my old Minolta my parents had given me for my sixteenth birthday. Thirty-five millimeter film. I actually developed them all myself, too."

"I'm so moved by this one," Kathryn said as she continued to look at the picture of the intertwined legs.

"Yeah, they're the most *me* of anything in this house." Pam made her way over to the oversized armchair, sat, and propped her feet up on the ottoman.

"Is there a reason they're all of women?" Kathryn asked. Pam knew that question would come up eventually.

"No," Pam responded. She smiled when Kathryn's head turned and their eyes locked. "I'm not secretly a lesbian, if that's what you're thinking." The words came out of Pam's mouth before she even had a chance to register them. If those pictures were the most *Pam* thing in the house, that line she'd just muttered was the least *Pam* and also, probably, a lie.

Kathryn let out a laugh that was followed by her shaking her head. "Geez, Pam," she commented as she turned around and plopped down on the couch next to Pam, "I didn't say that, although it does beg the question."

"Ha ha ha."

Kathryn came back with "I'm just *teasing*," her eyes smiling. "You're most definitely not a lesbian. No worries."

Pam watched as Kathryn brought her own glass of scotch up to her lips. She cocked an eyebrow. "Your hand is shaking. Why?" Pam asked coyly.

"Just a nervous tic."

"Do I make you nervous?"

Kathryn's eyes went wide as she stared at Pam over the glass. She slowly pulled the drink away from her mouth and swallowed the liquor. "I think, *um*, what?"

Pam felt her mouth turn up into a grin. "Do. I. Make. You. Nervous?" she repeated, making sure to end each word with a firm staccato.

"There's a logical explanation. I, um—"

Pam watched Kathryn's chest fill as she took a deep breath. It was obvious that Kathryn was trying her hardest to not react, to not let her guard down. Pam hated to admit it, but Kathryn had every reason to be guarded, because without the influence of wine and scotch and witty banter, would they be in this present situation?

Kathryn smiled before finally replying with, "Kinda? I mean, you didn't when we first started hanging out. Not at all, actually. But now? Yeah, you kinda do."

"Why?"

"I guess I just *really* like you."

"I thought all you wanted was a friendship."

"That *is* all I want," Kathryn said.

"Then why would I make you nervous?" Pam knew why. But selfishly, she wanted to hear it. She wanted to hear Kathryn say it.

Kathryn wrinkled her nose and shrugged. "I honestly have no idea," she answered while avoiding eye contact.

Pam watched Kathryn lean forward, prop her elbows on her knees, and sigh. Pam mimicked her as she looked over at her. "What is it? Am I doing something to make this harder than it needs to be?"

"You're not doing anything wrong, Pam. You're doing everything perfectly. I just—" Kathryn paused and broke eye contact. "I'll be okay."

"I feel like you're not telling me something," Pam said, her eyes moving back and forth between Kathryn's, studying her face, noticing for the first time the small scar above her lip. She could tell that she was fighting with something inside herself. She knew that this friendship meant more to Kathryn than it probably should have after only knowing each other for such a short time. But Pam felt the same way, which scared her, too. And she really did want to talk about it.

Pam moved her hand slowly and placed it lightly on Kathryn's back, feeling the heat radiating through Kathryn's clothing. "But I'm not going to push you into telling me. When you're ready, you'll tell me."

Kathryn looked over at Pam. "You think so?"

Pam nodded before she put her arm around Kathryn's shoulders. "Tell me the truth eventually, though."

Kathryn chuckled. "I promise to tell you eventually."

❖

I made it home.

Pam rolled onto her back, clutching her cell phone while reading the text that had just arrived. *Good,* she typed out and quickly added, *Were the roads bad?*

She waited and waited, her hands gripping her phone like a lifeline.

Not anything my trusty steed couldn't handle.

A smile came to Pam's lips and she tapped away a response of *Your black beauty, eh?*

Yes, black beauty indeed.

Pam propped her head up a bit, focused on the screen, watched the bubble indicating that Kathryn was typing something, and almost held her breath while she waited.

Do you remember the first time you saw someone that took your breath away?

A smile spread across Pam's lips, because ironically that person for Pam was Kathryn. *Yes,* she answered, without even thinking.

Remember how you felt afterward?

Scared, excited, freaked out. Like a million scattered puzzle pieces had finally found their way together?

Kathryn's next text came across the screen, and it shocked Pam when she read it.

You make me nervous because you're all I think about. And that feeling? How you felt after seeing that person? That's how you make me feel.

She read it again.

And again.

And *again.*

The bubble reappeared, and Kathryn's next text of *I'm sorry* appeared, and those two words made something inside Pam's chest tighten.

Kathryn, Pam typed. She pressed Send and then without a second thought typed out *You are not alone in these feelings. At all.* Her thumb hovered over the Send button, and then without another hesitation, she pressed it.

Okay, Kathryn responded.

Pam smiled. *Go to sleep. I'll see you tomorrow.*

Good night.

Night.

Pam put her phone on the nightstand and then leaned back onto her pillow.

What the hell was she doing?

She had absolutely *no* idea. All she knew was that this woman made her happy.

And that was literally all that mattered.

CHAPTER EIGHT

So, how was the show last night?"
Sydney, Kathryn's best friend through thick and thin, was perched on the center island in Kathryn's kitchen, her legs swinging back and forth like a child's. Her short bleach-blond hair was messy from the knit stocking cap she had been wearing, but she didn't care, which was often the case with Sydney and her hair. She had arrived bright and early, like she always did on Saturday mornings. It had become their best-friend ritual shortly after Kathryn moved into the brownstone. She would drink coffee, fix them both a bowl of cereal, and they would talk about each other's nights. The only difference was that this time, Kathryn wasn't awake and she was sleeping alone. After all, she hadn't left Pam's house until almost two in the morning, and even then, she didn't want to go.

"It was so awesome," Sydney started after she took a sip of coffee. "Packed house. Both shows were sold out. I keep reading the reviews about how this Second City ensemble is the best the critics have seen in years and I literally have to pinch myself. I cannot believe I'm a part of this."

"That is so awesome, Syd. I am so proud of you. I knew you'd make it. I really did."

"I know, babe. You're the only person that believed it, though. So thank you for that."

"Well, you know. That's what best friends are for, right?" Kathryn happily munched on her bowl of cereal while Sydney filled her in on last night's show. She spoke a million miles a minute, and it was wonderful because Kathryn didn't want to talk about her night. She knew the minute she opened her mouth Sydney would judge her or try to convince her to run away from Pam, which Kathryn knew was probably the right thing to do. But she should have known better than to assume Sydney wouldn't sense that something was up.

Sydney was studying Kathryn after she finished the retelling of her evening, complete with play-by-play detail of the bedroom action with the insanely hot chick she took home. "Okay," Sydney said.

"Okay what?"

"Something's going on," Sydney commented matter-of-factly.

"Why would you think that?" Kathryn asked from one of the stools around the island before she put a spoonful of her second bowl of cereal into her mouth. Kathryn knew Sydney understood things, almost as if she had a sixth sense when it came to Kathryn. It was awesome sometimes, but other times it was a giant pain in the ass. Kathryn had met Sydney in college. While Sydney was studying theatre, Kathryn was majoring in broadcast journalism. They hit it off instantly and, yes, did their fair share of being friends with benefits while trying to find themselves. Their friendship had lasted through almost every obstacle a friendship could go through, including when Sydney stole Kathryn's fencing coach right out from under her nose.

"You weren't at the show last night, so you weren't out partying with us, and now you're not telling me to keep my voice down because some woman is still asleep in your bed. All of that means you probably didn't have sex last night, which means I'm the only one that did and," Sydney pointed at Kathryn with her spoon, "*you're* the one that's glowing."

"I am not," Kathryn said around a mouthful of cereal and then swallowed, "glowing."

"Yes, you are." Sydney slid off the counter and walked over to Kathryn. "Who are you seeing?"

"Is it still snowing out?" Kathryn asked.

"Yes, there are five inches on the ground. Now, who are you seeing?"

"I'm not seeing anyone," Kathryn protested.

Sydney eyed Kathryn. "Yes, you are. Now answer the fucking question."

"God, no, I'm not." Kathryn stood and walked over to the sink. "I'm not seeing anyone. Why do you think that?"

"Because. If you weren't out with me, then you had to have been out with someone else. You're not out until…what time was it when you got home last night?"

Kathryn sighed. "You mean this morning?" she asked sheepishly.

"Seriously?" Sidney huffed. "*Morning?* What the heck, Kath?"

Kathryn looked away from Sydney. "I was with Pam."

"Pam?" Sydney thought back. Kathryn hadn't mentioned a specific woman in a long time. "Who is that?"

"Remember? Pam? I gave her my number after—"

"Oh yes," Sydney interrupted. "The hand-massaging straight woman. I remember now."

Kathryn rolled her eyes. "Yeah, that's the one."

"So, wait. You're actually *fucking* this woman now?"

"Jesus, Syd. I said that I wasn't seeing anyone or *fucking* anyone, for that matter." Kathryn turned around and leaned against the island. "Why is everything about sex with you?"

"Um, because everything *is* about sex," Sydney said in a joking tone. "You're telling me that you don't want to sleep with this woman?"

"No, I don't."

"Well, that's even worse."

"What the hell are you talking about?"

Sydney took a long drink from her cup of now-lukewarm coffee. "If you don't want to sleep with her, then you're getting close to her, which we both know you don't do."

"Shut up," Kathryn said, laughing. "You're not allowed to pull that."

"Oh, yes I am, because I know you. And I know you don't let yourself get close to people, especially pretty women."

Kathryn glared at Sydney. She was right. She was always right, but she didn't need to know that. "I just want to be friends with her."

"And you don't think that's a problem?"

"No, I don't."

"Kath." Sydney took a deep breath and looked around the kitchen. "Do you remember the last woman that broke your heart? The one I so lovingly refer to as Heartbreaker?"

Kathryn rolled her eyes.

"She was straight. And you were a hot, hot mess for a very long time. And ever since then, all you ever want is to fuck 'em and forget 'em. But now you're telling me you want to be friends with this woman? Don't you see how this could be a problem?"

Kathryn reluctantly nodded. "Yeah, I see why."

"Do you really think it's a good idea to get mixed up with another woman that might just break your heart at the end of the day?"

"Sydney, I know it's hard to believe, but I'm watching myself. I just want a friendship. That is all. And besides—"

"Besides what?"

"She's like, older, or whatever."

"You really think that makes a difference?"

"Yes, I do!"

"Kath, Heartbreaker was forty-one." Sydney smiled. "And Joann was thirty-eight and Kelly was forty. Shall I continue?"

"No. You shan't," Kathryn replied with a laugh.

Sydney eyed Kathryn and said, "I seem to recall that this Pam woman just buried her husband. Am I right?"

"How do you remember these things?"

Sydney crossed her arms over her chest. "Because I listen to you, Kath, my dear."

"I'm not falling for this one."

Sydney picked up her messenger bag and walked over to Kathryn. She put her hands on Kathryn's shoulders. "I worry so much about you, Kath."

"I know you do. But really, you don't have to. This one's

different. She's enjoying the company. And you're right, I haven't been able to get close to someone in a very long time, so I'm being careful. Believe me, this is really different." Kathryn smiled. "I know what I'm doing this time."

"As long as you're sure."

"I am. I promise," Kathryn lied, hoping she'd reassured Sydney without her seeing right through the lie.

Sydney leaned in and kissed Kathryn on the lips. "You drive me nuts, you know that, right?"

Kathryn started to laugh, "Yes, I know."

"I love you, babe. I'll see you tonight," Sydney said as she turned to leave.

"Um."

"Oh, my God, you're going to miss Girls' Night Out?" Sydney threw her arms up sarcastically.

Kathryn blushed as a grin graced her lips. "We're supposed to get together over here tonight."

"And so it begins."

"Syd, don't try to make me feel bad."

"Fine, I won't. Call me, though. I want to know how much you *aren't* falling for her."

"Oh, fuck off," Kathryn said with a laugh as Sydney left the kitchen.

"'Bye, babe."

"'Bye." Kathryn heard the front door close. She tied her robe a little tighter, already nervous about her evening with Pam. She knew Sydney was right. She was falling for this woman. Hell, she had fallen for Pam the second she saw her that day in Skin. The fact that she was forming a friendship with Pam was shocking. Nothing that Kathryn wanted this fervently ever happened to her. That had to mean something. She had no idea what, though.

❖

Kathryn felt anxious the entire day. It would be the first time that Pam was at her place, so she felt like she needed to clean every inch of it. Even if she knew that they were only going to be watching a movie.

All she kept thinking about was her texting conversation with Pam the night before.

And her stupid *confession*.

And Pam's *response*.

It was so surreal and not at all what she had planned on happening.

Well, she did plan on it. But did she think it would actually happen? Hell no!

She knew she needed to put the brakes on. There was no good to be had from letting this whole thing get out of hand.

No good at all.

Except those lips. And that smile. And, God, that *body*. And that *hair*.

Kathryn was in so far over her head, it was absolutely ridiculous.

When seven o'clock rolled around, she was freshly showered with her hair pulled back into a braid, wearing yoga pants and a Chicago Blackhawks sweatshirt. She did not look cute at all. She made sure of it. She didn't even put makeup on. She was going for the whole "I don't give a shit" look. Hopefully, it wouldn't backfire.

Pam arrived bearing a twelve-pack of Goose Island 312 and a cinnamon sugar strudel. "It was the last one at Corey Brothers," she said with a small smile. "I hope you like it."

"How could anyone not like cinnamon and sugar?" Kathryn asked as she relieved Pam of the beer and opened the door for her to step inside.

"I'm not sure," Pam replied. "We'd seriously have to reevaluate our friendship if you didn't like it, though. So I'm glad that you do."

"Oh goodness, this is serious. I can see it now, 'An argument over cinnamon and sugar ruined our friendship.'"

"Right? That would be awful." Pam looked around at her surroundings. "Your place is great. I love these built-in bookshelves," she said as she motioned to the shelves along the left-hand side of the foyer. "The character in these older buildings is awesome."

"Why, thank you," Kathryn replied. "It really is an incredible house." They walked through the hallway toward the kitchen, and Kathryn pointed out the guest powder room, motioned up the stairs toward the three bedrooms, and then told Pam about the rooftop deck that wasn't usable this time of year, obviously, but was still pretty awesome.

"You'll have to take me up there," Pam said as she slid her coat and purse off and hung them on one of the center island stools before leaning against the counter.

"Oh, for sure." Kathryn handed an opened beer bottle to Pam and then took a long drink from her own bottle. She noticed that Pam's zip-up sweatshirt was an old Purdue one that probably had seen better days. The cuffs were frayed and ripped, and it made Kathryn's heart smile that Pam held on to something that clearly meant a lot to her. Kathryn reached out and touched the sleeve. "Worn this a couple times?"

Pam gave a hearty laugh. "A few," she replied through the laughter. "It's probably as old as you are."

"Funny!" Kathryn raised her beer bottle. She asked Pam how her day had been. Pam proceeded to tell Kathryn how she hadn't been able to sit still so she'd reorganized her closet, gone through a bunch of clothes, and made piles to donate. She'd made chicken stock and frozen it, but also made soup for the next couple of nights. Kathryn felt insanely guilty that the only productive thing she had done was not drive herself crazy with worry. That and she managed to pick movies for their movie night that would hopefully not bore Pam.

"So..."

"Yes?" Kathryn asked. She watched Pam's mannerisms, the way she was fidgeting with the beer label and the look of nervousness that had replaced the laughter in her eyes.

"Why don't you have a girlfriend?" Pam asked and then inhaled sharply. "I'm so sorry."

"Why are you apologizing?" Kathryn asked as she mirrored Pam and leaned against the opposite side of the counter.

"Because we're having a great conversation and I ruin it by asking stuff that is honestly not my business."

"But it is your business." Kathryn smiled. "You're my friend, Pam. Why shouldn't you be allowed to ask questions? Why wouldn't you deserve to know?"

Pam looked down at her sock-covered feet. "I don't know."

"Well, it's not a big deal anyway. I just don't have one."

Pam looked up at Kathryn. "Why?"

"Because I haven't been able to get close to anyone in a long time." Kathryn turned and busied herself with a bag of microwave popcorn. She honestly hated talking about why she didn't have a special person in her life. The whole story was not worth retelling or reliving. "It's just easier to not care, I guess."

"Wow."

Kathryn sighed. "Yeah, pretty pathetic, huh?"

"Not at all," Pam replied with a warm smile. "How many girlfriends have you had?"

"How much time do you have?"

Pam's laughter echoed throughout the kitchen. "That many, hmm?"

"Well, there've been a few." Kathryn looked up at the ceiling. She quickly did a tally in her head. "I've had five girlfriends."

"That's not bad. Any one-night stands?"

Kathryn almost choked on the swallow of beer she had in her mouth. She wiped her lips with the back of her hand and smiled. How in the world did she answer that? "One-night stands?"

"Yeah, y'know, take someone home, sleep with them, never talk to them again—one-night stands."

"I know what they are, Pam." Kathryn snorted. "Thank you for clarifying, though."

"Well? Inquiring minds want to know."

"Pam, honestly, why do you want to know?" She watched Pam shrug her shoulders. "I don't know. A few? There, are you happy?"

"Not really, but I'll take that answer. For now." Pam grinned when she saw Kathryn's face fall.

"Great," Kathryn said with an eye roll. She poured the freshly popped popcorn into a bowl and put it on the counter next to Pam. There was a part of Kathryn that wanted to be mad at Pam for standing in her kitchen and asking all of these questions. But an even bigger part of her wanted to savor every second, because these were the moments Kathryn wanted. She wanted to know Pam, and more importantly, she really wanted Pam to know *her.* It was frightening, of course, because Kathryn had made it her job to not let women get close to her. She didn't want the questions. She didn't want the heartache. But Pam was breaking through the self-built walls around Kathryn's heart, and all it was doing was making it harder and harder to tell herself to stop falling for this woman. "How about you?"

"I've never had a one-night stand. Or a girlfriend."

Kathryn stuck her tongue out as she threw a piece of popcorn at Pam. "You know what I meant!"

Pam was laughing as she picked up a handful of popcorn and started to eat it. "I only had Harold."

"No one before him?"

"Nope."

"And no one after him."

Pam shrugged. "I've never even been attracted to another man."

"Seriously?"

"As a heart attack," Pam replied. "I settled for what was in front of me."

"Do you ever regret that?"

"All the time. Except for—"

Kathryn noticed that Pam looked like she didn't think she should say whatever it was that she wanted to say. "What? Say it."

"I don't regret it when I think about how everything that has happened has led me here. To you. To our friendship or whatever it should be called."

"God," Kathryn breathed. In that moment, it took everything in her to not grab Pam and kiss her deeply.

Pam crossed her arms and looked down at the dark gray tile floor. "Kathryn, about your texts last night—"

Kathryn froze, and instant regret washed over her. "Can't we just pretend those didn't happen?"

"I can't," Pam said, barely above a whisper. "I can't just forget how they made me feel."

"They weren't supposed to make you feel anything," Kathryn lied. She wanted to fake being ill and tell Pam to leave.

"Well, they did make me feel something," Pam protested. "And you knew I would feel something."

Kathryn shook her head. "No, I didn't."

"Don't lie," Pam replied. She locked her eyes onto Kathryn's. "Do you care about me?"

"Jesus, Pam."

"Answer the question."

"Are you insane?" Kathryn placed her palms on the cold granite counter. "Do you really need to ask that?"

"No, I don't need to ask, but I want to hear you say it." Pam moved over to where Kathryn was standing. She gently touched the back of Kathryn's arm. "Tell me."

Kathryn could feel how close Pam's body was to her back. *This isn't happening. This can't be happening.* "Yes, Pam, I care about you. Way more than I should."

"Why?"

"Why do I care?"

"No," Pam said. "Why more than you should?"

Kathryn turned, slowly, so that she was facing Pam. There wasn't much of a height difference between the two women, so they were looking directly into each other's eyes. *God. Look at her.* That blond hair, that white shirt under that ratty zip-up sweatshirt, those beautiful breasts. Kathryn sighed as she tilted her head downward. "You know damn well why."

"Kath," Pam whispered. "Talk to me."

"I just," Kathryn said, her voice shaking, "I don't want to cross that line."

"Which line?"

"You know, the 'line,' the 'we're friends/we're more than friends' line." Kathryn tried to smile, to lighten the mood, but it wasn't happening. "It's me, though," she continued. "I don't ever realize how blurry it is until I'm right up on top of it, reaching across it, trying so very hard to not tackle you as I come charging over it."

"Ohhh." Pam smiled. "*That* line."

"Yeah, that line. And all I really want is a friendship, because I know that's all I can have, so I have to keep reminding myself of that." Kathryn made sure to stress the fact that she really was only in this for the friendship. Even though last night those texts said everything but that, and every last inch of her wanted more with Pam, she knew it was uncharted territory for her. Kathryn seriously didn't need to start a relationship with yet another woman who wasn't a lesbian. She wondered how long she could keep this charade up, though. Her feelings were real, but she felt like every time she turned around she was lying to Pam, which might have been to protect Pam, but it was only hurting her in the end.

"What if I told you to cross the line?"

"Pam," Kathryn started.

Pam swallowed. "What?"

"You aren't serious."

"I might be. I honestly don't know anymore."

"I mean, last night you said I'm not alone. What the hell does that mean?"

"It means everything you're feeling, I'm feeling it, too," Pam explained, her voice trembling.

Kathryn focused on Pam as she stood there, fear and desire clearly mixed in her expression. "What do *you* think is happening between us, Pam?" Kathryn closed the distance between them.

"I don't *know* what's happening," Pam answered. She had backed up so far that her back was now pressing against one of the kitchen walls.

"I'll tell you what's happening. I shouldn't have to keep telling you that all I want is a friendship, but I feel like every time we are together I have to somehow reassure you of that."

"Maybe you're just reassuring yourself," Pam offered.

Kathryn was crumbling like a weak foundation under Pam's persistence. Letting Pam know that she was right was not a good thing. "You aren't a lesbian, Pam," Kathryn said firmly.

Pam smiled and looked seductively at Kathryn. "How do you know?"

"This isn't a joke!"

Pam's smile faded quickly. "I never said it was a joke, Kathryn. I'm old enough to make my own decisions," she replied.

"You can't just *decide* to love another woman."

Pam slowly brought her hands up and placed them on Kathryn's cheeks. "It just *happens*, doesn't it? It just happens when you least expect it?" she asked, her voice so soft that it made Kathryn's knees weak.

Kathryn closed her eyes. "Why are you doing this?"

"Because."

"Pam—" Kathryn stopped as she opened her eyes. She reached up, put her hands over Pam's, and then moved them so she could press them against the wall above Pam's head. She then bent her head down within an inch of Pam's face. "You don't know what you're doing," she whispered.

"Yes, I do."

"Do you?" Kathryn asked as she bent her head a little farther down and brushed her lips against Pam's. She could smell the sweet smell of hops from the beer mingling with the scent of Pam's peppermint lip balm. Kathryn breathed in sharply and then took in the expression on Pam's face. *She wants this. This incredibly beautiful woman wants this.*

"Kathryn," Pam whispered hoarsely. "Kiss me, *please*."

Kathryn let go of Pam's hands and backed away from her. "I can't do this again."

"But this is what I want!" Pam pleaded.

"I...I can't," Kathryn stammered.

"God!"

Kathryn was stunned by the frustration and the tone in Pam's voice. "What?"

"Why can't you?" Pam asked, her voice dripping with irritation.

"I just can't, Pam."

"Y'know, you are driving me nuts! I'm practically begging you for this, and all you can do is stand there and tell me that you *can't.*" Pam moved away from Kathryn. "I'm just as scared as you are, Kathryn. Just as scared. Probably more, because as you've so delicately pointed out, I'm not a lesbian, and before you, I have never even considered this. But nevertheless, I want it. I have never wanted something or someone so much before in my entire life. Yet it's just dismissed because even though you know you want me, too, you just *can't*? And you think I should be okay with that answer? Are you fucking kidding me?" Pam turned and glared at Kathryn. "Why won't you just admit that you want this, too? That you want me so bad that it makes your hands ache and your stomach fill with butterflies? That when you see me it takes everything in you to not press me against that fucking wall and make out with me?"

"Pam, you don't understand. You'll never understand."

"Why won't you at least tell me? Give me a chance to understand instead of just dismissing my feelings!" Tears fell from Pam's eyes when she took a couple of steps closer to Kathryn.

Kathryn looked up at Pam, at her tears, at her eyes. Pam bit her lip. Her chin trembled. It was obvious that Pam didn't know what to do with her hands. They were clutching at her clothes one moment and then gripping her arms the next. Kathryn knew she was hurting Pam, and it was killing her inside. She looked down at Pam's feet. "I can't," she finally answered.

"Well." Pam frantically wiped away her tears. She took two steps and boldly grabbed her coat and purse from the kitchen counter stool. "Call me when you can."

And with that, she left, leaving Kathryn speechless.

CHAPTER NINE

So, I was standing there, getting ready to interview Bob Saget, when this moron comes charging up to me, and he says, 'Are you Mark Jones?' and I calmly reply with a simple nod."

Pam had no idea why she had let Judy talk her into a blind date with Mark Jones, but alas, there she was. Pam was upset about what had happened with Kathryn the weekend before and she needed to take her mind off it. And Judy's cure for all that ailed was a night out on the town and hopefully hot, sweaty sex at the end. Pam didn't operate like that, but Judy was persuasive. And Pam hated to admit it, but she was sort of hoping that maybe, just maybe, this man would make her realize she didn't really want a woman.

But as Pam sat across from Mark Jones at Murphy's Pub, watching him eat and drink and talk about himself, she vowed to never again let Judy talk her into anything, especially if it concerned a man and his penis.

Pam was praying that her cell phone would ring. Someone somewhere had to need her for something, right? Why hadn't Judy called her like they had discussed? What had happened to the escape plan? "But you won't need it," Judy had said smugly. If she only knew. Pam was getting angrier and angrier as she sat there. Judy was trying to sabotage her! That was the only explanation.

The restaurant was ridiculously dark and even more ridiculously loud, and thankfully it wasn't super obvious she was on a date. For some reason, she kept thinking everyone was staring at her, though.

But the booth was discreet with high walls, tucked away in a corner with only an electronic candle on the table top illuminating them.

"Pam?"

Pam jerked her head when she heard her name. "Huh?"

"Poignant reply."

Pam grimaced. "I'm sorry."

"Are you all right?" Mark asked. He really did have kind eyes, even if the rest of him made Pam's skin crawl.

"Yeah, I'm fine." Pam picked up her beer and drank two long gulps of the cold liquid.

"You don't seem fine. I may be extremely self-absorbed," he winked at her, "but I do know when someone isn't having a good time."

Pam scoffed, "Mark, I'm fine."

"Really? What's wrong?"

"Oh, my God, why do you want to know?" Pam asked, her voice filled with irritation. The last thing she wanted to do was talk about something important with quite possibly the most egotistical man alive. She was going to wring Judy's neck.

Mark smiled as he leaned back in his seat. He propped his arm over the back of the old booth, an air of arrogance rising off him. "There's someone else."

Pam felt her jaw drop a bit. "What?"

"Yes, there is someone else you're wishing that you could be with."

"I have no idea what you're talking about."

"Judy warned me."

Pam rolled her eyes, leaned her head to one side, and asked, firmly, "What did she say?"

"Just that you might seem a little distracted and to keep talking because eventually you'd come around."

Judy was definitely going to get it now. "Well, she's wrong. I'm not distracted."

"Pam, you haven't heard a word I've said."

He was right. She hadn't heard a word, just the part about Bob

Saget, and really, who wanted to listen to someone talk about *him*? Pam tried so hard to not break under the pressure. "Would you be terribly offended if we just called it a night?" she asked.

"Maybe we could pick it up another night?"

"Um, probably not. I'm sorry."

"I understand."

Pam looked down at her hands. "It's just that, well…" She took a deep breath. Maybe it wouldn't hurt to talk about it? "You were right. There *is* someone else. But it's not going to happen, which is why I'm upset. But I don't want to date you. I'm sorry."

"Why would you say that?"

"Because I honestly do not want to date you. Why else would I say that?"

Mark let out a deep laugh, one that made Pam's ears hurt. "No, no, that's not what I meant," he said, waving his hand. "I mean why do you think it's never going to happen with this person you like?"

For the first time that night he seemed like a human being. Pam shook her head, embarrassed. "Well, because I'm the one that walked out. It's just not going to happen. It can't happen."

"Do you want it to happen?"

Pam's gaze drifted upward to meet Mark's. *Yes.* She wanted something to happen. At this point she *needed* it to happen if for no other reason than her own sanity, so she nodded.

"I know I don't know you very well, Pam, and honestly, telling you to leave is only going to leave me sitting here alone, but if you really want to be with this person, you should probably go after him."

"Her," Pam corrected, her eyes not leaving Mark's. She was shocked when his facial expression didn't change.

"Then go after her. You only live once."

Those words instantly brought tears to Pam's eyes as she remembered Harold saying that as they white-water rafted for the first time six months before he passed away. She needed to talk to Kathryn. "You're absolutely right." She slid to the end of the booth. "I'm sorry."

Mark started to laugh as Pam tried to leave a twenty-dollar bill on the table. He pushed the money back into Pam's hand as he stood. "Don't worry, Pam. Good luck."

She waved at him as she ran out of the restaurant, praying the entire time that she knew what she was doing.

❖

Pam had only been to Kathryn's house the one time. She really had no right inviting herself over, especially since she had left the ball in Kathryn's court. And she hadn't heard from Kathryn, so obviously things were over. Whatever was there had to be over.

But as the days passed and the thoughts crept into Pam's mind about Kathryn's smile and her eyes and the gentle way she would laugh, Pam was finding that she *needed* Kathryn. Even if it meant traveling into completely uncharted territory, Pam knew she had to take that chance. And the need she felt drove her to do things that she had never fathomed.

"Oh, for Pete's sake, Pam," she said out loud. "You didn't drive to Wrigleyville so you could turn around and go home. Just ring the damn bell." She took a deep breath and very gently pushed the doorbell. She listened as it rang on the other side of the door. Everything after was completely silent. She pressed her hands on the glass next to the door and peered inside. She saw Kathryn's boots and coat lying on the floor next to the door. Her laptop bag was sitting next to the heap of winter clothing.

Pam looked up at the birdhouse that was hanging above her head. She remembered laughing with Kathryn one time over coffee about getting locked out of their houses. Pam told Kathryn about the frog statue next to her door. Kathryn told Pam about the birdhouse. Pam looked around her and then stood on her tiptoes. She pulled a key out of the birdhouse, glanced at the door and then at the key. "Screw it," she said with a brazen attitude as she slid the key into the lock. She walked into the house, closing the door behind her.

"Kathryn?" Pam called. "It's me." She scrunched her face at how stupid she felt. "I mean, it's Pam." She rolled her eyes at herself as she slid her snowy shoes off. She stepped over Kathryn's heap of clothing and looked around the house. There was a small lamp on in the study off to the left, but that seemed to be the only light on. She stepped a little closer to the stairs and stopped to listen. "Kath?" Still no answer. She slowly started to ascend the steps, carefully trying to make her presence known and to not scare Kathryn if she was home.

Pam stopped on the second floor and called Kathryn's name again. She could see Kathryn's room from the stairwell. The door was open slightly. Pam walked over and placed her hand on it, listening to it creak as it slowly swung the rest of the way open. Kathryn was lying in her bed, a bare foot hanging out from under the down comforter that was thrown over her. Pam heard a sniffle as she stood at the end of the bed and saw Kathryn move under the covers.

"Kathryn?" she asked, her voice barely audible.

Kathryn's voice was muffled as she moved slightly. "Oh, God."

"Kathryn, sweetie, what's wrong?" Pam's heart sank.

"You shouldn't be here."

Pam walked closer to the armchair that was near the bed and sat. Kathryn was facing away from her. "Okay." Pam sat in silence watching Kathryn's back for what seemed like a good ten minutes. She was worried.

"I'm sick," Kathryn finally said, breaking the silence.

"Kathryn, what do you mean?"

Kathryn rolled over, pulling the comforter with her. "I have the flu, Pam. You're gonna get sick if you stay here."

"Jesus, Kath, you can't say things like that!" Pam clutched at her chest and shook her head, anger flooding her features.

"Like *what*?"

"Like that! 'I'm sick,'" Pam mimicked. "What the hell? You realize that's how I found out about Harold? You have the *flu*. You aren't fucking dying, for Christ's sake." She took a deep breath and looked down at her feet. Her left leg was bobbing up and down, a common nervous reaction. "I'm sorry," Pam whispered. "But you can't do that to me."

Kathryn sniffled. "I thought you didn't say that word very often."

"Yeah, well, you pissed me off."

"Ditto," Kathryn whispered, a smile following. "Why are you here?"

"I wanted to see you," Pam said. "For some stupid reason."

"You did?"

"Yes." Pam tried to not let the sight of Kathryn being wrapped in a comforter like a burrito make her laugh. It was almost too adorable. "I was worried."

"Even after how I behaved the other night?"

"*Especially* after how you behaved the other night," Pam answered.

"You must like it when I play hard to get," Kathryn said in a joking tone.

"Actually," Pam said, "I must."

"Pam," Kathryn whispered. "You really shouldn't be here. You're gonna get sick."

"Don't tell me what to do," Pam responded as she gathered her hair and pushed it over her shoulder. She slid her parka off and draped it over the back of the armchair.

"What are you doing?"

"I'm going to lie down with you," Pam explained. "Stop protesting this and shut up." She crawled onto the bed and placed her head on the pillow next to Kathryn's.

"Fine," she said, finally relenting to Pam's demands.

Pam slid a hand between the covers and felt Kathryn's face. "Do you have a fever?"

"Your hand feels amazing," Kathryn whispered.

"You're very warm." Pam moved her hand and placed it on Kathryn's neck. "How high is it?"

"A hundred and one," Kathryn answered, her voice still a whisper. She closed her eyes and said quietly, "Listen, Pam, I'm so sorry about the other night."

"It's okay. I understand."

"You do?"

Pam smiled. "Believe it or not, I understand a lot more than you give me credit for."

The edges of Kathryn's mouth turned upward into a small smile. "Yeah?" she asked.

"Of course I do." Pam cleared her throat. "Harold had an affair. It takes a while to make yourself believe that everyone isn't out to get you."

"He had an affair?" Kathryn asked; her eyes shot open.

Pam took a deep breath and nodded. "With his twenty-three-year-old secretary." She let out a laugh. "On his five-thousand-dollar couch at his office. Where I walked in on them."

"Fuck," Kathryn whispered.

"It's just not something you forget or get over. Believe me, I know how hard it is to trust someone."

"I wish I would have known you then," Kathryn replied, her voice soft, sincere.

"So you could have said 'I told you so'?" Pam sighed, looked at Kathryn, and tried to remain strong.

"No," Kathryn said, "so I could have helped pick up the pieces."

"Kath—"

"I fear I would have just fallen for you even sooner," Kathryn murmured.

Pam's heart clenched in her chest. "Well, I fear I would have been the one having the affair if I knew you back then," she calmly explained, a smile following her words. When she saw tears forming in Kathryn's eyes, she changed the subject. "Guess where I was tonight."

"Hmm, let's see," Kathryn started. She eyed Pam and then leaned in closer to her. She breathed in deep and then exhaled as she pulled away. Pam's eyes were wide as Kathryn responded with "On a date?"

"What gave me away?"

"The makeup."

"Not the perfume?"

"I just wanted to see," Kathryn answered.

"See what?"

"If my memory had failed me."

"And did it?"

"Not at all."

Pam felt herself blush. The look on Kathryn's face was almost too much for her to handle. "Yeah, I was on a date."

"How'd it go?"

"Well, halfway through a conversation about Bob Saget, I got up and left."

"Are you serious?"

"Yes," Pam said, laughing right along with Kathryn. "It was terrible. I've never in my whole life been with someone so self-absorbed. I mean, Harold was bad, but this guy. I wanted to stick my fork in his side."

"Sounds romantic." Kathryn chuckled.

"Oh, yeah, *real* romantic. You've ruined me."

Kathryn's face fell in mock alarm. "What? *How?*"

"By being amazing," Pam whispered as she stroked Kathryn's cheek and ran her fingers down along her jawline. "I don't think I want anyone else."

"That's a pretty big declaration."

"You should feel really honored, then. I don't typically make big declarations."

"Oh, well then, I *do* feel honored."

"Good." Pam rested her hand on Kathryn's and lightly squeezed it. "Get some rest. I'm not going anywhere."

Kathryn did as she was told and closed her eyes. Pam's heart was smiling as she watched Kathryn drift to sleep. It wasn't exactly how she planned on spending her evening, but it was definitely acceptable.

CHAPTER TEN

Pam pulled down a face wash. "Our new line of cleansers is absolutely amazing. I've been using this particular one for the past month, and I can totally tell a difference in how my skin looks and feels."

"Wow, really?"

Pam nodded at the customer she was talking to. "Absolutely. I wash morning and night with this, moisturize with this—" Pam saw Kathryn as she walked into the store. A smile spread across her lips when their eyes met from across the store.

The customer looked at Pam. "And then what?"

Pam snapped her head back toward the customer and laughed. "Oh my gosh, I'm sorry. I zoned out for a moment there."

The customer smiled. "It's okay, dear. It happens all the time to me."

"Hi," Pam said after she finished with the customer and made her way over to Kathryn. She touched Kathryn on the back of the arm.

"Hey there," Kathryn replied. "How has your day been?"

"Oh, all right, I guess. It suddenly took a turn for really great, though." Pam looked down at the ground. She was flirting like a high-schooler, but at the same time, she couldn't fight off her blushing mechanism. She often wondered who this person was that she turned into around Kathryn.

"Can you get away for lunch? Or coffee? I can get something for you so you don't have to waste time standing in line."

"It wouldn't be wasting time," Pam said quietly.

"You know what I mean."

Pam looked around. "What time is it, anyway?"

Kathryn reached down and put her hand on Pam's wrist. She gently lifted Pam's hand up while tilting her watch so she could see it. "It's four thirty." She breathed in deeply. "God, you are so beautiful."

Pam could tell that her smile was more than likely as big as it could be. She didn't know how to respond, though. She always found herself speechless when Kathryn complimented her. It was as if everything in her body momentarily swooned, especially her speech capabilities. She put her hand on Kathryn's arm again. "Let me go tell Abby that I'm going to lunch. I'll be right back." She rushed toward the back of the store and into the employees' lounge. "Abby?"

"So that's Kathryn?" Abby asked as she poked her head around the lockers.

Pam smiled. "Yes."

Abby leaned over and looked in the little mirror that was on the side of one of the lockers. She quickly fluffed her short, black hair before she turned around and said, "She seems very nice."

"Yes, she is."

Abby cleared her throat. "She's been in here a number of times recently."

"Yeah, she has." Pam didn't know what else to say. She surely couldn't deny it. Abby kept track of customers like they were her children. All the employees teased her, saying that if she started charting visits, none of them would be surprised. Pam took her purse out of her locker and shut the door. She clocked out and then looked over at Abby. "I'm going to lunch."

"Pam?"

Pam started to laugh. "Yeah?"

"How come you've not introduced us to her?"

"Because you're normally not around when she's in the store," Pam answered quickly. Almost too quickly.

"Uh-huh." Abby took a couple of steps closer to Pam and leaned against the lockers. "She's a newer friend, right?"

Abby's cute personality was hard to ignore. It didn't matter what she asked a person, she almost always got the answer she was looking for. She batted those eyelashes, flashed that grin, and voilà—the answer was delivered on a silver platter. Thank goodness Pam was impervious to Abby's devices.

"You know, she's not a scarf or a new pair of shoes. I didn't just purchase her at Nordstrom or something."

"You know what I meant, Pam." Abby reached up and fixed a piece of Pam's hair. "Does she work around here? She seems so familiar. I swear I've seen her somewhere before and I just can't place it," Abby explained.

"Well," Pam said as she hung up her apron on the outside hook on her locker, "she has a movie review show."

Abby's face lit up. "Oh yes, I remember now. *Windy City Now!* That's a great show."

"Do you want her autograph?" Pam asked sarcastically. Abby stuck her tongue out at Pam as she left the staff lounge. "I'll be back in a bit." What in the world was the inquisition all about?

She took a deep breath and quickly located Kathryn at the front of the store. She was standing by the doorway, leaning against the wall, one leg crossed in front of the other. Pam took in the view. Kathryn wearing heels and tight black pants was always a welcome sight, but today her heels were red and her pants were extra tight and she had on a vest with a loose-fitting skinny black tie. It was almost too much to handle. Not to mention the fact that her hair was down and wavy and flowing and— *Jesus. Get your shit together, Pam.*

She tried to shake the deep red out of her cheeks as she approached Kathryn. "Ready?" she asked as she put her hand on Kathryn's back.

"You don't want me to go get it first?"

"Nope, we're fine. I can take an hour today, no worries."

❖

Kathryn could barely see straight. She wanted to ask Pam if she knew what she was doing. This woman was playing footsies with her. And it had catapulted Kathryn into shock. *Chill out, Kathryn. Chill the fuck out.* Everything that was happening was exactly what she wanted. But it was going to be hard getting used to getting what she wanted. No other woman had ever been able to render her practically speechless the way that Pam so expertly did. Kathryn hated to admit it, but a part of her was very happy Pam had mastered the feat.

"So," Pam started. She picked up her Diet Coke and sucked gently on the straw. "My best friend wants to meet you."

Kathryn laughed. "Why?"

"I'm not sure why."

"Pam," Kathryn said with a grin.

"What?"

"I know you're lying. Just tell me why."

Pam shook her head. "She wants to make sure you're not going to hurt me."

Kathryn's eyes grew large. "What? *Why?*"

"You have to understand, Kath." Pam paused. "She has been my best friend for twelve years. She has been through a lot of shit with me. I think she just wants to make sure that you're an okay person with whom I am spending my time."

"Ohhh, okay. So she's, like, your mother?"

Pam started to laugh. "Exactly."

"Got it," Kathryn said through her laughter. "Okay, when should we get together?"

"Can you tomorrow? I'm off. We can meet at Water Tower Place on Michigan Avenue." Pam leaned forward. "And then we can go back to your place afterward and watch a movie or whatever."

Kathryn stared at Pam over her forkful of rice. "Sounds perfect."

"Then it's a date."

CHAPTER ELEVEN

S o." Pam leaned back on the bench in the middle of the crowded Water Tower Place shopping mall and continued to people-watch to keep her mind occupied. As usual, there were quite a few tourists and fancy rich people out shopping in the middle of the day. The stores were all decked out in autumn decorations even though winter had arrived with full force, and the mall itself had wreathes complete with different-colored leaves hanging from the faux lampposts.

Judy had not stopped staring at Pam for the past ten minutes.

"You have to stop staring at me like that." Judy had bugged her just enough that she finally relented and told Kathryn to meet them for lunch. She could tell that Kathryn wasn't thrilled about the idea, but she also knew that at this point it was inevitable that they would start introducing each other to the important people in their lives. The only issue with introducing her to Judy was that her dear best friend had already come to her own conclusions about the relationship. And it was honestly a little frustrating.

"What? I didn't even say anything!"

"I know, but I can tell what you're thinking."

"How?" Judy huffed.

"Because I've known you for twelve years. And I can read you like a freaking book."

"Okay, then, what am I thinking?"

Pam laughed as she ran her fingers through her hair. "You're thinking that I'm nervous. You're thinking that this woman is just a big lesbian that wants to jump my bones. You're thinking that—" Pam stopped talking when she saw Kathryn approaching. "There she is."

"Where?"

"I was right about all of that, wasn't I?" Pam asked as she eyed Judy.

"Yes and no. Now, which one is she?"

"She's walking toward us."

"*Judy?*"

"Oh my God, Katie!" Judy jumped up and ran over to Kathryn.

Pam's eyes almost bugged out of her head. She stood as she watched the exchange between the two women.

"What are you—" Judy stopped herself and glanced between Pam and Kathryn. "Wait. *You're* Kathryn?"

Pam watched as Kathryn swallowed what seemed to be a giant lump in her throat.

Kathryn bounced on her toes. "Um, yeah, I guess I am."

Pam could feel her mouth hanging open. "You two know each other?"

"Um, yeah. Katie and I worked—" She cut herself off and looked at Kathryn. "I can't believe that *you* are the woman that Pam can't stop talking about."

"Small world," Kathryn said with an uncomfortable laugh. She motioned between herself and Judy. "We used to work together."

Judy shook her head, a laugh spilling from her. "I am just shocked."

"That makes two of us," Pam commented, sarcasm dripping from her words. Jealousy washed over her as she watched Kathryn and Judy's interaction. It was clear something was amiss, but Pam could not put her finger on it. "Well, should we go?" She took a couple steps in the direction of the restaurant she had picked. "Food. This way. Come on, you two."

As the three women walked toward the Mediterranean restaurant, Kathryn wrapped her hand around Pam's forearm and pulled her closer. "Quit worrying," she whispered into Pam's ear. "I'll explain about Judy."

Their faces were only an inch apart. "You bet your ass you will," Pam said boldly. No way she was going to let her out of this without some serious explaining.

Okay, so maybe there was a reason to be jealous. The chemistry between Judy and Kathryn was ridiculous. Pam was getting more and more suspicious as she sat there sharing small plates of dolmades, spanakopita, and chicken shawarma with Judy and Kathryn. Or was she just incredibly envious that Judy had known Kathryn longer than she had? Either way, she was mad at herself for letting whatever link these two women shared bother her. Pam heard a lull in the conversation. She looked from Kathryn to Judy to her plate of food and then back to the two women. She was so irritated she could barely eat.

"So, how do you two know each other again?" Pam dropped the question and sat back a little in her chair. She watched Judy's eyes as they flitted over to Kathryn, who was clearly uncomfortable.

"Well, I worked at the radio station with Judy for about two years," Kathryn replied. Pam wanted to say she heard a quiver in Kathryn's voice, but she knew she was just being hypervigilant now. Pam kept her eyes glued to Judy, though, watching for some sort of sign as to what the hell was going on.

"Two and a half," Judy corrected her, with a hint of sadness.

"*That* long, eh?" Kathryn's voice was definitely different.

Pam clenched her fists under the table. "You seem to know each other fairly well," she said coolly.

Kathryn's eyes were wet, far too wet to be anything but the formation of tears.

Judy motioned at the waiter for the check. "Well, I'll get lunch." She pulled a credit card from her purse, never making eye contact with Pam. Or with Kathryn.

And that was when Pam realized what had happened between the two women. Pam abruptly slid her chair out and stood. She could feel bile rising in the back of her throat. She was getting ready to lose what little she'd eaten of her lunch all over the table.

"I'm going to the restroom." She rushed toward the back of the restaurant and the door that led outside. The cold air hit her like an answered prayer. She took a deep breath and tried her hardest to not let the tears and the vomit come all at once. But as she exhaled, she knew she couldn't hold it in any longer. It hit like a wave. She bent over and retched and cried and cursed for even caring.

When she was finished and had composed herself as much as possible in the frigid air, she pulled the door open and made her way to the bathroom, where she tried to finish pulling herself together. She wiped her mouth with a paper towel, washed her hands, looked in the mirror. She wanted to cry all over again. But why? Did any of what happened between Kathryn and Judy really matter?

Pam closed her eyes and again took in a very deep breath. She knew all of this was too good to be true. She just knew it.

Kathryn watched Pam almost run away from the table. Her heart was in her throat. She could not fucking believe this was happening. Here she was with the woman she was falling in love with, sitting across the table from the woman who had shattered her heart into a million pieces. It was a scene right out of a movie. A movie Kathryn swore she would never star in. Yet here she was, and she knew every line of the script.

"What the *hell* are you doing?"

Kathryn heard Judy's hissing question and she almost stood and walked away, but of course, because she was so fucking stubborn sometimes, she engaged. "What the *hell* are you talking about?"

"You know damn well what I'm talking about. *Pam?*" Judy jerked her thumb toward the back of the restaurant.

Kathryn's laugh was so loud that it almost sounded like a bark. "You have a lot of nerve."

"But she's *my* best friend!"

"Judy, it's really not your call here." Kathryn leaned back in her chair, a confident air surrounding her.

"It *is* my call when it concerns Pam. She's my responsibility."

"No, she's not. She's a grown-ass woman." Kathryn crossed her arms. "Besides, I didn't want a relationship with her. *I* wanted a friendship. Why is it so hard to believe that the one that wanted more wasn't me?"

"You mean she's the one that wanted more? She actually asked you for *more*?"

"Does it really matter, Judy?" Kathryn replied. She made sure to make her voice sound as irritated as possible even though she was practically dying inside. Everything about this conversation was making her want to get drunk and forget about life for a very, very long time.

"You can't do this, Katie. She just lost her husband. You can't waltz in here and make her happy and then hurt her."

"Oh, you bitch," Kathryn gasped. She knew it was futile to try and control her anger too much. "*You're* the one that hurt *me*! So don't even—"

Judy reached across the table to try and put her hand on Kathryn's arm, but Kathryn pulled away. "Don't," she said under her breath. "You need to step back and realize that this is none of your *fucking* business." She took a breath and hoped that she sounded convincing. She looked down at her lap and tried to settle down. "I can't believe *you're* the spastic lunatic that made Pam realize that I was gay."

Judy cocked her head. "You slip her your phone number on her tip? I mean, come on, Katie. That's the oldest trick in the book."

"Oh, yeah?"

"Yes. I can't believe she's falling for you."

Kathryn leaned forward and propped her elbows on the table. She raised her eyebrows. "*You* fell for me."

"Yeah, well, don't expect everything to be as easy with her."

Kathryn rolled her eyes. "Oh, yeah? Why?"

"You think you won't have any competition. Like it'll just be smooth sailing for you and your new crush. Well, good luck with that." Judy cocked an eyebrow and went to stand. "Tell Pam I'll talk to her tonight."

Judy walked away just as Pam emerged from the bathroom looking like she had seen better days.

"Where did Judy go?"

"She said she would talk to you tonight."

"Yeah, well, you and I have some serious talking to do. So you can either come to my house or I can go to yours. But," Pam glared at Kathryn, her eyes clearly red from crying, "we are far from okay."

And with those words, she turned and marched out of the restaurant, Kathryn following behind like a lost puppy dog.

❖

"Hold on one second."

Kathryn was sitting on her couch looking at Pam as she continued to walk back and forth between the bay window and the fireplace. She could tell that Pam was freaking out. She had been silent since they left the restaurant and walked to the train station together. During the entire ride to Kathryn's brownstone Pam hadn't said a word. Kathryn wasn't sure what to do. She kept trying to swallow the lump that had lodged in her throat the minute she saw Judy before lunch, but she was quickly learning that the lump was there to stay.

"Whenever you're ready," she said.

"So, you're telling me that—" Pam stopped, her back to Kathryn. She pushed her hands through her hair and pulled down on it. "I can't even."

Kathryn crossed her legs and bent her head down. She was waiting for Pam to explode.

"You and her…"

Kathryn continued to sit there silently.

"God, I think I need to sit down," Pam said through labored breathing.

Kathryn started to stand to help Pam, but she wouldn't let her.

"Don't!" Pam exclaimed through her breathing. "I'm *fine*." She walked over to the overstuffed armchair next to the television stand and sat, her back ramrod straight. "You and Judy," she said. She brought her eyes up to look at Kathryn and then quickly looked away again. "I knew something wasn't right when Judy kept eyeing you over lunch. I mean, I knew she wanted to get a good look at you, but *dammit*. I just, I never thought in a million years that this was the reason." Pam paused. "When did this happen?"

Kathryn cleared her throat. "Four years ago."

"When Judy and Tom were going to get a divorce," Pam whispered. "How long did it go on?"

"A little over a year." Kathryn couldn't take her eyes off Pam. She was hoping with everything in her body that the change in Pam's tone was a good sign.

"She almost left Tom for you."

Kathryn nodded slowly in agreement.

"Why didn't she?"

"The kids," Kathryn easily answered. "And maybe Tom? I'm not sure. But I know it was the kids. She didn't want to leave them even though I would have..." Kathryn's voice trailed off. She shrugged. "It doesn't matter. It just didn't work."

"I remember her talking about you. Well, I didn't know it was a woman. I was fairly certain it was a man." A smile spread across Pam's lips. "She was so happy then. Even through all the drama in her marriage. She was *happy*."

"It didn't work out for a reason, Pam."

"Did you love her?"

Kathryn nodded.

"Do you still?"

Kathryn shook her head.

"She's the reason, isn't she?"

"That I don't let myself get close to anyone?" Kathryn didn't need a response. She knew that was what Pam was asking. "But I'm not sad it happened anymore. Even though it hurt and I was a hot mess for a long time, I'm glad it happened." She nudged Pam's shoulder. "So, are you too freaked out to like me anymore?"

Pam moved her hand and intertwined her fingers with Kathryn's. "Is it weird that I like you even more now?"

Kathryn wondered if Pam could hear her heart beating. It sounded like a bass drum pounding inside her chest. "Sort of," she whispered, a smile on her lips. Kathryn let the weakness in her knees ground her. "I'm sorry that you had to find out this way."

Pam smiled. "It wasn't exactly a good introduction."

"So," Kathryn looked away from Pam, "that picture of the legs?"

Pam started to laugh. "Yes, those are Judy's legs."

"I thought they looked familiar." Kathryn felt a smack across her arm, and she let out a laugh. "Hey, I was just kidding."

"You'd better be," Pam said. A silence fell between them.

Kathryn reached up with her free hand and gently pushed Pam's silky blond hair behind her ear. "This is going to change everything," she whispered.

"I'm counting on it," Pam replied quietly.

Kathryn leaned forward as Pam's eyes slid closed, and she gently pressed her lips to Pam's. As first kisses go, which sadly Kathryn had a lot of experience with, it was the most amazing one she had ever experienced. She hated how clichéd it sounded to say she felt the hair stand up on the back of her neck and her toes curl, but fuck, those things actually happened. Kathryn knew the instant Pam's lips parted and the slickness of Pam's tongue pressed against her that this was going to be a kiss she would remember for the rest of her life.

And as she heard Pam's heavy breathing and the mumbled *oh, my God* between the kisses, she was positive Pam felt the same way.

Chapter Twelve

P am knelt in front of the fireplace at her house. She picked up the poker and gently moved a spark that had popped out back into the fire. Judy sat on the floor, leaning against the ottoman where she normally camped out and drank wine.

"Thanks for coming over."

Judy tilted her head to one side. "We needed a girls' night."

Pam nodded and settled in against the opposite couch. She slowly glanced over at Judy and studied her best friend's features, her nose, her eyes, the curve of her lips. She hadn't been able to stop thinking about what happened between Kathryn and Judy, and it was starting to drive her insane. Pam wanted some answers. The only problem was she had no idea what she was curious about. Did she want to know about Judy's side of the story? Or was she really interested in finding out more about what was going on in Judy's head about Kathryn? Pam had been best friends with this woman for twelve years, and she never once had an idea that maybe Judy liked women. She let out a soft laugh as she pulled her gaze away from Judy.

"What are you thinking about?"

"Nothing," Pam quickly replied.

"Oh, whatever! You're not allowed to say that to me."

Pam cocked an eyebrow. "It's *my* house," she said, sticking her tongue out to drive her point home.

"Just tell me."

"You really want to know?" Pam asked, and she watched as

Judy shrugged. "I was thinking about you and Kathryn," she said matter-of-factly. "Or Katie, or whatever *you* call her."

"Oh."

"Yeah." Pam pulled her legs up to her chest and wrapped her arms around them. "Can I ask how it happened?"

Judy lowered her head. "Do you really want to know?" she asked, a heavy sigh showing her lack of enthusiasm.

"Well, not if you're going to act like that," Pam answered with a huff.

"Pam, it's not that I don't want to tell you."

"You're a hypocrite, you know that?"

"Why? Because I told you to watch out for this woman? You realize I said all of that because I've been down the *exact* same path you're heading down. Why does that make me a hypocrite?" Judy set the glass of wine down and sighed. "I had to interview her."

Pam pulled her legs into her chest and propped her chin on her knees. "Why?"

"I was on the hiring committee to find a new reporter."

Pam listened as Judy described a young Kathryn, *Katie*, fresh out of college, eager and ready to take on the world. She had interned at a big station in Milwaukee, so she had the background that the radio station was looking for. She was fierce, animated, assertive. She was Judy fifteen years ago. Pam's eyes traveled over to Judy as she talked. She watched as Judy reached up and pushed her bangs away from her forehead.

"We hit it off right away. I liked her style. I liked her portfolio. I liked the way she presented herself, which, by the way, was as Katie Hawthorne, *not* Kathryn." A smile appeared on Judy's lips. "She was a great hire. And I told the news directors that. So they hired her.

"Then I was appointed as her mentor, which I was totally okay with because we were so much alike. I passed down my very first antique tape recorder to her. Told her to keep it for good luck. And she did keep it. She carried it in her bag with her at all times." Judy's eyes moved from the fireplace to her hands. Pam noticed they were trembling.

"She asked me out for coffee. Then I asked her out for lunch. And then it escalated to dinner on our late nights together." Judy paused and gently touched her fingers to her mouth. "She kissed me one night, in the restroom, backed me up against the paper towel holder and kissed me like I had never been kissed before. Freaked me the hell out."

Pam's heart felt like it was being smashed inside the walls of her chest. "I'm sure it did," she whispered as she tried to remember how to breathe.

"Yeah, it definitely did. Needless to say, I didn't sleep a wink that night. I tossed and turned. Tom tried to have sex with me to make me sleepy. I tried telling him that sex makes *him* sleepy, not me. All it did was make me—" Judy stopped.

"Make you what?"

"Make me want her to kiss me again."

Pam felt her entire body heat up as she remembered the night before, when she and Kathryn had made out for hours and hours on Kathryn's couch. She knew exactly what Judy was talking about. The need to feel Kathryn's lips again was so real.

Judy covered her face with her hands and breathed out. "Katie kissed me more times in the two weeks that followed than Tom had kissed me in our entire marriage. And every single time we kissed, it was amazing. And every single time she touched me, my body would overheat. And every single time she would look at me, I would melt into a puddle." She paused again, her eyes not making contact with Pam's. "We made love for the first time on my fortieth birthday."

"Oh, well, shit. No wonder you didn't want to go out that night!" Pam laughed as she stretched her legs out. Judy mimicked Pam's laughter, which oddly made the conversation more tense instead of more relaxed. Pam wanted so badly to ask how it was. She wanted to know. She needed to know. But the idea of Judy and Kathryn doing things to each other's bodies...The thought was making her skin want to crawl right off her body. And before she knew it, she was opening her mouth and asking, "How was it?"

Judy didn't hesitate to answer with, "*Amazing.*" A look washed over Judy's face when she locked her eyes on Pam's. "She knew exactly what I wanted…how hard I wanted it…how fast I wanted it…how long I wanted it. I've never felt so completely loved before."

"Even now?"

"Especially now," Judy replied.

Pam kept looking at Judy. "You almost left Tom for her."

"I had my bags packed, Pam," Judy said quietly as she looked up. "They were *packed*. I had written the kids a letter. I didn't even write Tom one. I was so ready to get out of that marriage. And, God," Judy's eyes were moist with unshed tears, "and away from the kids."

It was breaking Pam's heart to see her best friend so emotional over someone she, too, was feeling so many emotions for. She scooted herself over to Judy's side and patted Judy's leg. "What made you change your mind?"

"Josh."

Pam smiled. Josh was Judy's middle child and definitely a big mama's boy.

"I was standing in the middle of my bedroom, looking around, wondering if I had forgotten anything, when he came into my room and hugged me. For absolutely no reason whatsoever, he just wrapped his little arms around my legs and hugged me."

Judy chuckled before she explained how she had almost collapsed from the emotion. Five minutes earlier Judy had been ready to leave her entire family. She was going to walk away from sixteen years of marriage and the kids, the three people she seemed to love more than herself, which was saying a lot when it came to Judy. It was so unreal, watching Judy talk about this time in her life.

Pam knew that if she had been faced with leaving Harold for Kathryn she wouldn't have hesitated. The thought rolled through her mind that maybe it wasn't such a bad thing that she'd never had kids.

"I started sobbing," Judy whispered through tears. "Y'know when you're crying so hard you can't breathe?"

Pam nodded. "The kind when you can barely talk?"

"I'm sure I scared the shit out of Josh." Judy laughed through her tears. "Later that night I called Katie and told her that I couldn't do it. I was sitting on the floor of my closet crying my eyes out on the phone with her, wondering if my heart would ever stop aching. We were both crying. I felt like I was dying. Katie seemed to take it fairly well. I think she knew I wouldn't go through with it. She had told me so many times that she was ready and willing to be with me *and* the kids."

"I know," Pam commented. She knew exactly where Judy was going with that last sentence. Telling people that you're a lesbian can't be easy. And then telling the kids? Pam felt her stomach tie into a knot.

"She ended up transferring from radio to the newspaper and now, as you know, she's a movie critic. It was a good move for her." Judy tilted her head and looked into Pam's eyes. "Why are you so interested in this?"

"Because it was a huge part of your life and you never shared it with me," Pam replied, hoping that Judy believed her.

Judy smiled. "Nice try."

"What?"

"Pam."

"*What?*"

"What is happening between you and her?"

Pam looked away from Judy. "Nothing."

"Mark told me that you left dinner halfway through."

"How did you find out—"

"He told me the next day. I just didn't talk to you about it. I wanted to meet this girl and was shocked out of my mind when it was *Katie*."

"I know you're going to tell me not to do this," Pam said. "But it's not going to matter what you say or how many times you tell me to stop."

"Pam—"

"No, Judy." Pam pulled air into her lungs and looked at Judy. "We kissed. And I loved every second of it."

"Pam."

"I went home with her after we all went out for lunch," Pam said as she motioned to Judy. Pam's entire body was on fire, including her face, which she could tell was beet red.

"Pam, what the hell are you doing?"

"You're not even going to ask me how it was?" Pam was shocked. Judy was supposed to want details just like *she* had wanted details. Judy wasn't supposed to be the sane one in this situation!

"I *know* how it was. Were you not listening for the last hour? I've been there, I've done that, and a hell of a lot more times than once. And in that same *fucking* bed!" Judy looked around the room, and then a chuckle escaped from her throat. It sounded almost maniacal. "What the fuck are you thinking, Pam?"

"What do you mean?"

"You know damn well what I mean." Judy took a deep breath. "She's a *lesbian*."

"Oh, really? I had no idea," Pam replied sarcastically.

Judy rolled her eyes. "No, Pam. You don't understand. She is *gay*. She wants a relationship with another woman. You, on the other hand, are not gay. You want a relationship with a man."

"Judy, do you think that I'm stupid?"

"I'm starting to wonder."

"Shut up. I'm not. I understand what I'm doing."

"Do you?"

"Yes! Why is it so hard for you and Kathryn to realize that I'm not two years old? In my forty years on this planet I have developed an ability to make my own choices. To follow my heart if I want to. And right now, I want to follow my heart on this one. Just because I was a little hesitant doesn't mean that I have absolutely no idea what I'm doing. I realize that she's gay. I realize that my having feelings for her could mean that I'm gay. Or bisexual. But you know what? I don't give a damn. I *like* being with her. And I don't want to stop just because it means that I'm a lesbian."

"I hope you are prepared for this."

"Prepared for *what*? Why do you think there are always consequences?"

"Because there *are* always consequences!" Judy huffed.

"Judy," Pam started, followed by a heavy sigh. She looked

down at her lap as she pulled her hair over her shoulder and tied it up with a hairband.

"Pam, I've been there! I know what happens."

"Yeah, Judy. You know what happens. You blew your one chance to be completely happy. Good job." Pam gave Judy a mocking thumbs-up.

"Oh, shut up, Pam."

Pam leaned forward. "I was unhappy for most of my life with a man that I didn't love. I was treated like an employee rather than a wife. I've learned to not expect much from other people. But Kathryn?" Her mind flashed back to the night before, when Kathryn had told her how beautiful she was between their kisses. She could almost feel Kathryn's lips, her hands, her breath. Her palms immediately started to get clammy.

She sighed. "I trust her."

"I get it."

"Then I need you to trust *me*," Pam urged.

Judy still looked as if she was going to cry. "I do trust you, Pam," she whispered, tears starting to fall from her eyes. "I trust you more than I trust myself."

"Good." Pam smiled as she leaned in and kissed Judy on the cheek. "Thanks for looking out for me, though."

Judy wiped at the tears on her face and shook her head. "You are infuriating," she whispered through her tears and a small laugh.

CHAPTER THIRTEEN

On Pam's next day off from Skin, she decided it was time to start decorating for Christmas. Thanksgiving was right around the corner, and according to her coworkers, her schedule was only going to get crazier and busier. She thought she would take advantage of her good mood, one that was absolutely Kathryn's fault. Before Kathryn happened, Pam figured she wouldn't want to decorate for Christmas. She'd known it would be too hard after losing Harold.

And then Kathryn waltzed into her life and quite literally changed every single thing about it, including her desire to celebrate the holidays.

As the days passed, one by one, Pam found herself feeling better—revived, as if the hole that was left empty after years and years of a loveless marriage was healing. There was a part of her that wanted to blame it all on Kathryn. After all, she was the reason Pam felt like getting up every morning. But Pam also knew that none of this would have happened had Judy not pushed her to take advantage of the opportunity.

Pam turned around and observed the pile of boxes she had taken out of the basement closet. "Overdo it much?" Her words echoed through the empty basement. She heard Dorothy's tags jingle as the dog stood and walked over to the stairs. "What is it, girl?" Pam listened and heard the doorbell ring.

"What would I do without you?" she asked Dorothy as they raced up the stairs and approached the front door. Pam peered out the peephole, immediately feeling her stomach fill with butterflies. She quickly pushed back the errant strands of hair that had fallen from her messy ponytail before she opened the door. She smiled when she saw Kathryn standing there, red cheeks and eyes bright.

"Now, this is a pleasant surprise. What brings you to the suburbs?"

Kathryn chuckled as Dorothy ran outside to greet her and then bolted for the fresh snow. She leaned against the door frame. "Truthfully? I wanted to see you." She smiled, her hands shoved into the pockets of her parka.

Pam pulled her wool cardigan tighter around her body. She held her hand out for Kathryn to take. "You're all snowy," she said.

Kathryn walked inside, Dorothy right behind her, and Pam closed the door behind them. Pam took Kathryn's wool cap, then unzipped her parka.

"I hope I'm not bothering you," Kathryn said in a soft voice.

"Kathryn." Pam laughed as she hung up the hat and coat on the rack next to the door. She bent down and dried the snow off Dorothy, who was patiently waiting next to Kathryn. "You have never bothered me," she said before standing. "Now, I hope you aren't completely turned on by my amazing hairstyle and complete lack of makeup." Pam crossed her arms over her chest. "I clearly wasn't expecting company."

"You look adorable," Kathryn replied as she took a step closer to Pam. "I like this look."

"You're a great liar." Pam looked down at her feet with a smile far too large to hide. And before Pam knew it, she was up against the wall in the foyer, Kathryn's lips pressed firmly against hers. Pam felt Kathryn's hands move from her face to her sides and then to her backside, and then the kiss deepened.

Pam found herself not wanting to stop, not wanting to pull away, not wanting to live her life without this feeling. It was all too fast for her. But at the same time, it wasn't fast enough. When she finally parted from Kathryn, breathless and very aroused, she whispered, "Wow."

"You were saying?"

"I have no idea what I was saying," she mumbled, kissing Kathryn between her words. "No idea at all."

Kathryn slid her hands down Pam's backside and gripped her ass. "I can barely handle this without wanting to rip your clothes off," she whispered against Pam's lips. "But I know neither one of us wants to rush this."

Pam agreed before kissing Kathryn again. "I want you to know that this is taking everything in me to stop, though."

"I'll take as much as you give me."

Pam leaned her head back, exposing her neck, delighting in the feel of Kathryn's lips as they latched onto the soft skin there. "God, I feel like a teenager again. Except this time, I'm actually enjoying it."

Kathryn slid her tongue down Pam's neck to her bare collarbone, which showed from underneath her white V-neck T-shirt. She placed a kiss there and then said, "We can make out in my car, too, if you want. Really make it like high school."

Pam slid her hand under Kathryn's chin and guided her face so they were looking at each other.

Kathryn smiled. "What?"

Pam's heart was clenched in the walls of her chest. All she wanted to do was tell this girl that she was falling in love with her. But she froze. "Nothing," she replied, her voice cracking. She leaned forward and kissed Kathryn again.

"So, do you miss him?"

"Sometimes." Pam looked up at the ceiling of the living room. "Other times, I'm happy he's no longer suffering."

"Cancer is a real bitch."

Pam nodded and then felt Kathryn's hand cover hers as they curled up on the floor of the living room in front of the warm fire. Their heads were propped on pillows, they were two glasses into a second bottle of wine, and Pam's decorating plans had fallen by the wayside.

Kathryn rolled onto her side and said quietly, "You know it's okay to cry in front of me, right?"

"I don't like crying about him," Pam whispered.

"I know," Kathryn replied, "but if you ever need to, you can."

"I don't need to." A small smile spread across Pam's lips. "You have helped with that, you know?"

"Well." Kathryn let out a soft chuckle. "Look at how awesome *I* am."

Pam mimicked Kathryn's position on the floor. "You're *amazing.*"

"Pam—"

"No, Kathryn. You are." Pam pushed Kathryn's dark, wavy hair behind her right ear. "I look forward to every minute we spend together. And I dread when you tell me that you'd better head home. It's so incredible to finally understand what it feels like to want someone else so badly that it makes my insides ache. Even my *hands* ache when I think about you."

"I never thought this would happen with you, Pam," Kathryn commented tenderly.

"I'm so happy it did." Pam cleared her throat. "Can I ask you a question?" Kathryn nodded and Pam proceeded. "So, remember when you said that the smell you remember the most was the smell of your friend Elizabeth's carpet? Can I ask why?"

"I haven't talked about this in a really long time," Kathryn replied, her voice low.

"You don't have to."

"No, it's just, I considered a lot of things after Judy. A lot of things." Kathryn paused. "I fell off the grid and my friend Elizabeth came over one day, made me get myself together, took me to her house. This will probably sound really dramatic, but she saved me." Kathryn closed her eyes. "Those first days at Elizabeth's were pretty rough, though."

"Kath." Pam's stomach fell to her knees. She understood what Kathryn was saying without even saying it. The idea of Kathryn being so heartbroken and distraught was too much. But then to also imagine that it was over *Judy*? Pam's mind was reeling.

"I was lost." Kathryn rolled onto her back again and looked up at the ceiling. A tear slowly slipped out of her eye and ran down her cheek.

"It's so strange to think that Judy, my best friend for all these years, was living this secret life. With you. Sometimes I sit there and think about it and wonder how this all happened. How twisted this all is. You know she lives right there?" She pointed toward Judy's house.

"She does?"

"Yes, did you not visit her there?"

"No. Not once. I guess I should have known when she wasn't inviting me over that things weren't going to be good for me." Kathryn sighed. "She fucked me up, Pam. Really, *really* badly."

"I won't do that to you." Pam intertwined her fingers with Kathryn's. "Ever."

"Don't make promises you might not be able to keep."

"I'll keep that one."

"I would rather you just communicate with me. You've already let me in a lot further than she *ever* did."

"What do you mean?"

"I mean, she was with me for over a year, and I barely knew anything about her." Kathryn paused, clenched her jaw. "Honestly, I was the idiot for thinking it was anything more than what it was."

"Honey," Pam soothed. "She really loved you. Like, *really* loved you. Even if you don't think she did. I can tell you that whatever you felt, she wasn't lying to you. She was happy, she was in love, she was everything she said she was with you."

Pam moved closer to Kathryn. "She just didn't have the courage to leave. That's all. And truthfully," she continued, her voice lower, "I'm really happy she didn't, because I wouldn't have you now."

A smile spread across Kathryn's lips. "Silver lining, eh?"

"Always," Pam replied, leaning forward to place her lips on Kathryn's. "Now get up and help me go make some dinner."

❖

"A library? Did you really read all of these books?"

"Well, not the law school books. But I did read about ninety percent of the books in here. I was a housewife for most of my marriage, remember?"

Pam watched as Kathryn would reach forward and pull one of the books off the shelf, thumb through it, then slide it back into its spot on the mahogany shelves. Her hair was wavy, more so than normal, and Pam was loving how it looked. Watching Kathryn from this position was a thrill for Pam. She never thought she'd actually enjoy the act of admiring another person. But here she was, enjoying every second.

"*The Notebook?*" Kathryn asked as she turned, holding a leather-bound book, her eyebrow arched.

"One of my favorites."

A laugh bubbled from Kathryn's throat as she spotted a row of yearbooks. "Oh, yes!" she exclaimed, quickly moving toward it. "This is going to be good."

"Noooo," Pam exclaimed as she rushed over to Kathryn. "There is no way in hell that I'm letting you look at these."

"Um, *why?*"

"*Um*, because. No way!" Pam was guarding the shelves, her back to them, her arms outstretched, her hands gripping the shelves.

"You realize," Kathryn said as she leaned in toward Pam and got within centimeters of the skin on her neck, "that this position is doing nothing but turning me on?"

"As long as it distracts you from the yearbooks, I don't really care," Pam responded, her voice low, seductive. Kathryn placed her hand firmly on Pam's hip and then slid it slowly up, up, up, until her fingertips were on Pam's waistline.

"Excuse me?" Pam asked.

"Yes?" Kathryn asked in a tone that implied she had no idea what Pam was referring to. "Is everything okay?"

"Yes," Pam breathed, her voice barely audible.

Kathryn's fingertips started to roam farther up Pam's T-shirt. Then she leaned forward and placed her lips ever so lightly on Pam's neck, pushed her thigh between Pam's legs, and pressed against her center.

"Holy *shit.*" Pam's voice came in a whisper. "What are you doing to me?"

Kathryn giggled as she slowly pulled away. "Distracting you," she said against Pam's lips and then turned around, a yearbook in hand, and galloped away.

"You ass!" Pam yelled with a laugh. "That was not fair!"

"I think it was." Kathryn sat on the leather chair in the library. She watched as Pam approached and sat on the arm of the chair.

"You can't make fun of me," Pam quickly said, placing her hand on the cover of the book. "Not even my bangs."

"You had bangs?"

"Kathryn!"

Kathryn started to laugh. "Okay, okay. I promise." And with that, Pam moved her hand and Kathryn opened the book.

Pam watched as she turned the pages that were littered with *Buffalo Pride!* and *Make sure to stay in touch!* and *Stay cool!* and *You are so much fun, Pam, never change!* There were phone numbers and random dates and crazy sayings. And there were pictures of Pam. Tons and tons of pictures of Pam.

Kathryn smiled when she found the club pictures: Future Business Leaders of America, the volleyball team, drama club, the bowling team, classroom mentors, track and field, choir. She glanced up at Pam. "You were quite involved," she commented.

Pam tilted her head and tried to gauge if that was sarcasm or not. "Yeah," she finally replied. "Not much to do in New Buffalo, Michigan, but join things."

Kathryn looked back down at the page in front of her, an eighteen-year-old Pam staring back at her. "I wish I would have known you then."

"You would have been ten." Pam laughed.

"You know what I mean." Kathryn smiled. "I would have had a crush on you even then, I'm sure."

"You think so?"

"I know so."

Pam reached down, placed her hand underneath Kathryn's chin, and tilted her face up. She bent down, and an overwhelming feeling of love came over her. "Thank you," Pam whispered against Kathryn's soft lips.

"For what?"

"For being you."

Kathryn smiled into their kiss, the book quickly forgotten.

CHAPTER FOURTEEN

When Kathryn had first mentioned the idea of meeting both sides of the family on Thanksgiving, it *seemed* perfect. They would go to one house and then the other. Kill two birds with one stone, right?

But as Pam sat in the passenger seat of Kathryn's Jeep, her stomach in a giant knot, she started to wonder if she really knew what she had agreed to.

"Thanks for coming with me today, Pam. I mean, you didn't have to. I hope you know that."

Pam looked over at Kathryn and smiled. "I know. But I totally agree with you. I think it'll be good. And then we can go over to my parents' afterward."

"Is this too soon, though? I mean, we haven't really been together or whatever for very long."

The word "together" made the knot in Pam's stomach get bigger. "Well, maybe a little." Pam reached over and moved a loose curl away from Kathryn's face. "But it'll be nice to get it over with." She was hoping she was coming off as easy-breezy and not giant ball of nerves.

Kathryn started to laugh. "You do have a point there."

"Of course I do."

"You're not nervous at all?" Kathryn asked, glancing over at Pam.

"Oh, nooo," she answered. "I'm as cool as a cucumber."

A laugh escaped from Kathryn's throat. "You're a horrible liar. You know that, right?"

"Shit," Pam sighed. "I'm so nervous to meet your mother that I think I might need you to pull over so I can throw up."

"Pam!" Kathryn was laughing. "I know I've painted a really terrible picture of her. I promise we won't stay long. We'll say hi, we'll say 'bye, and then we'll get the fuck out of there."

Pam was laughing when she turned her head back toward her window. Kathryn's mother was really the only person she was nervous about meeting. Her stepfather and half siblings seemed like they would be nice enough, or at least Kathryn made them sound fairly nice. They were all meeting at Kathryn's parents' house in Oak Brook, one of the more affluent suburbs of Chicago. Pam had received a warning fairly early that Kathryn's parents were filthy rich. Not only did her grandparents have money, but Virginia Striker's second marriage was to a man that was a CEO of one of Chicago's most prestigious financial brokerages. Pam remembered Kathryn telling her that the only reason she was able to afford the brownstone in Wrigleyville was because her stepfather bought it for her as a college graduation gift. Some people got watches or jewelry, or even a car. But not Kathryn. She got a house. A really nice house, at that.

After hanging out with the Rockefellers—Pam's nickname for Kathryn's parents—they were going to go to Pam's childhood home, which was more like *Little House on the Prairie* in comparison. Thankfully indoor plumbing had been put into the house years earlier and the outhouse was just used to tease her smaller cousins.

Pam was taking Kathryn to her family gathering, armed only with the knowledge that Pam had a sister. She had no idea that Pam's mom had five brothers and four sisters, or that her father had six brothers. And all of those siblings had wives or husbands and children, and every last one of them was invited to spend Thanksgiving on the farm. It was bound to be a madhouse.

Shockingly, Kathryn seemed really excited about it all. As with everything else that had anything to do with Pam or her family, Harold had never really cared. They usually ended up spending most of the holidays with his family. It was going to be a lot of fun finally being able to see her family on the holiday.

"Do your parents know anything about me?"

Pam looked over at Kathryn and smiled. "They know that you're a good friend."

"Ohhhh," Kathryn replied calmly. She let out a small laugh.

"What?"

"Oh, nothing."

Pam playfully smacked Kathryn on the arm. "Tell me!"

Kathryn looked over at Pam. "Do you kiss all of your 'good friends'?"

Pam felt her entire face get hot. "You're gonna get it."

❖

Kathryn glanced over at Pam. "They're like dogs, Pam," she whispered, leaning into Pam. "They can smell fear."

Pam let out a puff of air and tried to act nonchalant. Kathryn was right: Pam was as nervous as she ever had been. She could barely feel her knees. "What do you mean?"

"Oh please, you really think you're fooling me? You're scared shitless. You're one step away from barfing in the bushes."

Pam groaned and shook her hands, trying to get the nervousness out of them. "I know, I know. I'm sorry. It's just—"

"*So* nerve wracking?" Kathryn finished Pam's sentence. "I promise we won't stay long."

"Okay." Pam reached over and briefly intertwined her fingers with Kathryn's. She took a deep breath. "I'm ready now."

Kathryn smiled as she opened the door to her parents' house and walked in. "Mother?"

Pam figured her mouth was more than likely hanging open. The entryway to the house was immense. Marble floors, grand staircase, beautiful woodwork. The house was gorgeous. "Kathryn," Pam whispered. "This is amazing."

"I know. Can you believe this place? I've never liked it. It has always made me feel insignificant."

"Katie."

Pam looked over at the deep voice. A tall, balding man had come out of a dimly lit room off toward the right. He was holding a tumbler with what looked like scotch in it. Pam glanced at Kathryn so she could gauge her reaction to the man. She didn't seem repulsed, so that was good.

A smile spread across Kathryn's face, and it actually looked genuine. "Hi, Richard," she said as the man opened his arms and hugged Kathryn.

"Your mother is upstairs. Still primping."

"Of course she is."

"It's good to see you."

"You, too. I figured Mother would never let me live it down if I didn't at least make an appearance." Kathryn motioned toward Pam and smiled. "Richard, this is Pam. Pam, this is my stepfather, Richard Striker."

Richard smiled broadly, showing off perfectly capped teeth. "It's really nice to meet you, Pam."

Pam shook Richard's outstretched hand and returned the smile. "Likewise," she answered. "I've heard a lot about you."

"All good, I hope."

"Of course." Pam hoped that she sounded convincing. It wasn't that she heard a lot of horrible things about him. The truth was she hadn't heard much of anything.

"Well, you two are welcome to join me in the study until Virginia finishes." Richard headed toward the room where he first emerged. "I'm watching *Planes, Trains, and Automobiles.*"

"Oh gosh, I haven't seen that in ages," Pam said with a grin.

"Come on then." Kathryn reached back and pulled gently on Pam's arm but then stopped and glanced up the staircase. Pam's gaze followed Kathryn's, and she realized instantly that it had to be Kathryn's mother.

Pam watched the slender, gray-haired woman as she made her way down the staircase. She was dressed impeccably, from her navy-blue slacks to her orange silk top. Her hair was pinned back on one side, but the rest, which was long and wavy like Kathryn's, flowed freely. She was a beautiful lady, from the clothing to the way her skin looked as if she wasn't a day over fifty years old. It was clear who Kathryn took after, even though Pam had never met Kathryn's dad. Pam was just happy that she'd worn black pants and a nice gray top, because obviously it was not a casual affair.

"You're looking ever so grungy, Kathryn."

Pam felt her hands tighten into fists. There was nothing about Kathryn that was *grungy*. In fact, Pam thought she looked absolutely adorable in her cream turtleneck sweater, skinny jeans, and tall brown boots.

"And you're looking ever so phony." Kathryn's eyes darted over to Pam's and she winked. "Mother, this is Pam. Pam, this is my mother, Virginia."

"I'm sorry," Virginia said, her hand on her chest over where a heart presumably resided. *"Pam?"*

"Yes, Mother. *Pam*. It's not hard to pronounce."

"Lovely to meet you, *Pam*," Virginia said semi-sarcastically.

Pam felt her insides churn when she heard Virginia repeat her name for the second time. "Yes, it's nice to meet you, as well."

Virginia took a drag off a long, skinny cigarette. "Can I see you in the kitchen, Kathryn?"

Kathryn sighed. "Sure. Pam, do you mind?"

"Not at all. I'll go watch the movie with Richard."

"Jackson and Jessica are in there, too."

"Are those the half siblings?" Pam whispered.

"Kathryn, *now*."

Kathryn glared at her mother's back as the woman walked through the swinging door into the kitchen. "I hate her. Oh, my God, I hate her."

Pam reached up and put her hands on Kathryn's cheeks. "You don't hate her. It's okay, sweetie. I promise. Besides, your stepfather seems very nice."

"The devil himself would seem nice compared to my mother." Kathryn let out an exasperated breath, and Pam tried to stifle her laughter. "I'll be right back, okay?"

"Okay." Pam watched Kathryn rush in the direction that her mother had gone. She wondered before she retreated to the movie room if Kathryn's relationship had always been like this or if it was a product of her being a lesbian. Either way, Pam was thrilled they weren't staying very long at the Striker residence.

❖

Virginia puffed away on her cigarette as she studied her daughter. She was clicking her acrylic nails on the marble countertop.

Kathryn's teeth were set on edge by the sound, and she knew her mother was only doing it to be an irritating bitch. It was working. "So, how have you been?"

"I finally recovered from turning fifty-one. I've decided that it's nothing to be ashamed of. So I'm fifty-one years old. Big deal, right?"

Kathryn cringed. *Pam is only eleven years younger than my mother.* "Yeah, Mom, *big deal.*" Her gaze landed on her mother's fingernails. They were drumming away incessantly. "I see Richard bought another piece of Kandinsky art?"

"Yes, he just had to have it."

"I'm sure." Kathryn leaned back against the counter and crossed her arms. She watched the chef that her mother always hired for their Thanksgiving brunch. Kathryn had no idea why Virginia needed to have the best of everything all the time. What ever happened to turkey and gravy? And Stove Top stuffing? "How is everything else?"

"Fine." Virginia took a deep breath. "Have you seen your *father* lately?"

"Yes, of course. He actually makes an effort."

Virginia pushed the butt of her cigarette into the ashtray. She blew the smoke sideways out of her mouth. "And I don't?"

"I didn't say that." Kathryn sighed.

"Didn't you?"

"Mother, stop. Please."

"Fine." Virginia tilted her head to the side. "It's not like hearing from me would make you happier. I didn't make your father happy, and I most certainly do not make you happy."

Kathryn said, "Don't even start." She could barely look at her mother recently without wanting to slap her. It was an impossible relationship to deal with. Kathryn often wondered how she managed to not go ballistic.

"Well, it's true."

"It's your own fault that you two couldn't find a happy medium."

Virginia pushed a long lock of gray hair that had fallen out of her barrette behind her ear. Her fidgety hands quickly reached forward and pulled out another cigarette. She lit it and inhaled. "Your father and I," she started, the smoke billowing from her mouth, "we're better off apart."

"I agree. Wholeheartedly."

"Then what's the problem, Kathryn?"

"That you're heartless and don't give a shit about me."

Virginia sighed deeply. "Why must we always argue?"

"Because you're intolerable."

"Yes, but it's *Thanksgiving.*"

"Like that has stopped you before?" Kathryn replied, her eyes rolling almost involuntarily. As much as Kathryn couldn't stand her mother, she did admire her ability to never back down when she thought she was right about something. It was infuriating most of the time, but every now and then Virginia actually *was* right. Kathryn liked to think that she'd inherited that trait. Whether or not it was true did not need to be confirmed.

A smile was displayed on Virginia's thin lips. "Tell me, Kathryn," she started with a voice that said only one thing: *ever heard of the Spanish inquisition?* "Have you found a boyfriend yet?"

"Mother."

"Okay, fine. A girlfriend?"

"Do you not remember meeting the woman I brought with me today?"

Virginia glared at her. "Yes, I remember." She added, "Her name is a cooking spray."

"Mother!" Kathryn hissed. "You've *got* to be kidding me."

"How old is she?"

Kathryn felt the air in the room get thick. She closed her eyes. "She's forty."

"Oh, for Christ's sake."

"What?" Kathryn glared right back at her mother. This was not something she was going to back down from.

"*Forty?*"

"Yes, forty!"

"Kathryn Scott Hawthorne. What the hell do you think you're doing?"

Kathryn let out a laugh. Maybe this was more fun than she had imagined. "I'm spending time with someone I like a lot. What's wrong with that?"

"She's only eleven years younger than I am!"

"So?"

"Kathryn!"

"Mother, seriously, what is the big fucking deal?"

"Don't you take that tone of voice with me! You might be thirty-two, but you are still my daughter."

"Whatever," Kathryn said.

"Kathryn."

"What?"

"Why does she have to be *forty?*"

Kathryn sighed. "You realize she can probably hear you."

"I don't care," Virginia said arrogantly. "This is *my* house."

"Stop."

"What?"

"Stop right this instant. Do not be like that to her."

Virginia took a sip of her drink. "What does this woman do?"

"She works."

"Where?"

"Why does it matter?"

"Because it always matters." Virginia flicked the ashes from her cigarette in one of the many ashtrays that were scattered throughout the immense house. "Now, *where?*"

"At a high-end boutique downtown."

"You have got to be kidding me. She works in retail?" Virginia shouted, shocked, her laughter bubbling around her words. Her voice was smothered with arrogance.

"Oookay."

Virginia inhaled sharply, trying to cover her laughter. "I'm sorry."

"Mother. *Please.* Just give her a chance."

"Why?"

"Because it would mean a lot to me." Kathryn looked into her mother's eyes. "I don't ask for much."

"Okay. Fine."

"Thank you."

Virginia watched as Kathryn turned to walk out of the kitchen. "Kathryn?"

Kathryn stopped in her tracks, not bothering to turn to face her mother. "What?"

"Nothing," Virginia answered. Kathryn rolled her eyes and walked out of the kitchen.

❖

Pam soon realized that Thanksgiving brunch at the Striker household consisted of a wide range of fancy hors d'oeuvres and lots and lots of alcohol. The conversation seemed lively enough, and so far, Virginia had only managed to stare at Pam from the end of the extra-long dining room table. For a second, Pam thought she was going to get away from the afternoon without having to answer any questions.

"So, Pam?"

Pam looked down the table at Kathryn's half sister, who had addressed her. "Yes?"

"Where do you work?" Jessica asked.

"It's called Skin. It's a high-end boutique on Michigan Avenue."

Jessica let out a gasp. "Shut up! I love that store. I shop there all the time!" Her hands were moving wildly as she launched into a story about the body scrubs and lotions that she loved from Skin. Her long, dark hair was exactly like Kathryn's, full of waves and beautiful. Her eyes were her mother's, though: bright blue and full of something Pam couldn't put her finger on. It was almost as if her eyes were doing the talking, as weird as that sounded.

"Jessica is always asking for gift cards from there. I think she has tried everything in the store," Kathryn explained with a laugh. "She has no willpower when it comes to expensive beauty products."

"Sounds like someone else I know," Pam said as she winked at Kathryn.

"Hardly. I had no willpower when it came to *you*," Kathryn whispered. She leaned into Pam and slid her hand onto Pam's leg. It was such a gentle touch, but Pam loved Kathryn's attempt to lighten the mood. The gesture was small but meant the world to Pam.

"Did you go to college?" Virginia interrupted from the end of the table, her voice echoing off the walls of the expansive dining room.

Pam felt the temperature rise in the room. Oh, great, the questions were starting. How bad would they get? "Yes," she answered after clearing her throat and finding her voice. Something about Virginia speaking to her made Pam want to get up and run from the room screaming. "I went to Purdue."

"Really?" Richard said with a laugh. "I did, as well."

"What a small world." Pam grinned. "And what was your degree in?"

"Business. Both of them. You?"

"Same, as well." Pam laughed.

"And how do you feel about Harry's Chocolate Shop?" Richard's question was followed by a smile as he obviously reminisced about something. He raised his tumbler of scotch and finished his thought with, "Did you frequent that fine establishment?"

A smile spread across Pam's lips as she leaned back in her chair. "'Go ugly early,' right?" she asked, quoting the motto of the famous college bar. "After every test. Before some of them, as well," Pam added. She could tell Richard was definitely a fan of hers after that confession.

"Ahh, the memories," Richard laughed with Pam. "Jackson here is a fellow Boilermaker."

Pam looked over at Jackson. His blond hair had fallen across his forehead and he barely looked old enough to drive, let alone be in college. "What are you majoring in, Jackson?" Pam asked as she swirled her drink in the glass.

"Mechanical engineering," he replied.

"And? How's it going so far?"

"It's a lot of fun. I have straight As right now. Although I do feel like some of the professors don't really know who I am."

Pam leaned forward, placed her elbows on the table, and smiled. "You'll be noticed, I'm sure of it." Her heart warmed when Jackson smiled at her. He looked so much like Kathryn in the face even though he was only her half brother. He had that same crooked smile and those same dark eyes.

Kathryn grinned. "Aww! Jackson's growing up!"

Jackson's cheeks turned a deep red as he lowered his head. "Oh, shut up, Katie," he said playfully.

"And what school do you go to, Jessica?" Pam asked as she swirled her vodka and soda in her glass. The drink was strong thanks to Richard's bartending. She was thankful for it now, though, as she knew it was the only thing that was calming her down.

Jessica glanced at Kathryn and smiled. "Columbia College. Same school Katie went to."

"Oh, wow. I didn't know you went there," Pam said, looking at Kathryn, who was leaning back in her chair with her left leg crossed over her right and her hands folded in her lap. Kathryn looked so beautiful, so at ease, even though Pam knew she was probably hating every second of being this close to her mother. And sadly, Pam was starting to understand why.

"You never asked," Kathryn said as she winked at Pam and lightly rubbed the back of her arm.

"Well, shame on me," Pam said, a grin stretching across her lips.

"Why do you work at a retail store if you have a degree in business?" Virginia's voice cut through the laughter like a chain saw.

Kathryn glared at Virginia from her seat at the table. "Mother." "I'm just asking, dear. Am I not allowed to ask questions?"

"Kathryn, it's fine," Pam murmured. Virginia's tone was so fake and full of shit that Pam found herself fighting back the urge to roll her eyes. She looked around the room. How did she begin to tell this group of people why when she herself didn't know some days? She worked at Skin to escape who she had become, but was that really Thanksgiving hors d'oeuvres conversation?

"Well," she started, her eyes now glued on Virginia's. "I was married for twenty-one years to a very successful lawyer."

The sound of the ice clinking in Virginia's tumbler was almost deafening.

"Oh, Jesus," Kathryn groaned. Pam saw her bow her head and take a deep breath as if she was praying to God for help.

"You were *married*?" Virginia asked.

"Shocked?" Pam asked, her eyebrow arched and her game face on.

Virginia cleared her throat. "Yes. Very," she answered matter-of-factly.

"Well, you aren't the first person to be shocked. Or the last," Pam said, the sides of her mouth turning upward into a smile. "Anyway, I didn't need to work." Pam waved her hand through the air as she explained the situation, how Harold had made so much money in his years at the firm and then after he made partner that her working wasn't a need. And Virginia seemed to understand, probably because she was in the same situation now. Pam wanted to make sure Virginia knew she wasn't some backwoods asshole that Kathryn was taking a chance on. Pam didn't know why she felt the need to impress Virginia, though. Maybe it was that Kathryn was quickly starting to be Pam's *everything*, and the idea of something getting in the way of that was too much for her to handle.

"So, after Harold passed away, I decided to get a job, even though I honestly never need to work again."

Virginia raised her hand to her mouth. "Oh, my goodness. He died?"

"*Mother*," Kathryn hissed.

"Kathryn," Virginia hissed back. "I'm not talking to you." She turned her attention back to Pam. "How old was he when he passed away?"

"Forty," Pam answered. She noticed that the entire room had grown quiet. Pam looked at Virginia and almost fell off her chair when the woman smiled at her. It was a genuine smile, too. All Pam could do was smile back. She felt like maybe, just maybe, she had become someone Virginia might like. Not right now, of course, but in the future.

Pam felt content, though. She'd stood her ground and stood up for herself. It wasn't a normal occurrence, but it felt good to not let someone else belittle her. And the outcome was positive. Thank goodness.

CHAPTER FIFTEEN

As Pam and Kathryn flew down I-94 on their way north to Michigan, Kathryn couldn't stop thinking about how amazing it had been to see Pam interact with her family. She had been so nervous about the afternoon because she knew her family could be a little ridiculous. But Pam had survived. Hell, she'd thrived. And the weirdest part? Her family seemed more *real* afterward. Especially her mother. Kathryn hadn't seen Virginia smile and interact with one of her love interests in forever. It was such a breath of fresh air, and all it did was make Kathryn fall further for this woman.

Pam cleared her throat, interrupting Kathryn's thoughts. "Turn left up there. Onto 300 North," Pam instructed, pointing toward the country road. "You've been fairly quiet," she said as she placed her hand on Kathryn's thigh.

"I'm just thinking."

"About?"

"You meeting my family," Kathryn said. "And how you so easily put my mom in her place." She glanced at Pam in the passenger seat, noticed the smile and the way her eyes were shining. "It was amazing."

"Well," Pam shrugged, "I guess I'm good with people."

"You really are." Kathryn looked back at the road.

"It wasn't as bad as you said it was going to be," Pam explained. "I mean, it was still nerve-wracking. Especially when your mother kept repeating my name—"

"I wanted to slug her," Kathryn interrupted. "She's so freaking snobby. She wasn't like that when she was married to my dad."

Pam smiled. "It's okay, Kath. Believe me, I'm used to getting treated like that."

"I'm so sorry, Pam."

"Don't be." Pam put her hand on Kathryn's arm. "I had a great time. Richard, Jackson, and Jessica are very nice. And your mother, once she realized that I'm not what she thought I was, warmed up to me. It wasn't nearly as awkward toward the end as it was in the beginning."

"You handled yourself like a professional."

Pam let out a laugh. "Well, twenty-one years of rude in-laws conditioned me for life."

"I'm glad you liked everyone, though."

"I did. I can say that honestly, too." Pam pointed before she ended her sentence. "That's it. Right there."

If Pam had been amazed by Kathryn's parents' house, Kathryn was equally taken aback by Pam's childhood home. It was a huge farmhouse, complete with a pole barn on the property.

Kathryn pulled up next to a minivan, turned the engine off, and looked over at Pam.

"This is amazing! It's so big! And the trees!" Kathryn got out of her Jeep and looked around. "You don't see things like this in the city." A bare oak tree towered over the house. There were boards nailed to the base of it, all the way up to a tree house. The boards looked very old, and the tree house itself had definitely seen a lot of wear and tear.

"Donna and I had so much fun in that tree house. It was our 'no boys allowed' clubhouse."

"I kinda like that motto," Kathryn said with a big grin.

"I'm sure you do." Pam threw her overnight bag onto the porch and then did the same with Kathryn's. "Come on. I'll show you around." They both started walking toward the pole barn, passing the chicken coop on the left. "Oh, here," she said as they walked over to a wooden structure with cells separated by chicken wire. "Close your eyes."

Kathryn smiled at Pam. "What are you going to do?"

"Nothing bad, I promise." Pam watched as Kathryn slowly closed her eyes. She swung open one of the cage doors. "Hold out your hands."

When Kathryn felt a large, fuzzy animal being placed into her hands, she opened her eyes and immediately said, "Awww!" It was a large black lop-eared rabbit.

"This is Queen Annabeth the Eighth."

"The eighth?"

Pam laughed. "Yeah, so Queen Annabeth was my very first bunny. The second Annabeth was my first first-place bunny in 4-H. And then, of course, every bunny after that had to be named Queen Annabeth. The name is good luck."

Kathryn stroked the soft fur of the bunny while Pam talked about her years in 4-H. She had raised two pigs, Oscar and Samuel, and one lamb, Jersey. It was obviously the thing to do in the hinterlands of Michigan. And Pam apparently had the time of her life doing it all.

"Sounds like you were quite the little ranch hand."

Pam playfully smacked Kathryn on the arm. "Shush." She locked Queen Annabeth back into her cage and then stopped. "Harold hated all of this," she said with her back to Kathryn.

It broke Kathryn's heart to hear Pam so sad about sharing such an awesome part of her past. She reached forward, placed her hand on Pam's hip, and leaned in. "Well, I really love all of this."

Pam turned around, reached forward, and put her hand on Kathryn's side. "C'mon, the goats are over here."

"You even have goats?" Kathryn asked, barely able to contain her excitement. "You had the best childhood ever, didn't you?"

"Yeah, I really did." Pam opened the barn door and let Kathryn walk inside. "I'm sure yours wasn't that bad," she said as she closed the door and then approached Kathryn from behind.

Kathryn let out a puff of air as she looked around the old barn. "I wouldn't say it was awful. But it certainly wasn't like this." She motioned around the barn. Her childhood memories included her parents fighting, her grades never being good enough, and her mother bringing another man into her life and not even caring that Kathryn was a hot mess still from the divorce. And then she had to welcome two half siblings into this world, figure out that she wasn't really into boys, and try her hardest to not hate her mother with every fiber of her being. The only good memories were her dad's unwavering support while she played as many sports as possible, joined as many clubs as possible, and even chose a career that followed in his footsteps. And he actually accepted Kathryn when she finally came out to him.

"You were probably an adorable little kid, though," Pam whispered as she placed a hand on Kathryn's hip and gently pressed her body against Kathryn's back.

"Of course. I was adorable. Look at how cute I am now." Kathryn laughed as she turned around and faced Pam. "Did you just bring me in here so you could kiss me?"

Pam laughed as she nodded.

"Were you really going to show me goats?"

Pam shook her head.

"So, you lied to me to get me where you wanted me?"

Pam nodded again and pulled Kathryn closer. "I just needed to feel you," Pam whispered.

"You…" Kathryn paused and rested her forehead against Pam's. "You are just so perfect."

"Yeah, well, you might not think that after you meet my family. They can be pretty crazy."

"Pam. Seriously? Do you not remember meeting my weird asshole family literally two hours ago?"

A laugh spilled from Pam's mouth and she leaned in to place a kiss on Kathryn's lips. "Well," she pulled away and grabbed Kathryn's hand, "we'll see how you feel in about five minutes."

❖

Kathryn followed Pam up the steps to the house. The deck had been shoveled off, but snow was quickly starting to accumulate again. Pam turned around and smiled at Kathryn when her hand landed on the doorknob. "Are you ready for this?"

"Ready as I'll ever be."

When the door opened, all Kathryn could hear was laughter, talking, shouting, and more laughter. Kids were running around, two dogs were chasing the kids, people were crowded around the stairwell, and more were packed in the small room that was directly to the right of the foyer.

Pam looked back at Kathryn and cringed. "Sorry, it's kind of a madhouse."

Just as Pam said that, all the people standing by the stairwell shouted, "Pamela!" and rushed over to her. Kathryn watched Pam hug every person, and she couldn't help but smile. Kathryn's mother was an only child and her dad had one sister who had passed away years earlier, so seeing this exchange was awesome.

"You guys, this is my really good friend, Kathryn." Pam reached back and grabbed Kathryn's arm to pull her forward. "She's going to spend Thanksgiving with us."

"Hi," Kathryn said with a shy smile.

Pam started to name everyone, starting with her cousins and then her brother-in-law, and finally her sister, Donna, whose dark hair was a stark contrast to Pam's blond locks. They were otherwise mirror images of each other with the same blue eyes, beautiful smile, and flawless complexion.

Donna reached out to shake Kathryn's hand. "How do you two know each other?" she asked, the inquisition starting before anyone else could get a word in edgewise.

"We met—"

"At the store," Pam interrupted, rescuing Kathryn.

Donna nodded, an eyebrow arched to her hairline. Kathryn could tell this woman was not buying the "friends" claim.

"Donna, we'll be right down. We're going to take our stuff up to the attic."

"Yeah, Mom said you called dibs on the attic. Thanks a lot, Pamela," Donna said with irritation.

"What's with the attic?" Kathryn whispered as she followed Pam up the creaky, narrow stairwell.

"You'll see."

Kathryn glanced at all the family pictures that lined the hallway walls as they climbed upstairs. The banister under her hand was smooth from many years of wear and tear. At the top of the stairs, throw rugs covered the wood floors, which creaked under their feet like the stairs had. The house was obviously old, but it was filled with character.

"Whoa, whoa." Kathryn stopped dead in her tracks as she got a closer look at a picture on the wall. "Is this *you?*"

"Oh, God."

"Pam, my word," Kathryn commented.

"What?"

"This doesn't look at all like the high school girl in the yearbooks."

"Yeah, well, college and a miscarriage and the start of a horrible marriage makes you look like shit," she explained as Kathryn studied a picture taken a couple years into Pam's marriage. "I hate that picture, but Mom loved it, so it stayed."

"Hey," Kathryn said, her voice low as she looked over at Pam. "You look absolutely incredible."

A small smile formed on Pam's lips as she said, "C'mon." She walked to the end of the long hallway and opened a door. As they started to ascend the stairs into a huge, open living space, Pam looked back at Kathryn. "This, my dear, is why Donna wanted the attic."

Kathryn stood at the top of the stairs and looked around the large attic. It spanned the entire length of the farmhouse. The slanted ceilings were lined with posters from Pam and Donna's childhood. An old television set was at one end of the room, and in front of it sat an old couch with a yellow and red crocheted afghan draped over the back of it. Behind them at the other end of the attic was a pullout bed near the windows that looked out on the acreage.

"Pam, this is amazing." Kathryn looked back at Pam, who was

smiling from ear to ear. "Did you spend all of your time up here when you were a kid?"

Pam bounced on her toes. "Yeah. Donna and I were up here every day after school. We had sleepovers with our friends all the time." She pointed to the window. "I smoked my first cigarette out of that window." She let out a loud chuckle. "Such a rebel."

Kathryn watched Pam talk about her relationship with Donna, her friends, Harold. The way he didn't appreciate the farmhouse, how he never liked coming here, how he never got along with her parents after the affair. There were many times that Pam would bring him up, obviously; he'd been a huge part of her life. But Kathryn had never seen Pam look so sad as she did as she talked about him here at her parents' house. It almost made Kathryn hate him, but she knew she couldn't hate someone who had loved Pam, even if it wasn't the way Pam should have been loved.

"Pamela!"

"Sounds like you're being summoned," Kathryn said as she nudged Pam.

"Are you going to come say hi to your mother?" The voice carried up the stairwell to the attic.

"That's Mom," said Pam. "I have to admit that I have missed that call. C'mon."

They descended, Kathryn a couple steps behind Pam. Kathryn saw an older woman standing at the bottom with shoulder-length gray hair and dark-rimmed glasses. She was the spitting image of what Pam would look like in thirty years.

"There's my girl," the older woman said with a smile that looked so much like Pam's it was almost scary.

"Hi, Mom," Pam said as she wrapped her arms around her mother. "I've missed you so much. Have you been behaving yourself?"

"I should be asking that of you!"

"Oh, Mom. You feel good," said Pam, squeezing her tighter.

"I know, baby. I'm just glad you're home." She pushed Pam's hair behind her ears and leaned back so she could look at Pam. "You look good, honey. Your skin looks great. Are you using something new? And your hair. I love this length. So silky. It's gorgeous."

Kathryn couldn't help but smile as she watched the exchange. It almost made her jealous that Pam's mom was pretty much the perfect mom and her mom was, well, *Virginia*.

"And who's this beautiful girl?"

"Mom, this is Kathryn."

"Kathryn, welcome. I'm Carolyn."

"It's so nice to meet you," Kathryn said as she held out her hand.

"Honey, we hug in this house. Come here."

Kathryn glanced at Pam and then took a step into Carolyn's arms. She smelled like brown sugar and butter, and it was the best hug Kathryn had experienced from someone she had just met.

"Thank you so much for having me over for Thanksgiving," Kathryn said when Carolyn finally released her.

"Oh, please. Thank *you* for coming! We are always thrilled when we get to see Pamela."

"Mom, you act like I never come up here."

"Well, dear, when was the last time we saw you?"

Pam rolled her eyes. "Last month?"

"Oh, whatever, that doesn't count." Carolyn waved away Pam's answer. She looked back at Kathryn. "We love anyone that loves our Pamela, so, Kathryn, you are always welcome."

"Well," Kathryn said, trying to not crumble like a cookie under Carolyn's gaze, "I love her to death."

"Good." Carolyn released Kathryn and whirled around. "Come downstairs, you two. The wine is being poured."

Kathryn felt Pam's arm around her bicep. "You love me to death?" Pam whispered as they got to the top of the stairs.

"Yeah," Kathryn whispered back as she looked into Pam's eyes. "I do."

❖

"Pamela?"

"What?" Pam asked from her squatting position as she fished around in the refrigerator for the mayonnaise. She could never find anything in her mom's refrigerator. It always looked like someone had tried to organize it but halfway through got bored. Pickles were with pickles, but a bag of brown sugar was shoved toward the back with a bowl of leftover meat loaf and two half-eaten jars of applesauce.

"Is this the girl you've been spending so much time with?"

Pam glanced over her shoulder at her mother. She sighed. "Why?"

"Just wondering."

"Yes, it is." Pam looked back at the unorganized mess. "Why can you not clean this thing properly, Mom?"

"Your father does that."

"Does what? Cleans it? Or messes it up?"

Carolyn cackled. "How 'bout both?"

"Mmm-hmm. That's what I thought." Pam moved the butter pickles aside. "Aha! Here it is." She pulled the mayonnaise from the fridge and stood. "That was insane. It should be right here on the door."

"Why don't you clean it out and organize it for me?"

"You gonna pay me?" Pam asked with a grin.

"Um, no. You're not twelve anymore, my dear."

Pam opened the mayonnaise and scooped out a big dollop. She stirred it into the spinach dip she was making and then transferred the dip to the round bread her mother had baked earlier that morning. "I can't believe I left Kathryn out there to fend for herself."

"Oh please, you really think our family is going to devour her?" Carolyn looked at Pam, who was just staring back at her with one eyebrow raised in a "you've got to be kidding me" stare. "Okay, okay. I can't believe you did either."

"See?"

Carolyn stood in front of the oven and peered in the window at the huge turkey. "She seems like a very nice girl."

"She is."

"Is she one of those *homosexuals*?" Carolyn asked, her Midwestern accent coming through all too clearly.

Pam dropped her mixing spoon. "What?"

"Well, your sister said something to me, and I was just wondering."

"What did she say?" Pam asked.

"Just something about you hanging out with this woman who's, you know…"

"What? Why would she think that?"

"Who knows? You know your sister. She's always trying to stir up something."

"Oh, for Christ's sake."

"Pamela! Your language, *please*. There's nothing wrong with it, of course. I remember when I had a rainbow flag up in our yard. I had it up for ages until your sister told me it was a 'gay thing.' Needless to say, I kept it up, partly to annoy your sister, but also because who cares? So it's about a different kind of love. As long as people keep loving, who cares?" Carolyn stopped basting the turkey and looked out the window. "It's starting to snow. That makes everything so holiday!"

Pam looked out the window and said "mmm-hmm," going right along with her mother's skillful subject change. She was a pro at jumping from subject to subject when the conversation got tense.

"We've had more snow this month than I think I've ever seen in November."

Pam knew her mother still wanted an answer about Kathryn. It was such a difficult question to reply to, though. Would saying yes make her mother wonder if she was a lesbian, too? Or would she even think twice?

"Kathryn is a lesbian, Mom," she said while trying to remain nonchalant.

Carolyn turned and looked at Pam. "Is that okay with you?"

"Well, yeah, obviously."

"I always wondered how two women could love each other like that. Without the equipment, so to speak."

"Mom!" Pam blushed as she looked across the island of the small kitchen at her mother. Her gray hair was now pulled back into a ponytail at the base of her head. She looked quaint with her glasses hanging from a chain around her neck, the sleeves of her light-brown cardigan—complete with elbow patches—pushed up, and her apron tied around her waist.

Pam wanted so badly to say something, to explain the depth of her connection and tell her what it felt like to be in love with a woman. To give her mother a hint of some kind. *I used to wonder the same thing*, she wanted to say. *I never understood homosexuality until now.* But right then and there was probably not the best time to tell her mother that she might very well be a lesbian herself. Thanksgiving might be the perfect holiday to spring a pregnancy or an engagement on the family, but not a change in sexual orientation. "I'm guessing it's the same reason why you love Dad so much. The heart knows what it wants."

"Whatever blows your hair back."

"Don't be rude to her because of this."

Carolyn gasped as she set the baster down on the counter. "Pamela Christine! I would never be rude to someone because of something like that." She slid the turkey back into the oven and then turned the knob to set the timer. "I may be a simple woman, but I am not entirely without class. Now, if she hurt you, I'd be rude to her. I'd be rude if *she* was rude. But I would never be rude because she's in love with you."

Pam's mouth fell open. "*What?*"

"Oh, Pamela," Carolyn said. "She said so herself."

"No, she didn't," Pam started, quickly trying to cover up Kathryn's earlier confession. "She just meant like a friend loves another friend. That's all."

Carolyn roared in laughter. "Honey, it's so blatantly obvious. Even your father noticed. She doesn't take her eyes off you." Carolyn walked over to Pam, stuck her finger in the spinach dip, and tasted it. "This is good, dear."

"Whoa, whoa. No way are you changing the subject. What do you mean it's obvious?"

"Pamela." Carolyn wiped her hands with a dish towel. She turned and leaned against the counter. Before she spoke again, she dusted some flour off her apron. "I talked with her for twenty minutes while you were helping your father set the tables. I've never heard anyone speak so kindly about another human being in all of my life."

"In twenty minutes, you decided that she doesn't just love me like a friend but she is *in love* with me?"

"Yes."

"What exactly did she say that made you come to that conclusion?"

"I'm seventy-five years old. You really think I don't remember?" Carolyn crossed her arms. "You'd better not be leading this girl on, because, Pamela, so help me."

"Mom, I *know*."

"She realizes that you're not into that kind of thing, right?"

Pam felt her stomach turn. She looked at her mother. "Yeah, she does," Pam replied, knowing she had just lied to her mother. And to herself.

Carolyn continued to look at Pam. "You do look good, though, Pam. I don't think I've ever seen you look like this. Like a breath of fresh air."

"Mom," Pam whispered, her voice cracking with emotion.

"Your aunt made your favorite pumpkin pie. The kind with the whipped cream whipped in already."

Pam dabbed at her eyes. What would she ever do without her mother?

❖

"Whoa, whoa, whoa. You put butter on your turkey?"

Pam looked over at Kathryn. They were sitting next to each other at one of the many tables that were set up through the dining room and living room. The house simply wasn't big enough for all the people that were there, but they always made it work. Kathryn's eyes were wide as she watched Pam pour melted butter over her turkey breast.

Pam smiled at her. "Yeah, why?"

"I've never seen someone do that before," Kathryn whispered.

"What haven't you seen before?"

Pam looked up at her cousin, Joe, and laughed. "Kathryn has never seen someone put butter on her turkey before."

David, another cousin, joined in with the laughter. "No shit?"

"David!" Grandma Gerrard shouted from across the dining room.

"My God, she still has good ears, doesn't she?" David's wife Rebecca whispered.

"Yes, I do! Now watch your mouth over there," Grandma Gerrard said jokingly. "There are virgin ears about." She motioned with her knife toward the children's table.

Pam looked over at Kathryn. "Here," she said as she stabbed a piece of turkey basted in butter with her fork and held it up to Kathryn's mouth. "Taste it." Pam cocked her eyebrow. "Seriously. You'll love it."

Kathryn's eyes locked onto Pam's. "Okay," Kathryn replied calmly. She opened her mouth and took the turkey from the fork. "Oh wow!" she said with a laugh, her mouth full of food. "This is really good. Pass the butter!"

The whole table erupted in laughter. Pam glanced back at her mother and father. They were both watching her, small smiles on their faces. It immediately made her feel uncomfortable, as if she was doing something wrong.

"Pam?"

Pam's head snapped around. "Huh?"

Donna chuckled. "Welcome back to reality," she said with a smirk.

"Don't start," Pam said and then stuck out her tongue at Donna.

"I want to talk to you after dinner," Donna mouthed.

"About what?" Pam asked through a mouthful of mashed potatoes.

"Swallow, Pamela," Carolyn said as she whisked past the table carrying a serving platter and headed into the kitchen.

Pam started to laugh. "I turn into a barbarian around these potatoes."

Donna laughed along with her. "You're always a barbarian. And *you* have to sleep in the same room with her tonight, Kathryn. Good luck with that!"

Kathryn glanced up at Pam and then quickly looked over at Donna. "Oh, I know. I'm already dreading it," she responded in a joking tone.

Donna almost spat out the mouthful of wine she had just taken. She managed to swallow the liquid and then burst into laughter. "Just wait!"

Pam could feel the entire room staring at them. She knew she was blushing. She was actually quite positive that she was so red, she might catch on fire. She looked over at Donna and glared teasingly at her. "You'd better watch yourself tonight."

Kathryn was laughing during the entire exchange. "Sibling rivalry. This is great."

Pam looked over at Kathryn. She was still so embarrassed. She wanted to crawl under the table and just hide there until Donna shut the hell up. She tried to smile, but all that came across her face was a pained expression.

"Don't worry," Kathryn whispered as she put her hand on Pam's thigh. "I'm looking forward to tonight."

Pam quickly glanced over at Donna, who of course didn't miss the exchange.

❖

"What?" Pam asked as she passed over another clean dish for Donna to dry.

Donna flipped her dark hair over her shoulder. "Oh, nothing."

"Don't give me that. Say what you want to say." Pam rolled her eyes.

"What are you doing with that girl?" Donna hissed over the sound of the running water.

"What do you mean?" There was no way that Donna could tell just by looking at Kathryn that something was going on between them. At least Pam hoped there was no way. Her mom seemed to pick up on it, though, so maybe? But Donna was far too quaint to realize something without being given a hint first. Right?

"She's so young! You're not supposed to be friends with someone so much younger than you are. That's unheard of. You're acting like a child."

And it was confirmed. Donna knew nothing. "Oh my God," Pam said while trying to contain her laughter. "You're joking, right?"

"No, I'm not."

"Donna! You and Bill have an age difference of fourteen years!"

"Yes, but we're married! And in love!"

Pam looked over at Donna and raised her eyebrows.

"Don't even."

"What?"

"You are not with *her*?" Donna could barely find the words she was looking for. She was stuttering and stammering like she just had the hell scared out of her. "She really is a lesbian?"

"Aren't you the one that outed her to Mom?" Pam handed over another dish.

"Pamela!"

"Donna!" Pam responded, mimicking her sister perfectly. "Aren't you?"

"Well, yeah, but I was honestly just guessing. I didn't think I was right! What are you *doing*?"

"I'm having a really great time with someone that I like a lot."

Donna walked away from the dishwasher and stood by the door to the kitchen.

"Get back over here. We're not finished."

"I can't, Pam. I've gotta get some air." And with that, Donna walked out of the kitchen, leaving Pam standing there with more plates to clean than she knew what to do with.

❖

While Pam was making the sofa bed in the attic, she kept hearing Donna's words echoing in her head. The way she said "lesbian." It sounded as if Donna thought it was a disease. The look on her face was indescribable. And Donna hadn't said another word to her or Kathryn the entire night. Pam sat on the end of the bed and leaned forward to put her head in her hands. Maybe Donna was right. Maybe Pam didn't know what she was getting herself into.

"What *am* I doing?" she asked herself, her voice barely above a whisper.

Pam flashed back to the first time she saw Kathryn, standing in the store, looking like she had absolutely no idea what she needed. And then the first time Kathryn looked into her eyes. She could vividly remember how her mouth went dry and her palms immediately started sweating.

Pam heard Kathryn walking up the attic steps. When Kathryn peeked over the railing at her, Pam felt everything in her body react. In that moment she realized it didn't matter if she didn't know exactly what she was doing. She didn't need to know all the variables. All she really needed to know was what she felt when Kathryn looked at her. It was a feeling she never wanted to lose.

"Okay, your turn for the bathroom." Kathryn stood at the top of the steps and leaned against the wood railing. "What's wrong?"

Pam cleared her throat. "Nothing. Why?"

"You sure?"

"Positive." Pam stood and walked over to Kathryn. She put her hand on Kathryn's stomach, rose onto her toes, kissed Kathryn, and then broke away. "I'll be back," she said, moving her hand across Kathryn's stomach. She headed down the stairs, glancing back at Kathryn, who was watching her. Pam smiled as she turned the corner at the bottom of the steps. The smile quickly faded when she made her way into the kitchen and saw Donna sitting at the little table in the breakfast nook.

"I thought you were going to bed?" Pam asked.

"I couldn't sleep," Donna answered without looking up from her book.

Pam sat next to her sister. Her dark hair was now pulled into a braid and her skin was clear of makeup. She had been crying. It was obvious. "Are you gonna talk to me?" Pam asked, breaking the silence.

Donna let out an exasperated sigh. "I hadn't planned on it."

"Donna."

"What?" she asked, placing the book facedown on the table.

"Talk to me. Tell me what's wrong."

"You know what's *wrong*, Pam." Donna went to stand and stopped when Pam grabbed her hand.

"Don't."

Donna looked into Pam's eyes. "There's nothing to talk about, Pam."

"Donna, God!"

"Don't 'God' me." Donna pointed her index finger at Pam.

"Fine. Don't talk to me. Leave for Colorado tomorrow and just don't talk to me."

"Pam."

"Yeah?"

"It's going to kill Mom and Dad."

Pam looked up at the ceiling and fought back tears. "Like seeing me married to an asshole for twenty-one years made them happy?"

"You know what I mean, Pam." Donna leaned back in her chair. "It's just not right."

"Why isn't it? Why is it wrong for me to be happy? Why have you always hated the idea of me being as happy as you are?"

"That isn't how I feel!"

"Then why do you always act like it is?" Pam asked, trying to not yell at her sister as she sat there in her pink bathrobe.

"Pam. This is going to take me a while."

"That's okay if it takes you some time, but you can't just shut me out. It's not fair."

"I just don't understand it."

"Do you think it was easy for me to understand?"

"You act like you're fine. Like this isn't even something you want to hide."

"I don't want to hide it," Pam said, a new bravery fighting to make itself known within her. "Not at all. But it's still hard because, in case you forgot, I worry. I worry all the time. I worry that the people I love the most are going to hate me the most."

"Like who?" Donna asked, eyeing Pam.

"Like Mom. Dad." Pam waited a beat. "You."

Donna took a deep breath. "I'm not going to hate you, Pam. You're my sister. I love you."

"Then why is this so hard for you to understand?"

"Because," Donna instantly responded. "Because you like men. You were married to Harold. And you were high school sweethearts. And this isn't *you*."

"But maybe it is me," Pam replied, shrugging her shoulders. "Maybe all of that wasn't me."

"Were you ever happy with Harold?"

"Maybe for a bit, when he got partner at the law firm and we weren't struggling at all financially and," Pam paused and thought back to those days, "and I barely saw him."

Donna's eyes grew wide. "I wish you would have talked to me more."

"Because you're so easy to talk to?" Pam asked with a laugh.

Donna started to laugh along with her. "Pam, I just don't want you to get hurt."

"I'm going to be fine. I promise you." Pam took a deep breath. "So, you really think Mom and Dad are going to disown me?"

Donna moved her hand so she could hold Pam's. "No," she said with a small smile. "Mom already knows. And so does Dad."

"Then why did you say it will kill—"

"Because I'm a bitch," Donna interrupted. "You know that."

Pam snickered. "You really are."

Donna looked down at their intertwined hands. "Mom pulled me aside earlier and told me she knows about you and Kathryn and that I better not be mean to you. Like I'm a child or something."

Donna took a breath. "Don't even say 'if the shoe fits' or I'll punch you."

Pam tried to cover her laughter.

"And then Dad walked up and said that he likes Kathryn and," she paused, "she's a lot nicer than Harold ever was." Donna's voice was an octave lower as she imitated their father's voice perfectly. "Our parents and their sixth sense."

Pam could feel her eyes welling with tears. "They aren't mad?" She watched as Donna shook her head. "Wow."

"They love you, Pam. And if you're happy," Donna paused, looked up at her, and smiled, "they're going to be okay with it."

Pam put her arms around Donna, pulling her into a hug. "I hope you're okay with it one day."

Donna squeezed Pam back. "I'll work on it. I promise."

❖

Pam climbed the narrow attic staircase after getting ready for bed. When her eyes adjusted to the darkness, she saw Kathryn curled on her side, eyes closed and her head nestled on a pillow. Pam could feel the butterflies in her stomach. She knew nothing was going to happen, but the idea of sleeping in the same bed as Kathryn made everything in her body do cartwheels. Pam smiled as she walked over to the bed. She watched Kathryn slowly open her eyes and smile as she lifted the covers for Pam to slide in next to her.

"Come here," Kathryn said seductively.

Pam eased between the sheets. She pulled the down comforter up around herself and let out a deep breath. "Hi."

Kathryn grinned as she put her arm over Pam's torso and pulled her closer. "Don't be shy now," she said, whispering near Pam's ear.

"God," Pam said through a loud exhale. She turned her head a little more and pressed her lips against Kathryn's, heard Kathryn's soft moan, and felt it reverberate through her lips. She pulled away gently. "Thank you so much," she whispered against Kathryn's lips.

"For what?"

"For being here. For coming with me. For everything." She

pushed Kathryn's wavy hair behind her ear. "You have no idea how much this means to me, that you came here with me."

"Today was really amazing," Kathryn replied. "Your family is so wonderful. I loved talking to your parents. Hell, you even managed to make *my* mother smile today. I don't think that has happened since the late eighties." The two women laughed. "I wouldn't trade this day for anything," Kathryn said.

Pam placed her hand on Kathryn's neck and lightly ran her fingers across her skin. She tenderly moved her thumb across Kathryn's lips. "Neither would I," she said through tears that had started to form. "Neither would I."

Kathryn wiped away a tear that had escaped from Pam's eyes. She leaned forward and kissed Pam again as she rolled onto her back. She parted Pam's lips with her tongue, sliding in gently and then pressing against Pam's tongue.

Kissing Kathryn was becoming as simple as breathing and just as necessary. And in the back of Pam's mind, all she could think about was wanting more. More kisses, more touching, more moaning, more skin, more, more, *more*. She moved her hand down Kathryn's arm, down her side, to the edge of her sleep shirt. She wanted so badly to move her hand up under the shirt so she could feel Kathryn's soft, warm skin. She wanted to slide her hand up to the expanse of Kathryn's breasts. She could feel Kathryn's breathing as it escalated. The urgency between them was starting to rise. Pam felt as if she was watching the thermometer climb on a hot day. One degree after another, it was getting hotter and hotter under those covers.

"Pam?"

Pam broke away from the kiss and gazed at Kathryn, breathless. "We need to stop, don't we?"

Kathryn let out an exasperated groan. "Yeah, or else."

"Holy hell," Pam said as she fanned herself. "Are we insane?"

"Yes, I think so." Kathryn started to laugh as she propped herself up with her elbow. "It's just, as much as I want this to happen—and, Pam, I want this to happen so much—I don't want it to happen *here*. Does that make sense?"

Pam brought her hand over and placed it on Kathryn's cheek. "It makes perfect sense." Pam could see the outline of Kathryn's figure in the moonlight that came in the window. "How did this happen?" she whispered.

"I'm not sure," Kathryn replied with a small laugh. "I'm still trying to convince myself that it isn't just a dream."

"Tell me about it," Pam replied. "I feel like I want to write a love song about you. Paint your picture! Or take a million photos of your beautiful body. Or maybe all those things."

"I'm sorry I almost didn't realize how amazing this could be." Kathryn looked directly into Pam's eyes. "I was so afraid that I was going to get hurt."

"Kathryn," Pam said, moving as close as possible to Kathryn, "I could never and I will never hurt you." She took a deep breath. Pam had never felt for someone what she felt for Kathryn. These feelings were taking over every part of her body. She was loving how she felt, too. What a strange feeling to actually look forward to being with someone else, especially someone of the same sex. "I do have something to tell you, though."

"Oh, no, what?"

"My parents know about us."

Kathryn swallowed. "Well, that was fast. How do they know already?"

"Donna told me that apparently they just *knew*." Pam smiled. "I guess you don't hide it very well."

"I never will," Kathryn replied. "I hope that isn't what you want."

"*You* are what I want. All of you," Pam whispered.

"Good." Kathryn put her head on the pillow and situated herself.

Pam scooted in closer to her. "I love you, too, by the way," Pam whispered when she closed her eyes.

"I know," Kathryn said with her arms around Pam.

CHAPTER SIXTEEN

Kathryn took a sip of her coffee and continued to read the paper as she sat at the breakfast nook waiting for Pam to come downstairs. The farmhouse was still quiet, thankfully, so Kathryn didn't have to deal with any questions yet.

"Well, good morning, Kathryn."

That was short-lived. Kathryn looked up at Carolyn, her heart instantly lodging in her throat. "Good morning," she finally responded after she had swallowed the lump.

"Did you sleep?"

"Yes, I did," she answered. "It's so quiet here. I love it. How about you?"

"I slept like the dead." Carolyn poured her coffee and whisked over to the breakfast nook. "Speaking of, are you reading the obits?"

"Nope." Kathryn chuckled. "They're all yours."

"When you get to this age you start seeing more and more of the people you knew in here." Carolyn tapped on the paper and then gasped. "Myrtle Townsend. Oh, dear."

Kathryn's face fell. "I'm so sorry."

"Don't be." Carolyn laughed. "She was a mean old woman. I just didn't know about her passing yet. You know, news travels very fast around these parts." Carolyn looked up at Kathryn. "So, should we talk about the elephant in the room?"

Kathryn sighed. "I guess so."

"Don't you hurt her."

"Mrs. Gerrard, I promise—"

"No, you listen to me," Carolyn said, cutting Kathryn off with a swipe of her hand. "We watched our daughter spend a lot of years of her life with a man that treated her horribly. And it didn't matter. She stayed. And stayed. And stayed. Because that's what she was taught. That you stick things out, especially when the going gets tough." She paused and took a deep breath. "I'm not very open-minded."

Kathryn continued to listen, not saying a word.

"But if Pamela is happy," Carolyn smiled, adjusted her dark-rimmed glasses, and slid them farther down her nose so she could make eye contact with Kathryn, "I just want her to be happy."

"I want that, too," Kathryn said firmly.

"Okay, then, we agree." Carolyn looked back down at the obituaries. "And you're a pretty girl, so at least there's that."

Kathryn started to chuckle and looked back down at the newspaper, as well.

❖

A lot had happened in the last twenty-four hours. Not only had Pam met Kathryn's ultra-rich parents, but she had just basically come out to hers. And all she wanted to do on the ride back to Chicago was talk about it. But every time Pam opened her mouth, she was instantly filled with nerves.

And the closer they got to her house, the closer they got to a bedroom…a bed…sex…and it was scaring the shit out of Pam.

She knew it was what she wanted. She'd thought about it all the time in the past couple of weeks. She thought about Kathryn's hands and how soft her skin was going to be and the way her lips would feel as she made her way down Pam's body. Pam was going insane with desire. And fear.

What if Kathryn didn't like her once she saw her naked? What if Pam didn't perform in a way that made Kathryn happy? She wasn't sure if she had the skills after all. And what if Kathryn didn't like the way Pam's body felt? Or the way she sounded? Or, Jesus Christ, what if she didn't like the way she tasted?

When they pulled into the driveway and exited the vehicle, there was a fleeting moment when she wanted to say good night to Kathryn and tell her she would see her tomorrow.

But Kathryn kept following her. Kathryn followed her all the way through the garage, inside to the house, through the kitchen, to the stairway. She took her coat off and took Pam's and it was everything Pam wanted her to do, but it was also everything Pam didn't know what to do with. She was nervous, scared, and so unsure of the inevitable. The very light research Pam had done online was not enough preparation for any of this.

Pam's hands shook and she wrung them before she turned around and finally locked eyes with Kathryn. "This is not, I mean, I don't...I just...Would you like some tea?"

Kathryn cocked an eyebrow. "No, I'm fine," she answered, her voice lower than normal.

Pam pulled air into her lungs. "I just, you know."

"Your first time with a woman?" Kathryn offered. She looked so adorable standing there, her hands shoved into her front jeans pockets with her hair still holding droplets of water from the now-melted snowflakes.

Pam nodded. "Yeah." She raked her fingers through her hair. "I just..."

"Don't know what to do?"

"Yeah." Pam shrugged. "I feel like—"

"A virgin?"

Pam nodded as she pulled her bottom lip into her mouth and bit down to try and distract herself from the embarrassment she was feeling. Her skin was two seconds away from crawling right off her body.

"Pam?" Kathryn placed her hand on Pam's clasped hands. "We do not have to rush this."

Pam wasn't sure what happened, but in that moment, every single ounce of nerves, trepidation, and fear left her body. It was like a switch had been flipped. She lunged forward, threw her arms around Kathryn's neck, and kissed Kathryn, tasting her lips, her ChapStick, her breath. It was so amazing. Every kiss they'd shared was mere child's play compared to this kiss. It was perfect and special and everything Pam had always wanted in a kiss. In everything, actually.

Kathryn wrapped her arms around Pam and, without any hesitation, backed her into the wall at the bottom of the stairs. Pam's hands were tight against the wall above her head, and Kathryn's knee was now pressing firmly between Pam's legs. It was so sexy and *hot* and everything Pam had never experienced with Harold. It was so perfect, Pam couldn't tell if she was dreaming or actually living this fantasy.

"Kathryn," she managed to get out between kisses. "I need you to," she kissed Kathryn again, deeper as she fought against her hands being restrained, "I want you to take me upstairs." Pam pushed out her words when Kathryn latched onto her neck and made her way to Pam's earlobe.

"Holy shit," Pam groaned when she finally broke away, breathless. "What are you doing to me?"

"Well," Kathryn said, her chest heaving, "I plan on fucking you, slowly."

"I don't know if I'll survive *slowly*," Pam murmured.

Kathryn leaned forward and grabbed onto Pam's earlobe again with her teeth. "I want you," she said quietly and then breathed deep, causing goose bumps to cover Pam's skin. She kissed her way back over to Pam's lips. "I want to taste you."

"God," Pam said into the kiss as she wrapped her arms around Kathryn.

"I want to make you scream."

Pam groaned.

"I want to make you come so hard."

"Kathryn," Pam whined, "stop talking about it and take me upstairs."

Kathryn did as she was asked and started walking up the stairs, leading Pam by the hand. Pam's heart was beating so hard she could feel the pulsing in her hands, in her stomach, in her knees. It was insane. The anticipation was so intense.

As soon as they walked into Pam's bedroom, Kathryn turned

around and pulled Pam into her arms. "I love you," she whispered against Pam's lips. "I love you so much."

Pam's eyes filled with tears as she touched Kathryn's face. "Oh, Kathryn." Pam leaned in and kissed Kathryn. "I love you, too," she said between kisses. "I'm so happy I decided to get coffee with you."

Kathryn tilted her head back and let out a laugh. "God, me, too."

"I almost didn't, you know."

"Well, you only live once, Pamela," Kathryn commented as she moved her hands to the hem of Pam's sweater. She started to pull the wool up. "Raise your arms," she whispered to Pam, who did as she was told.

Pam heard the sweater fall to the floor, and then Kathryn popped open her bra from the back. Goose bumps covered her skin when Kathryn slid the straps down her arms. She watched Kathryn in the dim lighting from the street lamps. She saw the way Kathryn was looking at her naked body. It was the most intense look she had ever seen on Kathryn's face.

Pam hated the idea of comparing what was happening now to what always happened with Harold, but it was almost impossible not to do, especially because the last time Harold had undressed her was so long ago she could barely remember it. Sex with him had become infrequent, and when it did happen, it wasn't something Pam ever enjoyed. And now here she was, getting ready to have sex with another person. A *woman*. And so far, Kathryn removing her sweater and bra was the sexiest thing that had ever happened to her. Pam was struggling over being sad about her lack of experience in being loved and adored yet feeling so completely lucky that she'd found this person who wanted to make her life worth living again.

When Kathryn's nimble fingers popped open the button of Pam's jeans, then hesitated, Pam gazed at Kathryn. "What?" she breathed. "Is something wrong?"

Kathryn shook her head. "Nothing is wrong. I promise." She pushed the jeans down to the floor and helped Pam step out of them. "I have to admit," Kathryn said as she knelt and hooked her forefingers into the waistband of Pam's panties, "I never thought this was going to happen."

It was Pam's turn to smile. "Imagine how I feel," she said.

Kathryn looked up at Pam as she slid the black panties down her legs. "Are you still nervous?"

Pam was standing in the middle of her bedroom, completely naked, with this woman who had managed to change every single thing in her forty-year-old life. She probably should have still been nervous. But as she looked down at Kathryn, all she could think was that she had never been more ready.

"No," she whispered. "But I need you to stand up so I can undress you now."

Kathryn's snicker as she stood was adorable. Pam immediately went after Kathryn's shirt, practically yanking it off her. She felt a twinge of embarrassment wash over her. "I'm sorry," she said quietly. "I've been imagining what your body looks like under these clothes since our second coffee date. I'm sick of waiting."

"Well, by all means."

Pam moved behind Kathryn and unsnapped her black bra. "Feel free to help me remove those tight-ass pants," Pam said against Kathryn's bare shoulder. She heard Kathryn chuckle and then watched as she undid the button and started to slide the jeans down her body.

"Jesus," Pam whispered when she noticed that Kathryn was wearing a black thong. "Are you serious?"

"What?"

"A thong?"

Kathryn turned around so she was facing Pam. "I can take it off," she said, her voice so low and seductive that Pam's legs almost turned to jelly.

Pam reached forward and placed her fingers on Kathryn's abdominal muscles. She outlined each one with a featherlight touch. "Your body is perfect," she commented as she took in Kathryn's perky breasts, her strong arms, and her toned legs.

"Pam?"

"Hmm?"

"Can I fuck you now?"

Pam's eyes went wide. "Oh, my God, yes, please."

Kathryn ran her fingers down Pam's stomach, and Pam hated to admit it, but she was slightly self-conscious after seeing Kathryn's body. But after she saw the way Kathryn was looking at her, like a starving woman that had finally found sustenance, the feeling was fleeting. Kathryn continued to move her hand down, down, until she found Pam's wetness and slid two fingers through it.

"Wow," Kathryn whispered. "You're so wet."

"Well, no shit."

Kathryn's boisterous laughter made Pam's nerves dissipate. "You're perfect," Kathryn whispered before she leaned down and pulled one of Pam's nipples into her mouth.

"Kathryn," Pam moaned.

"Are you okay?"

"Yes, my God, yes," Pam said through a moan. She wrapped her arms around Kathryn and leaned her forehead against Kathryn's.

Kathryn gently guided Pam back to the bed. "Lie down," she instructed, and Pam did as she was told. She watched Kathryn climb on top of her, straddle one of her legs, and then prop herself up with a hand on either side of Pam's shoulders. "You sure you're ready for this?"

Pam nodded. "I've never been so sure of something in my entire life." She felt one of Kathryn's hands slide between her legs and then through her wetness. Pam moaned Kathryn's name, and it sounded like a prayer as it left her lips. She could not believe how amazing this all felt. And then Kathryn slid a finger inside her. That was all Pam needed. She was floating and free, and for the first time in her entire life she felt *complete.*

As Kathryn slipped another finger inside her, Pam moved her hips, grinding along with the pumping rhythm of Kathryn's hand.

There was a second when Pam tried to talk herself out of coming. It was too fast, too soon. She didn't want it to be over so quickly! But the way Kathryn was filling her up, and stroking her, and latching onto her nipples, it was futile to resist the orgasm. It started in her stomach, building as she felt Kathryn's thumb brush against her clit on every pass. As the orgasm crept its way from Pam's stomach to the tips of her toes and the top of her head, she leaned her head back and repeated Kathryn's name over and over. And then, as if the entire scene wasn't hot enough, Kathryn spread Pam's legs, making sure to lock eyes with her before bending down and placing her mouth directly on Pam's center. It was quick, the whole process, but what Pam remembered the most was the way her orgasm crashed through her and made her feel like she was floating. It was incredible and scary at the same time. Incredible because she had never felt that way before, and scary for the same reason. How did she live her entire life and never feel this way?

Kathryn crawled on top of Pam. "You still with me?"

"Fuck," Pam whispered, her breathing still not at a normal level.

"I'll take that as a yes." Kathryn smirked as she situated herself next to Pam.

"I have never," Pam paused, took a deep breath, "felt like that before."

"Well, that wasn't even my best work," Kathryn commented in a seductive voice. "Roll over."

Was Kathryn serious? It wasn't over? There was *more*? Pam was beside herself with happiness because her past sex life had been one and done, and even then, it wasn't that great. When she got over the shock, Pam rolled over, her bare ass sticking in the air. Within seconds, she felt Kathryn's breasts as she dragged them down her back. She stopped at Pam's ass, kissed both cheeks, and Pam's body filled with excitement when Kathryn's hand lightly moved up the inside of her thighs. And then she felt Kathryn slip two fingers inside her wetness. A moan left her mouth involuntarily as she gripped the down comforter, and she spread her legs a little wider. A third finger slipped inside her, and another moan came from her mouth, this time Kathryn's name tacked onto the end. She felt Kathryn's mouth next to her ear.

"I fucking love hearing you moan my name," Kathryn whispered into her ear.

Pam propped herself up on her elbows and turned her head

so she could kiss Kathryn. "I am going to come again," Pam said breathlessly between kisses.

"Get on your knees," Kathryn urged, keeping her fingers inside Pam. She wrapped her arm around Pam once she was on her knees and started to rub her clit.

Pam's vision blurred as the second orgasm started to build. She found herself completely understanding why people become sex fiends. She never wanted this to stop. She wanted to be loved like this forever. And finally, when the orgasm hit, it was even more intense than the first one. She had never been loud during sex, but Kathryn was definitely bringing out another side of her. Pam could hardly believe those sounds were coming from her, and the sound she made when Kathryn slowly pulled her fingers from her throbbing center was no exception. She was slack against Kathryn, both women on their knees on the bed. Kathryn's hands were roaming over Pam's body, stopping on her breasts, tweaking her nipples. And within seconds, Pam felt another orgasm shoot through her—without Kathryn even touching her center. She shuddered against Kathryn and then a maniacal laugh raked through her body.

"What the fuck?" she asked, still breathless.

Kathryn smoothed her hands over Pam's torso and then rolled onto her back. "Do you want to ride my face?"

Pam let out a laugh. "What? Wait. Seriously?"

Kathryn smiled. "Yes, seriously. Have you ever done it before?"

"No." Pam shook her head.

"Put a knee on either side of my head," Kathryn said. "Here and here. You put your hands on the headboard to brace yourself. And then," she grinned, "I make you come so hard you will never be the same again."

"Kathryn," Pam laughed, a blush tinting her cheeks.

"Trust me."

"I do," Pam said quietly as she did as she was told. She looked down at Kathryn, gripping the headboard as soon as Kathryn's tongue slipped inside her. And that was it. She moved and found her rhythm on Kathryn's face, feeling when Kathryn would pull her clit into her mouth, roll it between her teeth, suck on it so hard that Pam thought she was going to cry. It all felt so fucking good. And just when Pam didn't think she could handle it any longer, her orgasm hit, like a rainstorm in a drought. Her entire body shook, from her head to her toes and every other spot in between. She came so hard that she almost blacked out. She wondered if she would be able to walk tomorrow, because she certainly couldn't walk right now. When she finally moved off Kathryn and rolled onto the bed next to her, she kept her eyes closed for fear that she would wake up from this amazing dream.

"Well?"

"You," Pam said, still breathless, "were right."

"About?"

"I'll never be," more breaths, "the same again."

Kathryn chuckled when she pulled Pam close to her. "Good." She kissed Pam on the cheek.

❖

Pam's eyes fluttered open and she tried to focus in the dark room. She stretched out her legs, feeling the soreness between her thighs. A smile appeared on her lips as she slipped her hand between the comforter and her body, feeling the still-wet area. She was sore but aroused, and as she flashed back to the amazing lovemaking she'd just experienced, all she wanted to do was wake Kathryn up. Pam looked over at Kathryn lying next to her. She was on her side, using her arm as a pillow. Her hair was still pulled up, but some strands had snuck out, making her look like she quite literally had sex-hair. Pam pulled the comforter back gently and took in the sight of Kathryn's breasts as she slept. She ran a finger over a nipple, watching as it slowly got hard. She ran her finger back over it and heard Kathryn's breathing start to deepen, so she leaned in and placed her mouth over the now-erect nipple. She flicked it with her tongue, tried to replicate what she liked when Kathryn did it to her. Of course, she liked every single thing Kathryn did to her, but she wanted so badly to make Kathryn feel like she had made Pam feel.

"Pam," Kathryn said through clenched teeth.

Pam lightly rolled the nipple between her teeth and sucked on it, which only elicited another breathless moan from Kathryn. "Someone's awake," Pam whispered against Kathryn's cleavage after she straddled Kathryn's legs.

Kathryn laughed as she lifted her head and looked down at Pam. "Yes, I'm awake, and *very* happy to see you," she commented, another laugh rolling through her body.

Pam looked up at Kathryn, a smirk on her lips. "Better than an alarm clock," she said, an air of cockiness coating her words.

"Fuck yeah, it is," Kathryn moaned, her hips rolling against the weight of Pam's body. "You feel so good on top of me."

Pam crawled up to Kathryn's face and smiled as she slipped her hand between Kathryn's thighs. The feel of Kathryn's wetness was almost too much for Pam to handle. She was surprised that she was affecting this woman like that. It had been so long since she had turned Harold on that it was almost as if she would never turn anyone on ever again.

"You're wet," Pam finally commented, her voice soft and unsure.

"You do that to me," Kathryn pushed out. "You make me that wet."

"Yeah?" Pam asked before sliding a finger through the wetness. "I make you this wet?"

Kathryn moaned in response, biting down on her lip.

"Tell me if I'm doing something wrong."

"You're fucking perfect," Kathryn said through short breaths. "I promise."

Pam chuckled as she slipped a finger inside Kathryn. The moan she was met with was enough of an answer, but she still asked, "So, this is okay?"

Kathryn smiled, her hips moving. "Yes, God, yes."

Pam pulled out, pushed two fingers in, and was met with another moan, this time her name on Kathryn's lips as a whisper. She continued to pull out and push in, thrusting slowly, feeling Kathryn clenching around her. It was one of the most amazing feelings she had ever felt in her entire life. Being this close to someone, being this trusted, being this in tune with another person—it was almost enough to make her cry.

"Pam," Kathryn breathed. "I love you so much."

And hearing that really was enough to make Pam cry. Tears welled in her eyes as she thrust. "I love you, too." She leaned down and kissed Kathryn, feeling Kathryn's arms wrap around her. Pam could tell that Kathryn was close. She heard Kathryn's breathing change, felt the change inside her, and then saw Kathryn's neck muscles tighten. There was a slight pause from Kathryn and then her orgasm hit. It looked like it literally started at her head and ended at her toes. Pam moved her fingers inside Kathryn and then felt her hand being clamped between Kathryn's thighs. A laugh bubbled from Pam's throat. "Is everything okay?"

"Yes, *fuck*, just don't move," Kathryn groaned, her orgasm still lingering, tears starting to spill from her eyes. "That was amazing."

When Kathryn unclamped her thighs, Pam slowly slid her fingers from inside Kathryn's wetness and smiled. "Are you crying?"

Kathryn snorted and lifted her head to look at Pam.

"Is everything okay? Are you okay? Did I do okay?"

"You're joking, right?"

"Well, no, I mean," Pam took a deep breath, "it's my first time. I want to make sure you're okay. And that I did okay." Pam's body was heating up, her blush filling her cheeks. "I'm sorry," she added.

"Pam," Kathryn said firmly. "You were absolutely amazing. You were," she took a breath, propped herself up with her elbows and gazed at Pam, "you were perfect."

A smile spread across Pam's lips. "I had a good teacher." She leaned forward and pressed her lips to Kathryn's. "A really, *really* good teacher."

Kathryn laughed through the kiss. "You're crazy, you know that?"

"Crazy in love with you." Pam wrapped her arms around Kathryn and pulled her with her as she rolled to the side. "Let's do it again."

"Again, eh?"

"Yes, again. And again. And *again*."

"I've created a monster," Kathryn teased as she straddled Pam's hips.

Pam moved her hands and let them roam over Kathryn's skin and up to her breasts, but Kathryn took Pam's hands into hers and pressed them above Pam's head. She leaned down and latched onto Pam's neck.

"I think I'll take my time this time," she said between kisses and nips.

Pam let out a low guttural moan and fought against the restraint. "Jesus," she breathed. She knew then it was going to be the longest and most amazing night of her entire life. And she was more than ready for every second.

CHAPTER SEVENTEEN

K athryn looked over at Pam as she continued to sleep. Her hair
was spread out on the pillow, and the sunlight coming in the
window caught the highlights in it. Her hand was across her chest
and her breasts were uncovered.

Kathryn smiled when she remembered the night before. Heat
shot through her body and ended between her legs. *Oh God.* She
was a little sore through her thighs, and her hips were aching. She
flashed back to how Pam had looked as she came, her neck and her
hands and, God, everything about her. Kathryn brought her hand up
to her mouth. She breathed deeply and was quite happy when she
realized that her hand still carried Pam's scent.

Needless to say, neither one of them had really slept. Every
time Kathryn closed her eyes, Pam would be right there, kissing her
or doing things to Kathryn's body that even she had no idea could
be done. Kathryn was shocked by Pam's eagerness and abilities. She
was a natural, and it made Kathryn feel amazing. The last time she'd
been excited about making love was with Judy, and even then she
knew it wasn't going to last. And now Pam was in her life, making
her believe in happiness again.

Kathryn moved her hand under the covers and onto Pam's
stomach, watching her expression the entire time. She pushed her
hand farther down, over the smooth mound between her legs. It
turned Kathryn on instantly when she felt how wet Pam still was.
She gently stroked Pam and smiled when her hips started moving.

A very soft moan, then Kathryn's name floated from Pam's mouth. She had Pam right where she wanted her.

"Jesus Christ, Kathryn."

Kathryn started to giggle as she looked up at Pam. "What?"

"Good morning to you, too," Pam said playfully. She gently flipped Kathryn onto her back and started to kiss her. Pam's lips still tasted like sex. Her mouth was warm, her body even warmer.

God, Kathryn, how did you get so lucky?

"Paaaaam?"

"What the hell"—Pam's eyes shot open—"was that?"

"Where are you?" came the voice up the stairs.

Pam groaned. "It's Judy. Shit."

"She just, like, lets herself into your house?"

"Yes," Pam replied. "She hasn't had to worry about bursting in on sex in a really long time." Pam jumped out of bed and grabbed her robe. She looked back at Kathryn as she was sitting there, breasts bare. She rushed back over to the bed, pulled Kathryn toward her, and pressed her lips against Kathryn's. "I'll get rid of her."

"I'll be right here."

"Good." Pam put her robe on and tied the sash. She closed the door to the bedroom behind her and rushed down the stairs.

❖

"I'm right here, Judes." Dorothy came charging with her tail wagging. "Well, hello there, Dorothy. How's my baby? Hmm?" Pam bent down and hugged the dog. "Thanks again for watching her, Judy."

Judy was standing in the doorway that led to the kitchen, eyeing Pam suspiciously. "You look like you've been through the wringer."

"I really need to change my locks."

Judy crossed her arms. "Were you going to call and tell me that you got home okay?"

"It slipped my mind." Pam rushed past Judy and into the kitchen. "Want some coffee?"

"No." Judy followed Pam into the kitchen. She put her hand on the counter and studied Pam. "Is she upstairs?"

Pam scooped two heaping scoops of coffee into the filter and pressed the Start button on the coffeepot. "Yes." She heard Judy sigh. "What?" she asked, keeping her back turned.

"Nothing."

"Judy."

"I'm leaving." Judy headed toward the front door.

Pam heard the door open and then close. She let out a deep breath and thanked God that she had escaped that question-and-answer session. And then all of a sudden, she felt a hand on her back. She turned around and Judy was standing there. "What..."

She felt Judy's hands land on her face and pull her forward, and then Judy's lips as they pressed against hers. Pam's stomach immediately clenched. She gripped the countertop, her eyes wide as Judy pulled away from the kiss.

Pam blinked once. And then again. "What the hell are you doing?" she managed to ask.

"I'm sorry," Judy said.

"Um, no, what are you doing?" Pam grabbed Judy's arm as she tried to walk away.

"I can smell her all over you, Pam," Judy hissed, jerking her hand away from Pam.

"And? Why does it matter to you?" Pam watched Judy's facial expression, her eyes, her lips as they trembled. "Answer me."

Judy turned around and rushed out of the house.

Pam looked around the kitchen. "What the hell just happened?"

❖

When Pam came back into the bedroom, Kathryn was sitting in the bed. Dorothy had found her way up and was snuggled next to Kathryn. She opened her mouth to say something to Pam about Dorothy when she noticed that Pam looked like she had seen a ghost. "What's wrong, Pam?"

Pam sat on the edge of the bed beside Kathryn. "Judy just kissed me."

Kathryn cocked an eyebrow. Did Pam really think she could fool her with that made-up story? Why would she even try? "Pam, come on. Don't be stupid. What's wrong, seriously?"

Pam's expression never wavered. She continued to stare straight ahead, never making eye contact with Kathryn.

"Pam, come on."

"Kathryn," Pam said, cutting her off. "I'm serious."

Kathryn let out a chuckle and then noticed that Pam was still completely motionless. She looked like she was barely breathing. "W-w-what?" Kathryn stammered. "Like, *serious* serious?"

Pam nodded, still not looking at Kathryn.

"I'll fucking murder her," Kathryn said through clenched teeth. "I'll murder her!"

"Kathryn, no." Pam put her hand on Kathryn's arm. "It's not a big deal."

"Oh, really? Because you look like you're ready to vomit and that's just because it's not a big deal?"

"Well, I mean," Pam said, "she's my best friend. I didn't really expect for that to happen."

"No shit."

Pam pulled Kathryn's hand into her lap. "I promise, it's fine."

"Um, yeah, it's fine because I'm going to fucking murder her." Kathryn knew she was beyond angry when she didn't even need to tell herself to stand up and get dressed. "I'm going over there," she said forcefully. She searched madly for her clothes, tossing random undergarments over her head as she looked for hers.

"Honey, stop." Pam stood and grabbed Kathryn's hand. "It's not worth it. It'll just make it worse. Just…stop…"

"Pam, I am not going to let this woman ruin my life again by fucking up the one thing that matters."

Pam pulled Kathryn closer to her. "Am I the one thing that matters?" Pam asked, her face lighting up.

"Yes, you asshole."

"Stop, then. It's not worth it."

"Just tell me one thing, Pam."

Pam moved behind Kathryn, pressing against her back. "Anything," she whispered.

Kathryn took a deep breath, feeling Pam against her, trying to keep her composure as Pam's hands started to wander. "What did you feel?"

"Nothing. I felt nothing." Pam walked around in front of Kathryn. "I love *you*," she said. "I want *you*." She placed her hands on Kathryn's face. "Please believe me," she whispered.

"I do." Kathryn wrapped her arms around Pam's waist. "I believe you." She rested her forehead against Pam's and took a deep breath. She needed to believe Pam if for no other reason than her own sanity. She knew how her brain worked, and she could feel the doubt creeping its way into the spaces that it shouldn't be allowed.

Chapter Eighteen

Pam was sitting on a stool at the bar in her kitchen, staring at the clock on the microwave.

5:57...

When Pam decided that she needed to talk to Judy about what happened between them, she'd called her at work and left a message on her voice mail. She hoped that Judy would actually accept the offer and come over after she got off that night. So far, Judy hadn't called, and the minutes kept passing by.

5:58...

Dorothy's ears perked up and she trotted over to the front door. Pam stood and followed, hearing a gentle knock as she put her hand on the doorknob. She opened it and looked at her best friend as she stood in her long black coat and New Balance crosstrainers. Her arms were crossed, her hat was pulled down around her ears, and her cheeks were red. Pam smiled, opened the door a little farther, and watched as Judy walked in and slid her shoes off.

"I was afraid you weren't going to come over." Pam made her way back into the kitchen. She headed for the coffeepot, poured two cups, and then added two spoonfuls of sugar and a dollop of hazelnut creamer into Judy's. She sat the mug on the center island and looked up at Judy, who was still standing awkwardly in her coat in the foyer.

"Judy, take your coat off and get in here." Pam watched Judy drape her coat over the stair railing and then she motioned toward the coffee.

"I don't really want coffee."

"Drink it and don't argue with me," Pam said with a raised voice.

"Fine." Judy picked up the mug and took a sip. "So, why am I here?" she asked as she set the mug on the counter.

"Oh Jesus, Judy." Pam sat on one of the stools. "You're kidding, right?"

"Well, Pam, what do you think we need to discuss? The fact that I kissed you? Or the fact that I don't know why I did it, so I think we should just move on and not talk about it?"

"You must have some idea as to why you did it."

Judy pursed her lips. "No, I don't."

"You're lying. I know when you're lying."

"How?"

"You do that thing with your lips where you press them together to stop yourself from telling me the truth." Pam smiled. "We've been best friends for twelve years, Judes. I know you better than you know yourself. Well, at least I thought I knew you."

Judy looked at Pam, a small smile appearing on her lips. "You do know me, Pam." She leaned against the counter and crossed her arms.

"Sit down."

"I'm perfectly fine standing."

Pam looked down at her hands and then up at Judy. "Judy, stop fighting this. Please." She pulled a deep breath into her lungs. She was so upset that this was happening. She wanted to know why Judy did it. Why did she think it was okay to ruin everything? She watched as Judy finally relented and walked over to sit on one of the stools across from her. Judy glanced up at her and then looked away immediately. Pam's stomach started to ache. She did not want this. At all. As if she wasn't confused enough! All she wanted now was to clear the air. Talk to her best friend. Figure out what to do next.

"Judy," Pam said. "Is what happened going to ruin us?"

"Probably." Judy shrugged. "I don't want it to, but it will. Eventually."

"Why?"

"Because, Pam. It just will."

"But *why*? I don't think that it has to."

"That's easy for you to say."

"I don't understand this, Judy."

Judy tore her gaze from Pam's and looked across the kitchen. "I've always loved you, Pam," she whispered, her voice cracking.

Pam's stomach immediately flipped. "I've always loved you, too, Judy."

"No, Pam." Judy looked back at Pam. "I mean, I've always been in love with you."

Pam felt her throat tighten and mouth go completely dry. "What are you talking about?"

Judy just stared down at her hands.

"Judy—"

"It's not something I'm proud of," Judy said, cutting her off. "I've hidden it and fought with it and struggled with it for years." She pushed back the strands of hair that had fallen out of her ponytail. "And then when Katie came into my life and swept me off my feet, and showed me what it felt like to be happy and in love, I realized why I felt the way I did around you. It was because I was in love with you. And it took Katie to make me see that."

"Wait." Pam stared hard at Judy. "You didn't leave with her because it meant leaving me?"

Judy finally locked her eyes on Pam's from across the island. "I didn't think I'd ever be the same if you weren't in my life. I loved Katie, I did. But…she wasn't you."

"You said it was the kids."

"It was always you."

Pam didn't know what to say. And as she sank further and further into a freak-out, Judy started to talk again.

"When you first told me that you two kissed, you have no idea how jealous I was. She got to hold you and kiss you, like I had wanted to do since the day I brought over that stupid store-bought apple pie after you and Harold moved in."

Judy got up from the stool, made her way over to the sink, and stood looking out the window. "The idea that you like women made me think that if you knew how *I* felt about you, you might..."

Pam turned on the stool and stared at Judy. "I might what?"

"Nothing."

"I might confess that I have feelings for you?" Pam asked. She realized again just how fucked up this conversation was. She used to be married. *To a man.* And now this? It was too much for her to get her mind around.

"Is that so wrong? Is it so wrong that I wanted you to know, Pam?"

"Judy." Pam walked over to Judy and cautiously put her hand on Judy's back. "I...I don't know what to say."

"Do you feel anything?" Judy asked, so softly that Pam almost didn't hear her.

Pam couldn't find her voice. She wanted to say that she didn't know. She wanted to say that this was too strange and complicated to talk about right then and there. She wanted to know why this was happening to her.

Judy looked over at Pam. "Are you in love with her?" she asked, a tear escaping from her eye and rolling down her cheek.

Pam answered honestly. "Yes." She quickly added, "But I do love you, Judy. I would die without you in my life. I don't want to *lose* you."

Judy placed her hands on Pam's hips and moved in closer. She moved her hands up Pam's sides before she slowly brought her gaze up and locked it onto Pam's. "God, Pam," she breathed out.

"What?"

"I want to kiss you."

"I know you do." Pam suddenly lost all the feeling in her hands. "But you can't."

Judy let out a frustrated groan. "This is going to be so hard." Her head dropped. "Do you have any idea how hard it is, to think you don't have a chance, and then when you find out you might, the person is *gone*."

"I know," Pam replied.

"I need to go."

Pam took Judy's hands in hers. "I don't want you to go."

"Pam," Judy whimpered. "If I don't leave, I'm going to kiss you."

Pam sighed as she let go of Judy's hands. "Okay. You can go." She watched as Judy stepped away from her and walked into the foyer. She slid her shoes on and picked up her coat. "Call me," Pam said after her.

"Okay."

Pam turned around before the door closed and placed her hands on the counter. She wanted to know how she'd gotten to this place in her life. And for a fleeting second, she hoped this was all worth it.

CHAPTER NINETEEN

O kay," said Abby, Pam's manager at Skin, as she leered across the table at Wildfire, the restaurant they'd picked for their Christmas dinner party. "Tell the three of us how you're enjoying your time at Skin."

Pam lifted her wineglass to her lips and nodded at Abby. "You really want to talk about work right now?"

"Well, of course she doesn't *want* to talk about work," said Samantha, another manager, motioning toward Abby with her wineglass. "She just has no idea how to function outside of that place. She's a workaholic."

"And a horrible one, at that," Melanie added. She was the owner of the store, and being out to dinner with her, as well as the other managers, was weird at best and nerve-wracking at worst.

Pam wasn't exactly sure how to act. Working with them was one thing, but actually hanging out with them? It was something else entirely. She had hung out with them numerous times, but she was always nervous, probably because she wasn't used to having friends outside of Judy. There had been a large part of her that had wanted to cancel. But she didn't. "So you're saying there's actually something else you want to talk about?"

"Yes," Abby answered for Samantha. "Samantha wants to know what's going on with you and that girl that keeps coming by the shop."

Pam wished she had canceled. "What do you mean? Kathryn?"

All three women let out low mmm-hmms and then drank from their wineglasses in unison.

"You all are ridiculous," Pam said while trying to suppress her nervous laughter. She glanced around the restaurant and tried to remain calm. The place was packed, 1920s music in the background, and the crowd was making it easier to pull herself down from the rafters.

"So, what's going on with her?"

"Nothing is going on with her," Pam answered quickly. Almost too quickly.

"You know," Melanie started as she swirled her pinot noir, "I don't really suggest friendships with the clientele."

"I don't think you have to worry about a *friendship*," Abby said under her breath, emphasizing her words with wide eyes as she took a bite of the bruschetta that they had ordered as an appetizer.

Pam took in Abby's small figure and how it looked even smaller while she held the giant red wineglass. "Excuse me?"

"Oh, come off it, Pam." Abby rolled her eyes. "We aren't blind. We all know what's really going on with you two."

"Oh, do you?"

"Yes," Samantha answered. She scraped the tomatoes off the bruschetta and pushed them onto Abby's plate. "Why won't you just tell us?"

"Maybe because it's my life, and I am a private person."

"So, you admit something is going on?" Melanie leaned in closer. "Just tell us."

"Tell you what, exactly?" Pam was getting more and more irritated with the pushing these women were doing.

"Pam, it's obvious that girl is a lesbian. We all know it. And so do you." Abby placed her hand on Pam's arm. "We care about you. We're just asking. It's not like we're going to think any less of you if you tell us you're fucking her."

Pam looked from Abby to Samantha and finally to Melanie. She took a deep breath. "Fine." She waited a beat. "I'm fucking her."

All sound left the air surrounding the table, and for a few

seconds, the silence was deafening. It was quite obvious that each woman, including Pam, was shocked that she'd admitted it so quickly and so defiantly.

Abby started to giggle, and boisterous laughs from Samantha and Melanie followed.

"Pay up, bitches!" Melanie held her hand out and waited for Abby and Samantha to hand over twenty-dollar bills. "I knew it!"

"Oh, Jesus. You guys were *betting* on it?"

Abby laughed. "Yes, we were. We're ashamed to admit it."

"I'm not ashamed," Melanie said.

Samantha grinned. "Neither am I."

They all looked at Abby as she sat there trying to keep a straight face. The sides of her mouth started to turn up into a smile when she said, "Me either."

Pam rolled her eyes. "I can't believe it," she said with a shake of the head. "I've been had."

Abby leaned forward. "Melanie bet that you'd tell us tonight. Samantha said it would never happen. And I said it'd happen closer to Christmas."

"Well, well, well…"

"Oh, don't give us that." Samantha handed her plate over to the server, waited for him to leave, and then said to Pam, "So, are you going to tell us about her?"

Pam felt her cheeks turn a deep red. "Are you serious?"

"Yes!" Melanie grinned. "We want to know. We've never had the pleasure of seeing you like this. We want to know the cause."

"Exactly," Abby and Samantha said in unison.

Pam sighed. "I can't believe this."

Melanie put her hand on Pam's shoulder. "Believe it. And spill."

Pam looked up at the ceiling of the restaurant. "Her name is Kathryn."

"She works for *Windy City Now!*" Abby said.

"Yes. She does."

Abby paused and glanced over at Pam, who was staring at her pointedly. "Okay, fine, you can tell them."

ERIN ZAK

"Thank you."

"Not a problem," Abby said while chuckling.

"She's a movie critic for the *Times*, and she does the movie review show on *Windy City Now!*" Pam paused. "She's very nice. And funny. We laugh a lot. And, well, she's really sweet. And really pretty. And honestly, everything I never knew I wanted."

"Have you met her parents?" Samantha asked before she sipped the freshly poured coffee.

"Yes, I did. On Thanksgiving."

"How was that?"

"It was weird," Pam said, looking at Abby. "It was uncomfortable, but at the same time, I couldn't believe how right it felt."

"Did you tell your parents?"

Pam started to laugh. "I guess kind of? They figured it out. And are actually being really cool about it all."

"So," Melanie leaned in, "does this mean that you're a lesbian?"

"Leave it to Melanie to be blunt," Samantha said.

"Well," Melanie said, "I want to know!"

"I think I am, y'know, a lesbian, or whatever." Pam glanced at each of the three women individually. "That's the first time I've said it out loud like that."

Abby reached over and put her hand on Pam's arm. "We're honored."

"Pam?"

Pam looked at Melanie. "Hmm?"

"Is the sex good?"

"Oh, my God!" Pam gasped. Samantha gasped as well and smacked Melanie on the arm while Abby just shook her head. "I love you, Mel," Pam said through laughter.

Melanie smiled broadly, making sure to stick her tongue out at Samantha. "I love you, too, Pam. Now, is it?"

"Pam, you don't have to tell us."

"Samantha, shush. Yes, she does," Abby hissed.

Pam looked around the restaurant. She took a deep breath and slowly let it out. "No, it's not good." Pam smiled. "It's better than good. It's fucking *fantastic*."

"Is it different than sex with a man?"

"Yeah, it really is." Pam leaned in and propped her elbows on the table. "Imagine being adored completely by a man. Remember how it used to be with your husbands? When you would have sex in the beginning, how everything was perfect? How he tried to please you, and even if he didn't succeed, he still tried. Now multiply those feelings and emotions by a million."

Abby pulled a deep breath into her lungs and let it out slowly. "Wow."

"Yeah," Samantha echoed.

"It sounds beautiful," Melanie said.

"It is." Pam smiled. "I've never been this happy before."

Samantha put her hand over Pam's. "Then that's all that matters, sweetie."

Pam couldn't believe what was happening. Each of the four women was unique; yet by working together, by going through the ups and downs of a great week in sales followed by a terrible one, by learning about each other, they had formed an amazing connection. Not even her startling news could break their bond.

CHAPTER TWENTY

Pam pulled a ball of dough out of the refrigerator and set it in front of Judy. She removed the Saran Wrap from the cold mass and smiled. "You are in charge of the sugar cookies."

"Um, no."

"Um, yes."

"Pam, you know I hate doing sugar cookies."

"I sure do. But I did them last year. And you've been all moody lately, so you *deserve* to be in charge of the sugar cookies." Judy stuck her tongue out at her. "Your kids love those, though, so you get to take more of them home with you."

"Oh, great. A sugar high followed by a sugar crash. Just perfect. Thanks, Pam." Judy sprinkled flour on the countertop and started to roll out the dough.

Pam had spent most of the day dreading this time alone with Judy. She wanted to ask Judy how this happened. How had she not realized that Judy wasn't just jealous that she was finding a friendship with Kathryn? And how had she never seen that Judy was harboring feelings for her? Pam hated that she was blind to the signs. Maybe she hadn't wanted to see them? Maybe deep down, Pam knew that understanding meant acknowledging, and acknowledging it meant having to deal with it...And she was not ready for that.

Judy worked with the dough. Her hair was pulled back into a ponytail and she wasn't wearing a lot of makeup, and Pam hated to admit it, but Judy was striking. Her eyes were so blue and her complexion was so perfect...beautiful, really, and her smile...It was as if Judy saved that smile for Pam. And only for Pam. Because Pam knew she never saw it around Judy's kids or husband.

Judy's runner's physique was apparent in the jeans she had put on and the tight shirt she was wearing. Pam used to get so angry at Judy because she never had to watch what she ate or work out to stay thin. And Pam was, well, a forty-year-old woman with a lifetime's worth of emotional eating. She never thought twice about her weight with Kathryn, though.

Kathryn...

Pam pulled her thoughts from Judy and instead flashed back to Kathryn from their morning together. And their shower together. And the way Kathryn so perfectly knew how to make her feel alive and loved. She didn't want to ruin what she had with Kathryn just to see what was going on with Judy.

"Earth to Pam!"

Pam's head snapped up. "What?"

"Where the hell were you?"

"Nowhere. I was right here." Pam cleared her throat. "What's going on?"

Judy eyed Pam from across the kitchen island. "I was just thinking that I have no idea what to get Tom for Christmas."

"Cologne."

"I always get him cologne."

Pam smiled. "Yes, you do. But you know he likes it."

"Yeah, that's true." Judy stopped cutting cookies and looked up at the ceiling. "Do you really think it was a good idea to be locked together alone for the entire day?"

"Do you honestly think we shouldn't be alone together anymore?"

Judy's eyes raked over Pam's body, and Judy quirked an eyebrow and nodded.

Pam rolled her eyes. "Quit," she said with a laugh.

"Quit what?"

"Looking at me like that!"

"Don't flatter yourself," Judy said with an air of confidence Pam had never heard from her before.

"Oh, whatever. I saw you looking at me." Pam started putting the ingredients together to make fudge. She turned the stove on and watched the butter melt in the pot. "Is this too hard for you?"

"Pam, you make it sound like I'm having the hardest time in the world controlling myself."

"Well, you sort of give off that vibe." Pam was ashamed. If one of them wasn't handling herself, it was actually Pam. And she had no idea why she was entertaining any of these ideas.

"Oh, whatever." Judy laughed. "I've been hiding my feelings for you for twelve years. I'm a goddamn professional."

Pam bit her lip and turned from the stove to look at Judy. "I hate that you never told me."

"What would I have said? How would I have said it?" Judy pulled a piece of dough off the counter and ate it. "Besides, it's not like you would have done anything about it."

"You don't know that I wouldn't have done something about it." Pam saw Judy perk up. "I just can't believe you kept such a secret from me."

"But it's not just any secret, Pam. It's not like I wasn't telling you that Tom only has one testicle or something."

Pam let out a cackle. "You're such a dork."

"You love that about me."

"You're right, I do."

Judy placed cut-outs of Christmas trees, angels, reindeer, and stars on the cookie sheets. Pam could see that her hands were trembling a little, and it made her want to hug her. She hated that the one person in the world that she entrusted everything with had held back such an enormous secret. It was frustrating and annoying and sad.

"Now what are you thinking about?" Judy asked, keeping her eyes glued to her project.

"I'm wondering why this had to happen to us."

Judy let out an exasperated sigh. "Do we really have to keep talking about this? Why keep beating a dead horse?"

"Because I need to talk about it. You can't just do what you did and then expect me to never want to talk about it again." Pam stopped stirring the fudge and took a drink of her wine. "And please don't act like we've discussed this numerous times, when you know damn well that we haven't." She pointed at Judy with the hand that was holding the glass.

"I don't understand why we have to talk about it at all. It's not like you're going to do anything about it."

"What the hell, Judy." Pam downed the rest of her wine.

"What?"

Pam looked away from her best friend's stare. She slid the fudge off the burner and turned it off. Pam heard Judy walk toward her and felt when she was standing right behind her. She turned around and studied Judy. They were only a couple of inches from each other. "I'm sorry."

And that's when Judy did it again. She reached up, and before Pam knew it, Judy's lips were on hers. Pam felt Judy's hands on her face and Judy's body pressed against hers. For the briefest of seconds, Pam kissed Judy back. She wanted to know what it would be like. Would she like it? Could she ever be happy with Judy? But in those seconds came Kathryn's face, and her hands, and it wasn't the same. Kissing Judy was like kissing *Judy*. But kissing Kathryn...was like finding heaven. It was indescribable. And *perfect*.

Pam placed her hands on Judy's shoulders and gently pushed her away. "Judy, I can't do this."

Judy's eyes filled with tears as she said, "I know."

Pam stood in silence next to the stove, trying to see if Judy was upset or mad or maybe a little of both. The silence was deafening.

"Is it going to be possible for us to be friends?" Pam paused. "Or is this always going to get in the way?"

"You have to understand why I needed to try again. I needed to be sure about your feelings for me...or in this case, the lack thereof."

"So this won't happen every time we're together?"

Judy cocked an eyebrow seductively. "Not unless you want it to."

"Judy," Pam groaned and threw an oven mitt at her.

"All right, all right. It won't."

"Okay."

"If you can handle it, I can handle it."

"I can handle it."

"You have flour all over your face."

"Oh, great." Pam grabbed the dish towel and wiped her face. "Thanks a lot, you bitch."

"Anytime," Judy said with a laugh. She moved around to the sugar cookies and started to roll the dough out again. Judy looked up from the dough at Pam. "You'd better finish the fudge before it sets in that pan."

"That'd be hilarious."

"Oh yeah, real funny. You'd probably send it home with me like you do all the other rejects."

"Your kids don't care what it looks like."

Judy smiled. "No, they sure don't."

❖

"It's not that big a deal. I figure she just needs her friends right now. She took a really huge step." Kathryn and her friends were drinking mimosas and Bloody Marys at their favorite Sunday brunch spot, Orange. The small, trendy restaurant was packed with hungover hipsters and small groups of stay-at-home moms desperate for a moment away from their children. Kathryn loved it, though, regardless of how crowded it was. It always reminded her why she loved Chicago so much. The hustle and bustle, the noise of the plates clattering, and the people talking and laughing at the top of their lungs. It all grounded her and made her feel alive.

Marcus, one of Kathryn's best friends, raised his mimosa in a mock toast. "Well, sure," he said, the sarcasm dripping from his words. His scruff was perfectly trimmed, and he of course looked better than all of them in his Chanel scarf and starched button-down. Even his skinny trousers were starched with a pleat down the front. He looked like he had just stepped out of a *GQ* advertisement.

"Yeah, you're right, Kath." Sydney coughed, her mouth full of hash browns. "Why else would she be spending so much time with her best friend that kissed her?"

"Jesus, Sydney, don't say that shit. And chew with your mouth closed, for Pete's sake." Elizabeth gently slapped the bill of Sydney's flat-brim Blackhawks hat. She looked back at Kathryn and smiled. "Kathryn, sweetie, you have to learn to trust Pam." She pushed her mass of curly auburn hair over her shoulder and propped her elbows on the table.

"I do trust her." Kathryn breathed a deep sigh. "It's Judy that I don't trust."

"I never trusted that bitch either, Kath," Marcus said matter-of-factly with his left leg crossed over his right. "Remember when she freaked out on *you* because her husband tried to have sex with *her*?"

"God," Kathryn said as she put her forehead in her hands. "That was such a fucking miserable time."

Sydney put her hand on Kathryn's back. "If you're so scared, why are you letting her hang out with Judy?"

"Because I have no right to tell her who she can and can't be friends with." Kathryn took the celery out of her Bloody Mary and bit off the end. "All they're doing is baking."

"So, is that what they call it these days?"

Kathryn glared at Sydney across the dimly lit table. "They do this every year. They start on Saturday and then finish up on Sunday. And they've been best friends for, like, twelve years. It'd be like her telling me not to hang out with you guys," she added between bites of the celery.

"You'd tell her to fuck off, right?" Marcus asked.

"Of course!"

"No, you wouldn't." Sydney chuckled. "Hmm, let's see. Really hot sex or friends that get me trashed at eleven thirty in the morning on a Sunday...I wonder what *I'd* choose."

Elizabeth quickly glanced around the dining area to make sure no one had heard Sydney. "Keep your voice down, Syd."

"Elizabeth, dear, you'd choose really hot sex, too," Marcus said calmly. "Hell, I know I would." The three women all gaped at Marcus with their mouths hanging open. "Sorry, honeys, but I would! It's been way too long since I've had a man."

"I *live* with a man and it's been way too long," Elizabeth lamented before taking a drink of her mimosa. The straight, married one among them always stuck out like a sore thumb.

"Well, I get hot sex anytime I want it," Sydney remarked as she sipped her Bloody Mary.

"You don't count, Sydney." Kathryn shook her head when Sydney glared at her. "You never count when it comes to matters of the heart."

"What the hell is that supposed to mean?" Sydney smoothed her hand over her backward ball cap and looked extremely hurt.

"It means that you have said time and time again that you don't fall in love." Elizabeth cleared her throat after answering for Kathryn. "And besides, you've been head over heels in love with me for years and have never done a goddamn thing about it."

They all erupted in laughter as Sydney leaned over and kissed Elizabeth on the cheek. "I know, sweetie, but you're married. Get a divorce and we'll see what we can do."

"Y'know, if you would grow a goatee, we might have something to talk about." Elizabeth placed her hand on Sydney's face and gently tapped her jawline.

Kathryn gagged. "I still can't believe that you like how that stubble feels!"

Marcus raised his eyebrows. "Oh goodness. There's nothing better than the feel of that roughness down my neck. *Swoon*," he said while fanning himself.

Elizabeth smiled. "Oh honey, I know. I like when Ken drags his chin down my back."

"God, I'm gonna ralph." Sydney covered her mouth and shouted through her hand, "This is gross!"

"Not that I don't love discussing men and their facial hair, but I gotta go. I have to meet my mother at my house in an hour." Kathryn reached for her purse.

"We got the bill, Kath," Marcus said as he waved away

Kathryn's money. "It's the least we could do before you go spend an afternoon with Satan."

Kathryn grabbed Marcus's face and kissed him on the lips. "You wish you could go with me and you know it!"

"Eww, girl slobber."

Kathryn leaned down and kissed Sydney. "Love you."

"Love you more," Sydney replied before she sucked down the last of her drink.

"I'll walk out with you, Kath," Elizabeth said as she followed Kathryn out of the restaurant. The cold December air hit them in the face, and both let out audible gasps. The temperature had dropped significantly in the last three days, making it almost unbearable to walk the streets of Chicago.

Kathryn turned and locked her sad eyes on Elizabeth's. They'd known each other through high school and met again when Kathryn interviewed her for a breaking medical story when she was still at the radio station. It was Elizabeth who first asked her about her relationship with Judy, and it was Elizabeth that was there when Judy ended it all. She'd picked up the pieces and even gone to therapy sessions with Kathryn. She was the kind of friend people hope they're lucky enough to have. "Everything okay?"

"Of course." Elizabeth smiled when she looked up at Kathryn. "We haven't had a chance to talk in a long time."

"God, I know. You're always so busy with that damn husband of yours."

"Yeah, well, you're all involved in a relationship right now."

Kathryn pulled out her gloves and slid them on. "I know…isn't it strange?"

"Yes! And no…It's honestly about time," Elizabeth replied. "So, you have to go meet your mom?"

"Elizabeth, she has been so weird recently. I'm almost sure that she's going to ask me for one of my kidneys or tell me that I'm out of the will or gosh, I have no idea, but it's weird."

"Maybe she had a revelation."

"About what?"

"Oh, who knows? Maybe she realized that wearing her pantyhose a size smaller was doing nothing good for her moods."

Kathryn laughed so hard that she had to lean against the outside wall of the restaurant to hold herself up. "God, Elizabeth, it's so crazy. It's just not *her*."

"Maybe she just realized how miserable her life would be without you."

"I love having you in my life. You're so wise. You always know what to say."

"Oh God. That's not being wise. It's because I'm three sheets to the wind at noon on a Sunday!"

"I know, right?"

"Hey, one more thing before you leave. You shouldn't let Sydney's remarks about Pam frustrate you. Take it from this straight woman. She obviously loves you if she decided to leave her old life behind her and start something new with you."

"Yeah, but—"

"Do me a favor."

"What?"

"Don't question me on this one." Elizabeth kissed Kathryn on the cheek, said 'bye, and walked back into the restaurant.

As Kathryn walked down Clark Street, her friends' remarks and opinions floated around her thoughts. She hated how she was feeling because she really did trust Pam. It frightened her sometimes. She had never trusted someone so easily before. But that little voice inside kept nudging her jealousy. She knew she needed to talk to Pam.

And to top it off, she was so skeptical about her mother lately that she didn't even know what to expect from a phone call with her, let alone a Sunday afternoon visit. At least when Virginia was always a bitch, Kathryn knew what to expect. She knew that she needed to go with the flow for the moment. Their relationship was never normal, and Virginia's recent behavior certainly reinforced that.

❖

Kathryn sat on the couch across from her mother. She sipped her coffee and looked up at the ceiling. *Oh God, there's a cobweb. Please don't see that…*

"Kathryn, there's a cobweb over there in that corner."

Sigh. "I'll get it later." The room was spinning ever so slightly. Kathryn knew then that she had drunk a little too much that morning.

"I'm concerned."

"About…?"

"That you're turning into your father."

"Oh, really?" Kathryn paused. "So, I'll have a heart *and* brains. I'm not quite sure what you're concerned about."

"I didn't mean *that*."

"Then what did you mean?"

Virginia shook her head. "I meant that you're allowing this woman to control you."

"What the hell are you talking about?"

"Where is she?"

"She's with her best friend."

"Why aren't you with her?"

Kathryn set down her coffee cup and leaned forward. "Because it's not necessary for us to spend every second together."

"So, you aren't the tiniest bit worried?"

"Mother, don't."

"Well?"

"Mother…"

"*Well?*"

"Stop!"

Virginia stood and walked over to the bay window in the living room. She brought her cup up to her lips. The clink as she rested it back on the saucer sounded loud in the quiet room. "The last couple times that I've spoken to you, she's been with this Judy woman, right?"

Kathryn put her forehead in her hands. She had never told her mom about what happened with Judy, nor had she ever wanted to. But she had for some reason started to talk more and more about

Pam to her mother, which was getting ready to bite her in the ass. "Why do I ever tell you anything?"

"Oh, Kathryn, stop being so dramatic." Virginia turned and sat on the bench seat by the window.

"Why do you even care? This is my life we're talking about here. Remember? *My* life. The one you don't really give a shit about."

Virginia moved her glasses down her nose and examined Kathryn over them. "Because you're *my* daughter, and I'm allowed to care whenever I damn well feel like it."

"Wrong answer."

Virginia sighed. "Why does it matter? I'm just being nosy."

"Bullshit."

"*Kathryn.*"

"Tell me what you really want to tell me."

"You really are just like your father." Virginia crossed her legs and huffed. "Okay, *fine*. I actually like this one, Kathryn."

Kathryn felt her heart leap into her throat. "You do?"

"Yes."

"Oh." Kathryn leaned back and crossed her legs. "Why?"

"I don't really know. She seems very down to earth. She's nothing at all like me, which means that she's perfect for you."

Kathryn smiled. "Ain't that the truth?" She eyed her mother. Her hair was lying perfectly. The black cardigan she had on was the one Kathryn had bought her for Christmas the year before. She always looked as if she had just stepped out of a Talbots advertisement.

"Mmm-hmm," Virginia said while swallowing a sip of coffee. "It still pisses me off that she's only eleven years younger than me, though."

"I knew you hated that."

"And I hate her name. I just hate it."

"Jesus, you're so shallow." Kathryn glared at her mother. "Virginia isn't exactly the prettiest name in the whole world. And neither is Kathryn. So quit being like that."

"Okay, okay. I'll stop with the name thing." Virginia readjusted her glasses and eyed the stack of magazines on the end of the bench. "Do you really need to have these gay magazines out like this?"

"Yes, I do, because everyone that knows me knows that I'm gay, and it doesn't matter to them, so stop letting it matter to you." Kathryn brought her hands up to her temples and started to rub her forehead.

"Fair enough," Virginia said. She cleared her throat. "Are you going to answer my question?"

Kathryn took a deep breath. "I'm not sure why she's been spending so much time with Judy."

"Well, you know what I think?"

"No, but I'm sure you're going to tell me."

"You bet your ass I'm going to tell you. You need to nip this in the bud."

"I can't tell her who she can be friends with."

"No, you can't." Virginia raised her coffee cup up to her lips and blew on the hot liquid. "But you *can* talk to her about it."

"But I want her to know that I trust her. I don't want it to be like it was with you and Dad."

"Kathryn, your father had every reason not to trust me." Virginia smoothed a wrinkle out of her gray trousers, completely leaving the admission in the dust. "All you have to do is ask her if anything is going on."

"But she hasn't given me a reason to believe that there is." Kathryn sighed. "Except for the fact that Judy kissed her a couple of weeks ago."

Virginia gasped. "Kathryn!"

"What?"

"Judy kissed *Pam*?" Virginia let out a puff of air. "This is great stuff. You need to write a book!"

Kathryn started to laugh along with her mother. It had been a long time since the two of them had a halfway-civilized conversation with each other. She wasn't sure if this was a good thing or a bad thing. "I'm not writing a book about this." Kathryn closed her eyes.

Virginia took in Kathryn's demeanor. "You have never seemed

happier. I was so used to seeing you mope around. And actually allowing me to come over? That hasn't happened in years."

"Well, Mom, I'm happy finally. And maybe I want you to be happy for me, too."

"Then why would you ever want to risk losing whatever has contributed to that change of pace and happiness?"

Kathryn looked up at the ceiling. "I fear talking to her about it will be risking it."

Virginia stood, walked into the kitchen, and left Kathryn sitting on the couch. "Talk to her, Kathryn," she shouted over her shoulder.

Kathryn rolled her eyes and followed her into the kitchen. "Don't light that in here," she said calmly as she motioned at the cigarette Virginia was holding between her fingers.

"I wasn't going to. I know you'd pass out or *die* or something equally dramatic."

"What is wrong with you today?" Kathryn asked through her laughter. "You're so nice…in that weird bitchy way you have."

"I was abducted by aliens last night." Virginia walked over to her coat, which was draped over the back of one of the chairs. She put it on, buttoned it, and walked over to her daughter. "Talk to her."

"I will."

"'Bye, Kathryn."

Kathryn watched as her mother walked out of the kitchen and toward the door. "Mom?"

"Yeah?"

"Thanks."

"Sure." She opened the door and looked back at Kathryn. "Your real mother will be back tomorrow."

Kathryn winked. "Thank God."

"'Bye, babe."

"'Bye," she said, chuckling. She heard her mother shout for a taxi. Kathryn had no idea what had happened to that woman over the past couple of weeks, but she was certainly happy about whatever it was.

Kathryn walked over to her cell phone, picked it up, and

quickly found Pam's contact information. "Hey," she said after the call connected. "Can you come over?"

❖

Kathryn heard the front door open and then close quietly. She swiveled on the stool and looked toward the sound of the noise. "Hey there," she said before she even saw who entered.

Pam poked her head around the corner and grinned. "God." She ran over to Kathryn and threw her arms around her neck. "I've missed you so damn much," she said before she pressed her lips to Kathryn's and kissed her deeply. She broke away from the kiss and laughed when she saw that Kathryn still hadn't opened her eyes. "You okay?"

"That was just what I needed," Kathryn said while opening her eyes. "You smell like vanilla and butter."

"Well, I should. I've been baking since seven last night." Pam laughed. "Judy had the kids come over today and help." She walked over to where she had set down her bags and pulled out a Tupperware container. She brought it over to Kathryn. "Here."

Kathryn pulled the lid off and started to laugh. "Oh, my goodness, look at these!" There were all different colors of sugar cookies in the container, and not a one of them looked like anything remotely resembling Christmas. "These are hilarious!"

Pam was grinning, "Oh yeah, I know. Judy had Joseph and Conlon help her frost them."

Kathryn looked up at Pam. "God, I haven't seen those kids in ages."

Pam put her hand on Kathryn's face and softly stroked her cheek. "They're getting bigger. Conlon is almost as tall as Judy."

"Wow," Kathryn said. She wasn't sure if she said it because of Pam's comment about the height of Judy's kids or because Pam looked so beautiful standing there in her dark-green sweater.

"Are you okay?" Pam sat on the stool next to Kathryn. "You sounded a little upset on the phone."

Kathryn looked down at her lap. "I'm not sure."

"Honey, talk to me."

"You have to promise," Kathryn paused as she raised her gaze and locked it onto Pam's, "to not get upset with me."

"Okay, I promise."

"I don't trust Judy," Kathryn said. She tried to gauge Pam's reaction.

"You have every right not to trust her."

"But…I mean that I don't trust her *at all*."

"And I understand why."

"No, Pam, you aren't getting this." Kathryn leaned her head down and rubbed her temples. She was getting more and more antsy and irritated with this conversation. "I think she's going to try something again."

Pam took a deep breath. "She already has," she replied, almost inaudibly.

Kathryn sat there a moment. Was Pam joking? Was she being serious? How was that possible? Kathryn didn't know if she should be upset or if she should just laugh it off. The worst part was she'd known that it was going to happen again. She knew Judy. She knew how Judy worked, how she thought, and how she moved. So the fact that Judy had actually done exactly what Kathryn knew she would was really sort of funny.

"Kathryn?"

"What?"

"Are you okay?"

"Pam…"

"Well, I know you are always worried when I go over to Judy's or she comes over to my house, and I know that you don't like when we spend time together."

"It's not that I don't like when you two spend time together, Pam. You've been best friends for years. You have to know that the only reason I get that way is because I hate the idea of losing you." Kathryn put her hand over Pam's. "I don't think you realize how amazing you are. People *look* at you, Pam, when you're walking down the street, or in the boutique, and it scares me."

Pam put her hand under Kathryn's chin. "You're so damn cute, you know that?"

"Oh, whatever. Your eyesight is failing." Kathryn was starting to get used to the idea that Pam could break her moods just by smiling at her. "I don't want to lose you," she said quietly.

"You're not going to." Pam leaned down and kissed Kathryn's forehead. She moved down and pressed her mouth to Kathryn's neck. "Do you hear me?" she said against Kathryn's warm skin. "I promise."

Kathryn gently moved her hands around to Pam's back and pulled her into a hug. "I missed you, too, by the way," she said with a soft laugh.

Pam chuckled as she leaned back and looked into Kathryn's eyes. "Oh, really?"

"Yes, really."

"Good, 'cause I'm staying the night." Pam stood and took Kathryn's hand. "Let's go watch a movie or something."

Kathryn stood and followed Pam, her eyes glued on Pam's backside. When Pam stopped in the middle of the foyer, Kathryn placed her hands on Pam's hips and pressed herself against Pam's back. Pam turned to face Kathryn, draping her arms over Kathryn's shoulders. "I choose 'or something,'" Kathryn said with a grin.

"Hmm?"

"You said, 'a movie or something.' I choose 'or something.'"

Pam cocked an eyebrow seductively. "What did you have in mind?"

Kathryn backed Pam up against the foyer wall. "Well, do you want me to tell you? Or would you rather it be a surprise?"

"I want you to tell me," Pam said quietly when she felt the wall against her back.

Kathryn slid her knee between Pam's legs and pushed it gently against Pam. "Why don't I just show you?" Kathryn leaned her head down and latched onto Pam's neck with her lips. She heard Pam's soft moan as she walked her over toward the stairs that led up to Kathryn's room. Pam pulled away and started toward the stairs. Kathryn stopped her. "No."

Pam looked back at Kathryn. "What?"

Kathryn pulled Pam back, placed her hands on either side of Pam's face, and kissed her passionately. When Pam reached down and started to tug Kathryn's shirt, Kathryn broke away from the kiss, let Pam get rid of the piece of clothing, and then immediately went back to kissing her. She slid her tongue into Pam's mouth and guided Pam against the stairs and down onto one of the steps. Kathryn lowered herself onto the step below Pam, gently moved Pam's legs farther apart, and situated herself right between them. "You're not going anywhere."

Pam pulled Kathryn's face down to hers. "You're too much."

"I know," Kathryn replied as she moved to unbutton Pam's pants. "I know."

CHAPTER TWENTY-ONE

K athryn sat back in the booth and looked around the restaurant. She could tell that the State Street Brewery was a gathering place for the after-work crowd because of all the suits and ties she saw in the bar area. She drummed her fingers on the table and wondered for the hundredth time why she was doing this. But when she saw Judy walk into the restaurant in her business suit and her heels, she knew that this conversation needed to happen.

"Hi," Judy said as she sat across from Kathryn.

"Hey," Kathryn responded from her spot in the huge booth. Kathryn felt like a child sitting there, scared out of her mind and hoping to God that Judy wouldn't make a scene. She waited for Judy to order a beer before she leaned forward. She watched her former lover as she scanned the crowd. It was hard for Kathryn to look at her sometimes without remembering everything they had gone through together.

"So," Judy started before she finally brought her eyes up to meet Kathryn's. "What did you want to talk about?"

"You and Pam," Kathryn said matter-of-factly.

Judy didn't miss a beat. "What about us?"

"You know what." Kathryn sucked down the last of her vodka and soda and motioned for another.

"What do you want to know?" Judy asked after she let out a deep sigh.

"Why you're suddenly making a point of being inseparable."

Judy took a drink of her freshly delivered beer and set it on the table. "We've always been inseparable."

"Sure," Kathryn responded sarcastically.

"Before she started telling you everything, Katie, she told *me* everything. And that hasn't changed." Judy took a deep breath. "And besides, what are you so worried about?"

"You kissed her, Judy."

"And she didn't kiss me back."

"Have you tried again?"

Judy looked at Katie. "No," she said, almost convincingly.

Kathryn pursed her lips. She looked away from Judy and glanced around the restaurant. It was getting even busier as their horrible conversation carried on. She wondered briefly if she should just let it go and tell Judy to fuck off. She shook her head and let out a very deep sigh. "You're *un*believable."

"What are you talking about?"

"Do you really think that she didn't tell me?"

"What?"

"Judy." Kathryn narrowed her eyes. "Pam told me about Saturday night."

Judy's eyebrow rose to her hairline. "I guess she really does tell you everything."

"I'm not sure why you keep trying."

"Why was it okay for you to steal me away from my husband, but it's not okay for it to be turned around on you?"

"So, you're admitting that you're trying to steal her?" Kathryn asked.

"Katie, don't be insane. It's just a question, and in case you forgot, she's my best friend."

"I know she is." Kathryn looked down at the drink the server had just delivered. "But normal people don't run around kissing their friends, Judy. I know something else is going on with you and your feelings for her. You act like I didn't spend a lot of time in my life getting to know you."

Judy's eyes locked onto Kathryn's. "Fine. I'm in love with her, Kathryn."

"Jesus *Christ.*"

"What? I am," Judy almost shouted.

"You're ridiculous."

"No, I'm not. I've been her best friend for twelve years. I deserve this more than you. And I cannot even believe this is happening. How is this even a competition?"

Kathryn was floored. She didn't know what to say next. She took a long drink of her beverage before she gathered the courage and said, "I want you to take a break from her."

"Are you serious?" Judy asked, her mug of beer halfway to her mouth.

Kathryn kept her head bent but moved her eyes so that she was looking at Judy. "Yes, I'm serious," she said calmly.

"Katie, c'mon. I'm not taking a break from her."

"Well, you either take a break from her or I tell her to take a break from you. You decide," Kathryn said forcefully.

"Fine. I'll talk to her."

"Um, no. That's not what I said."

"You know what, I can handle this. I can talk to my best friend about this." Judy rolled her eyes. "You realize your jealousy is not attractive, right?"

"It's not jealousy," Kathryn said through clenched teeth. "You know I'm right to ask this. You can't control yourself and you know it. You've proven that twice." Kathryn downed the rest of her drink, set her empty glass on the table, and then slid out of the booth. She buttoned her coat and slammed forty dollars on the table. "Have another drink on me." She turned and strode out of the restaurant.

❖

Pam walked up the steps leading to Judy's house wondering what the hell Judy must have wanted when she left such a frantic voice mail. Pam knocked and then heard footsteps and kids yelling.

Pam smiled when the door was flung open and Grace, Judy's oldest child, was standing there. "Pammie!"

"Grace!"

Grace wrapped her arms around Pam's waist and hugged her. "My mom's upstairs."

"Okay," Pam said, walking over to the stairs.

"Hey, Pam."

Pam turned as she climbed the stairs and looked behind her. "Tom! Hi there!"

"It's been a while," he said with a grin. He popped the tab on the can of beer he was holding. "How have you been?"

Pam leaned against the banister and laughed, all of a sudden feeling very self-conscious. "Not too bad. How about you?"

"Things have been pretty good. We're in the middle of the planning for our annual carnival for the steel workers union."

"Dad!" yelled one of Judy and Tom's three children.

Tom smiled. "Duty calls." He turned and walked back toward one of the kids' rooms. "It was nice seeing you, Pam!" he shouted behind him.

"Same here!" Pam took a deep breath and let it out. That was so awkward. She continued up the stairs. "Judy?" She waited for Judy's answer. "Judy? Where are you?" Pam walked into Judy's room and over toward the closed door to the master bathroom. She knocked. "Hey, it's me. Let me in." The door opened and Judy was standing there.

"Get in here," she said.

"Judy, what the hell is going on?"

Judy shut the door and leaned against it. "Katie talked to me today."

"About what?"

"About us. About our friendship." Judy looked down at the floor while she wrung her hands. "She doesn't want us to be friends anymore." She bit her lip.

"What? What are you talking about?" Pam asked as she moved closer to Judy. "When did you see her?"

"After work today. You were still at work. We met downtown at a pub." Judy looked up. "Pam…"

"What do you mean she doesn't want us to be friends anymore?"

"Exactly what I said. She doesn't want us to be friends anymore."

"But why? That doesn't sound like something Kathryn would say at all."

"Because she doesn't trust me."

Pam crossed her arms across her chest and took a deep breath. "Well, can you blame her?"

"Pam, stop."

"Well, Judy," Pam walked over to the tub and sat on the edge, "you haven't exactly been controlling yourself well."

Judy groaned. "I can't help it."

"You're going to have to if you want to be in my life, Judy." Pam leaned forward and rested her elbows on her knees. "Are you sure she said that we can't be friends?"

Judy nodded.

"This is so weird," Pam replied.

Judy slid down the bathroom door to the floor. She leaned her head back. "Why does she think cutting me out of your life will make things different?"

"Things aren't bad, though, so there's no reason for her to want anything to be different."

"Are you going to talk to her?"

"Yes," Pam said matter-of-factly. "And you need to get your ass out of this bathroom. Your family is running around down there like a bunch of lunatics." She stood and walked over to Judy, reached out her hand for Judy to take, and pulled her up. She was about to open the bathroom door when Judy moved in front of her.

Pam stepped back a bit and cleared her throat. "Judy," she said in a small voice. "What are you doing?"

Judy's eyes were sad as they searched Pam's. "I just, I don't want you to leave yet."

"But I have to. I need to go talk to Kathryn." Pam looked into

Judy's eyes. She was always shocked by how blue they were. "There can be no more kissing me, Judy."

"But, Pam…"

"Judy, no." Pam crossed her arms. "You have to stop."

"I'll try."

CHAPTER TWENTY-TWO

Kathryn stood on Pam's front porch, her hair blowing in the wind and her hands shoved into the pockets of her parka.

"Okay, we really need to sit down and talk," Pam demanded as soon as she flung open the door.

A determined puff of air came out of Kathryn's mouth. "Uh, yeah, we do, since I have no idea why you're so upset." She stepped into the house and removed her shoes and coat. "What's going on?" Kathryn bent down to pet Dorothy. "Hey, girl, how's it going?" Kathryn asked her, a giggle escaping from her throat when the dog licked her cheek.

Pam tried to remember to stay firm, but it was hard for her to focus with Kathryn being her usual fabulous self. Kathryn's hair was curlier than normal, and half was pulled back into a barrette. Tiny ringlets had snuck out of the clip and were making themselves comfortable along her temples and down the side of her face. It just wasn't fair for her to look that attractive when all Pam wanted to do was throttle her, and not in a good way. Pam tried once again to compose herself. But when Kathryn locked her eyes on Pam's, all Pam could do was flinch and then say, "Wow. You look terrific."

A blush washed over Kathryn's cheeks. "I was thinking the same thing about you."

Pam stood against the now closed door, her eyes clamped shut. "I hate this."

"What?" Kathryn asked, arms now crossed, guard as far up as she could muster.

"Being upset with you," Pam answered matter-of-factly and breezed past Kathryn into the kitchen.

"Why are you upset with me?" Kathryn asked as she followed Pam but made her way to the refrigerator and took out a bottle of water. She leaned against the counter and took a long drink.

Pam put a hand on the center island and hoped that the cold granite would ground her. She was having the hardest time not being moved by the fact that Kathryn acted completely at home whenever she came over. It made Pam's heart smile and her hands ache, and it was all too much.

"When did you go there?" Pam asked, motioning to the sweatshirt Kathryn was wearing. It said "Jackson Hole" on the front. Pam had always wanted to go there.

"When I was twenty-five I went with my friends on a road trip, and this was one of the stops." Kathryn cocked an eyebrow. "You really *did* pick up that subject-change technique from your mother, didn't you?"

"Actually, this is just more of a subject *avoidance* technique. Two entirely different things."

Kathryn leaned her head back and laughed. "I can't even wait to start fights with you if this is what they'll always be like."

"They won't always be like this."

"No?"

"Uh, no." Pam pushed her hand through her hair and gathered herself. "I can be a bitch if I need to be."

"Oh, I'm sure," Kathryn replied, her eyebrow raising to her hairline. "Now, what's going on?"

"Judy said that you talked to her today."

Kathryn licked her lips. "Yes, I did," she replied so calmly that it made the hairs on the back of Pam's neck stand straight up.

"Do you really think that was the best thing to do?"

"Well, seeing as how I didn't really do anything but ask her to take a break from you, yes, I do think it was the best thing to do."

"That's all you said?"

"Why? What did *she* say that I said?"

Pam walked over to one of the stools around the island and sat. "Well," Pam said, "she said that you told her that you didn't want us to be friends anymore."

Kathryn rolled her eyes. "You're kidding."

"No."

Kathryn stood in silence, one leg crossed over the other. "Well, she's certainly not going to give up."

"Give up on what?"

"Trying to steal you from me," Kathryn said bluntly.

"Jesus, Kathryn. That is not what she's doing."

Kathryn let out a frustrated laugh. "Pam!"

"What?"

"Are you blind?"

"Are you?"

Kathryn put the cap on her water, set it forcefully on the countertop, and walked over to Pam. "No, I'm not. That is why it's so obvious to me that's what she's doing."

"Kath, honey, no, she's not."

"Whatever."

Pam watched Kathryn walk over toward the dining room table. The desire to touch her was overwhelming. She was not enjoying this fight. Not that she'd thought she was going to, but when she fought with Harold it had felt good to release her anger. Now? Now all she wanted to do was say she was sorry and she didn't mean it and God, please don't be mad at her.

"Kathryn," Pam said, barely above a whisper. She was met with silence.

"Pam," Kathryn finally said after what felt like an hour, "don't act like she's not doing anything wrong here."

"Kathryn, come on. She isn't doing anything wrong."

"Are you serious?" Kathryn yelled.

Pam swiveled around on her stool and shot daggers at Kathryn. "Don't raise your voice at me like that. I put up with that for twenty years from my husband, and I don't plan on putting up with it from you or anyone else, for that matter."

"Don't you dare compare me to him, Pam. Don't even start that," Kathryn said, her voice quiet, with her back still turned toward Pam.

"I don't deserve this," Pam mumbled under her breath. "Let me repeat, I haven't done anything wrong here, Kathryn. Why are you making this such a huge deal?"

Kathryn glanced at Pam over her shoulder. "I don't trust her, Pam."

"Yes, but you can trust me." Pam stood and made her way over to Kathryn, where she placed her hand on Kathryn's back. She felt her heartbeat speed up, the feeling of Kathryn's body heat almost too much for her to handle. Pam was having a hard time dealing with the fact that even though she was angry with Kathryn at that particular moment, she still found herself completely and utterly attracted to her. She felt terrible for comparing Kathryn to Harold. They were nothing at all alike, and Pam knew that.

"Please. I need you to trust me," Pam whispered.

"I don't want you to be around her for a while, Pam. She needs to see that you're serious about me. About this. Aren't you? You're in this, right? This isn't just a fucking fling, is it?" Kathryn's voice cracked.

"Kathryn, baby, no, this is not a fling for me. You have to know that. You have to know that I'm serious about everything with you. This whole thing. You have to know that."

"Then?"

Pam shook her head. "I'm sorry, Kathryn. But I can't just ditch my best friend of twelve years because you think she might make another move on me."

"She'll try again. You can mark my words."

Pam took a deep breath as she moved her hand from Kathryn's back, tightening both fists next to her side. She could not believe this was happening. Of all the things to fight about, they were fighting over *Judy*? Pam was so done with the conversation. There wasn't anything left to say. "I need to go to bed," she said quietly.

"Are you mad?" Kathryn asked as she turned to face Pam.

"I'm certainly not happy with you right this second." Pam crossed her arms. "I don't like that you don't trust me."

"I do trust you, Pam. I just really do *not* believe Judy. I've been there, Pam. I've been you. I've been the one that was not interested and had her come back at me, time and time again. She ruined every relationship I tried to have after her. She doesn't give up. And when you say you're not interested, all it means is that she'll work harder. She'll flash that grin, and bat those eyelashes, and remind you of all the good times you shared together, because that is what holds the two of you together. And she *knows* that. She knows how to sway you, Pam, because she's swayed me. And I'm unswayable."

Pam clenched her jaw. "I need you to let me deal with this."

"She told me that she's in love with you."

Pam all of a sudden felt nauseated. "I know."

"How do *you* know?"

"She told me."

"She *told* you?"

Pam nodded. She could practically see Kathryn's heart breaking.

"She told you that she's in love with you?" Kathryn asked. "And you didn't feel the need to tell me this?" She moved away from the dining room table and away from Pam. "I like how I found it out from Judy and not from you. That's real fucking funny considering that literally two seconds earlier you were telling me to trust you. Do you even know what trust is?"

"Her saying that wasn't a big deal to me, Kathryn. And I didn't think it would be a big deal to you," Pam said, trying to convince Kathryn as well as herself.

"How could that not be a big deal?" Kathryn walked over to the front door and pushed her feet into her shoes. "Someone else is in love with you, has kissed you twice, and you don't think any of it is a big deal?" she asked, her eyes wild and angry. "Do you remember when I was so hesitant about wanting to jump into this relationship with you? How I kept telling you I didn't want it and I kept pushing you away? It was because I do not trust people. I always get fucked over. I always get walked all over. And here I thought you would be different. I took a chance on you, Pam. I thought you would never fucking hurt me like that." Kathryn walked toward the front door and grabbed her coat, her hand on the door handle.

"Kathryn, wait," Pam pleaded, a sob overtaking her voice. "Don't leave like this."

"I need to leave."

"Kathryn, please. I love you! Not her. Please don't go."

"Pam, I trusted you."

"Trusted? Not trust?"

Kathryn turned her head and looked into Pam's eyes. She felt like she was going to throw up. "Remember that time you left my house because I wouldn't give you what you wanted?"

"Kathryn."

"Now you get to see how it feels." And Kathryn left the house, leaving Pam standing there, so shocked she could barely see straight.

CHAPTER TWENTY-THREE

Y'know, Kath, not that I don't entirely love that you're holed up in my spare bedroom—"

Kathryn looked over at Elizabeth's husband, Ken, and smiled. "I'm leaving today, don't worry. I have a zillion Christmas movies that I should have screened by now. I hope they don't fire me." She had gotten way behind at work. Thank God, the season would be over soon.

"Elizabeth said that you're having troubles with your girlfriend."

"What?"

Ken sat next to Kathryn at the breakfast nook and positioned a Christmas-themed place mat in front of him. She knew then that he had been trained to do that or Elizabeth would probably murder him. He rubbed his hand over his salt-and-pepper goatee.

"Is it true?"

"Yeah," she muttered.

"You haven't talked to her in three days?"

"It's been four days now. And you don't need to act interested." Kathryn moved her gaze to the window and watched as the snow continued to fall. Chicago snow was usually erratic—it would snow and then the sun would shine—but today the snow was falling steadily. Of course. Even the weather wasn't as confused as Kathryn felt.

"Why do you think I'm asking? It's not an act. I am interested." Ken took a bite from his piece of toast. "Elizabeth loves you to death. She would do anything for you."

Kathryn had never actually sat and had a meaningful conversation with Ken before, partly because he always seemed a little put off by the fact that his straight wife always hung out with a group of gays. The couple of times when she did try to start a conversation with him, they always ended up talking about the Cubs or the Bears or the Blackhawks. But over the last year and a half, Ken had been trying.

"I know," she replied gently. And Kathryn decided to let him try. "I'm sorry."

"Don't be sorry," Ken said, tilting his head. He held his cup up to his nose and breathed in deeply, the hot liquid practically touching his nose. "This freshly ground French Roast is amazing."

Kathryn continued to look out the window.

"Ken, are you badgering Kathryn?" Elizabeth rushed into the kitchen wearing blue scrubs. Kathryn watched Ken's eyes rake over his wife's body and his lips turn up into a smile as Elizabeth finished pulling up her mass of curly auburn hair with bobby pins.

"Surgery today?" Ken asked.

Elizabeth poured a cup of coffee and walked over to the two of them. "Yeah, all day. I'm not even going to bother dressing up today. I'll clean up and put different scrubs on when I get there."

"To have the life of a doctor," Kathryn said.

"Saving lives and all that good shit," Ken mumbled through a mouthful of toast.

Elizabeth reached over and took the other piece of toast that was on Ken's plate. "You work tonight, Kath?"

"Yeah."

"Okay. But you know you can come over here afterward. I mean, it's Christmas Eve. I don't want you to be alone."

"I know. But really, I work until midnight covering for one of the reporters, so it'll just be easier to go home."

"You going to your parents' tomorrow?" Ken asked.

"They're in the Virgin Islands for another one of Richard's business functions, so no. I have no idea why that damn firm picks this week to send my parents out of town." Kathryn added, "Not that I like spending Christmas with them anyway. And I had already planned on spending Christmas elsewhere."

Elizabeth cleared her throat and glared at Ken for even bringing it up. "You can come here tomorrow, at least, if you aren't coming here tonight," she suggested.

"Wait a second here," Ken said as he held his hand up in the air. "What?"

"You were supposed to be with Pam and her family tomorrow for Christmas, weren't you?"

Kathryn nodded.

"Ken, don't butt in." Elizabeth put her hand on Ken's and shook her head.

"I'm not butting in. I'm wondering why you're acting like a four-year-old, Kathryn."

Kathryn gaped at Ken, her eyes wide. "What the hell do you mean?"

Elizabeth took a deep breath and let it out slowly. "Ken, please."

"Let me get this straight. You love this woman, right?"

"Yes, I do."

"And you want to be with her, right?"

"More than anything," Kathryn replied.

Ken snorted. "Then quit acting like a spoiled brat."

Elizabeth bent her head down and tried to hide her laughter. She looked sheepishly up at Kathryn. "You have to admit that he's right."

"This isn't about me being spoiled," said Kathryn. "It's about how she didn't tell me that Judy is in love with her. It's about the fact that she didn't even mention it to me. How am I supposed to trust her? Why doesn't she think it's as important as I do?"

"Kathryn, she didn't think it was important because it *isn't* important to her." Elizabeth reached over the table and put her hand on Kathryn's. "I have let you stay here for the past four days so you wouldn't have to deal with talking to her. I've let you mope around here because I know you don't like being told that you're wrong. But you have to realize that Pam is going through probably the hardest time of her life after losing her husband. She comes to the realization that, holy shit, she's in love with another woman. And then, like that isn't enough of a blow to the senses, she learns that her best friend, who, by the way, is also a woman, is in love with her. And that best friend also dated the woman that she herself is in love with! Her best friend is nothing at all like she thought she was. Imagine going through that, Kath. Imagine finding out that everything you thought was right and genuine in your life was actually all false. Imagine it...and then maybe you can see why we don't understand why you're not trying to work this out with her."

Kathryn's eyes filled with tears. "Fuck." She said it so quietly it was almost inaudible.

"Call her," Ken urged.

Elizabeth stood and grabbed her coat and purse. "Come on, we'll walk to the El together." She bent over and kissed Ken on the lips, then rubbed her thumb over the dimple on his whiskered chin. "I'll see you tonight."

"Thanks, Ken." Kathryn leaned over and hugged him.

"Anytime, kid."

The two women buttoned their coats and put on their hats and gloves as they headed outside into the cold air. Kathryn flung her duffel bag over her shoulder and trudged through the new blanket of snow that had accumulated overnight and early that morning. They made it onto the cleared sidewalk path and headed north toward the El tracks.

"You have to work almost twelve hours tonight?" Elizabeth asked.

"Yeah. I was supposed to get off at five o'clock and head to Michigan with Pam, but when the shit hit the fan, I told Bob Peterson that I'd cover the last part of his night shift."

"Are you going to call her?"

Kathryn didn't answer right away because she was torn. She knew she wanted to call Pam. And she knew that it was the right thing to do. But what she didn't know was how Pam would even consider forgiving her. Because Ken was absolutely correct. She was acting so spoiled. And selfish. And the argument that she was an only child for most of her life and didn't know any better would definitely not work this time with Pam. Kathryn leaned against one of the metal beams next to the tracks of the El train. She looked over at Elizabeth, who was waiting patiently for an answer. She squinted as she focused down the tracks, looking for the train.

"I don't know," Kathryn said when Elizabeth's gaze met hers.

"Kathryn."

"I know."

"Just call her," Elizabeth said. "You don't get the luxury of being the brat this time."

"Why do I love you so much again?"

Elizabeth leaned in and kissed Kathryn on the lips. "Because you know I'm right. Have a good day at work. And Merry Christmas, honey." Elizabeth stepped onto the Brown Line train and waved as the doors closed.

"Merry Christmas!" Kathryn shouted, a grin gracing her lips. Elizabeth's train left the platform and she thanked God when the Red Line train arrived. She rushed onto the train car out of the bitter, cold air, quickly found a seat, and leaned her head back. As a sigh escaped from her lips, she resolved right then to call Pam that night, even though it meant admitting that she had acted irrationally. And like a brat.

CHAPTER TWENTY-FOUR

A nd your total is $42.40," Pam said with a smile to Gertrude, a
very affluent, elderly customer that had become a regular over
the past couple of months. Gertrude pulled out three twenty-dollar
bills and handed them over with shaky hands.

"Is everything okay, dear?" Gertrude asked as she situated her
purse on her shoulder.

"Oh yeah, everything's fine." Pam handed the change back to
Gertrude, who waved it away.

"That's for you," she said with wink. "Merry Christmas, my
dear."

"Thank you so much, Gertrude. You have a Merry Christmas,
as well." Gertrude slowly made her way out the front doors. It was
the first time the store had been empty since she got there six hours
ago. It felt good to do absolutely nothing. It was Christmas Eve and
business had been better than ever, so they all relished the five or ten
minutes a shift when there wasn't a customer in sight. She turned
her head and looked over at Abby, who had been standing at the
register next to her. "How are we doing today?" Pam asked as Abby
started scrolling through the day's figures.

"It's picking up, thankfully, because we've only made four of
the five segments so far."

Pam smiled. "You're too hard on yourself. Four out of five is
really good."

Abby glanced over at Pam. "Mmm-hmm." She adjusted her
glasses. "You sure everything's okay?"

"You really do that eavesdropping thing well, you know that?"

"Honey, I raised two kids. I know how to eavesdrop with the best of 'em."

"I've found that out." Pam turned and began cleaning the back-counter area. She cleared her throat when she felt Abby staring. "Everything's fine."

"You're a terrible liar." Abby let out a laugh. "You've been avoiding questions about your personal life for the past couple of days. *We* don't avoid questions about our personal lives here. You need to get used to that."

"So, what are you guys doing for Christmas?"

"Oh my God," Abby said with an exasperated sigh. "No changing the subject, Pamela. Now, what the hell is going on?"

Pam leaned against the counter. "I haven't talked to Kathryn in four days." It hurt to say it out loud. She hoped she didn't start crying again. She couldn't stand the thought of crying again. She had cried so much since Kathryn left that she was sure she couldn't find another tear if someone paid her to.

"What? Why?"

Pam shrugged.

"*Pam.*"

"We got into an argument and she left mad. I've tried to call her about twenty times, but she won't answer my calls." Pam looked down at her shoes. "And my best friend recently told me that she's in love with me and has been for the past twelve years. Oh, and *she* also had a relationship with Kathryn about four years ago that she never told me about."

Abby stood there staring at Pam. "Wow."

"See? Everything's fine."

"Goodness, Pam. What the hell have you gotten yourself into?"

Pam shrugged again.

"So, wait. Let me see if I understand this. Your best friend—"

"Judy."

"Okay, Judy. Judy had an affair with Kathryn about four years ago." Abby paused and Pam nodded. "And then they broke up. And you met Kathryn and fell head over heels for her." Pam nodded again. "So then, when Judy sees you happy for the first time since she's known you, she decides to tell you that, oh, by the way, she's in love with you and has been since the first day she met you."

"Bingo."

"Wow."

"Oh, and did I mention that Judy is married and has three kids?"

Abby's jaw landed on the floor. "Holy cow," she whispered. "So, Judy's a lesbian."

"I guess?"

"And so are you."

Pam giggled. "Looks that way."

"And the two of you were both straight?"

Pam nodded.

"So, what's the problem?"

"What do you mean?" Pam crossed her arms.

"I mean, why don't you just get together with Judy?"

"Because I'm not in love with Judy."

"Then there's your answer."

"What was my question?"

"You were subconsciously asking what you should do. And I'm telling you that if you're in love with Kathryn, you'll do whatever you need to do to keep her."

"She doesn't trust Judy."

"Does she have reason not to?"

"Yeah, Judy has kissed me a few times in the past couple of weeks."

Abby howled. "I thought this kind of stuff only happened in romance novels."

"Believe me, I thought the same thing!" Pam put her hands on her forehead and rubbed it.

"Well, Pam, I'm going to give you my advice. Even if you don't want it, you're going to get it. You might not like hearing this, but I sort of think that Kathryn's right. I mean," Abby paused, "you're happy when you're with Kathryn. We've seen the way your face changes the second she walks into this store. We've seen the difference between how you were when you started here. God, Pam, when you started here, you were this woman that so badly needed to break out of her shell. You were happy then, but now, you're just," Abby laughed, "you're ecstatic. I love that I've been able to witness that transformation. And *that's* how Judy should be if she's really your friend."

"What do you mean?"

Abby glanced around the store quickly and then looked back at Pam. "Judy is being a bitch, Pam. Samantha, Melanie, me, *we're* happy for you. We're thrilled for you. And we barely know you. And Judy, your best friend in the whole world, is trying to ruin the first relationship you've had with someone that truly completes you. I can't imagine doing that to you." Abby took a breath. "That's what I mean."

"Shit." Pam could feel her legs shaking. Abby was absolutely right. "How do I fix this?"

"You go to Kathryn and you tell her that you love her and that you don't want to lose her."

"I think I already did lose her. She won't answer my calls. She doesn't trust me anymore."

"Don't be stupid, Pam. You know where she lives. Go over there. Sweep her off her feet."

"What if she doesn't want to see me?"

"Pam, use your head. Figure something out. Don't let a bump in the road ruin everything. Don't let *Judy* ruin your happiness." Abby gestured to show that there were customers in the store again. She cleared her throat. "Okay, back to work." She winked at Pam as she whisked past her. "Love you, babe."

"Oh, Abby, I love you, too."

Pam sighed when she thought about what she needed to do. She was afraid that she really had lost Kathryn. And there was really nothing she could do to fix it—except for one thing. And it just might work.

CHAPTER TWENTY-FIVE

Pam unlocked the front door to her house and opened it just enough for Dorothy to come outside. The dog came flying through the opening, immediately running off the front porch and falling into the fresh snow, playing as if she were a puppy again, rooting around with her nose and throwing the snow up in the air. "You are such a nut, Dorothy," Pam said with a grin. She bent down and packed a snowball to throw at Dorothy, who caught it in midair and then ran toward Pam, jumping on her and almost knocking her down. She was still laughing when she made her way into the house and removed her boots. She hung up her coat and then turned around. "Shit!" she yelled as she grabbed her chest and backed up against the door.

Judy chuckled. "I'm sorry."

"What the hell are you doing?"

"We haven't talked in a couple of days. I've been working, you've been working, and it has been crazy. I needed to talk to you," Judy explained. "I didn't mean to scare you."

Pam opened the door and let a barking Dorothy back into the house. The dog ran right for the mudroom where her kennel and blanket were. "It must have been too cold for her out there," Pam commented as she tried to calm herself down. Seeing Judy like this was not at all what she wanted right now. And she had no idea how to handle the impromptu visit.

"Well, it is freezing out," Judy said.

"It was so crazy at work today. I'm ready to pass out," Pam said as she tried to deflect and not let the subject steer toward them and their predicament. As she fidgeted with her hands, she breezed past Judy on the stairs and into the kitchen. Her heart was in her throat. She didn't want to get into anything with Judy, but she knew they needed to have a talk if she was planning on fixing things with Kathryn. As she pulled out a can of Diet Coke from the refrigerator, she felt herself chickening out.

"Weren't you guys supposed to go to Tom's mom's house for Christmas Eve?" Pam rolled her eyes at herself. She really was a scaredy-cat.

"We're going tomorrow morning since it's still snowing so badly." Judy had made her way into the kitchen and leaned against the center island. "I thought you were going to your parents' with Katie...I mean, *Kathryn*."

"Yeah." Pam swallowed a sip of her drink. "I haven't talked to Kathryn in four days."

"What? Why? Is there trouble in paradise?"

"Well," Pam said after she let out a very deep breath, "she doesn't trust you." Pam snorted when she saw Judy's face twist. "Don't even act like you don't know why."

Judy pushed out a very forced laugh. "I have no idea what you're talking about." She pushed her hair away from her face.

"Whatever," Pam replied. "She doesn't trust me now."

"Why?"

"Because I don't want to stop being friends with you." Pam watched as Judy started to make her way to where Pam was standing. She could feel the hairs on the back of her neck starting to rise.

"Pam," Judy whispered as she reached out and put her hand on Pam's.

"I think I've lost her, Judy," Pam said, her eyes welling up with tears. She didn't know why she was crying. Was she upset about Kathryn? Or was she afraid of how Judy would react? "And I know it hasn't been that long, but I can barely breathe when I think about not having her in my life."

"What about me?"

Pam let out a puff of air through her tears. "What are you talking about? What about you?"

"Pam, I *love* you." Judy moved in front of Pam and put her hands on Pam's shoulders. "I want to be with you."

"Judy," Pam started, but was cut off by Judy's lips. Instantly she tried to push Judy away, her voice muffled as she protested. "Stop it! Stop it right this instant! Quit being like this!" she shouted as she finally succeeded in getting Judy off her. She eyed Judy as she stood there, her chest heaving, her face flushed. "What the hell has gotten into you?"

"Why is this so difficult for you, Pam?"

"How many times do I have to tell you no? What is it about this that you can't understand?"

"Because I'm not sure that *you* understand it. I think there's more there than you want to admit."

"Why can't you just be my friend? Why all of a sudden is that not good enough for you?" Pam asked.

"I don't understand why you won't just love me," Judy yelled.

Pam took a step away from Judy. "What the hell is wrong with you? Don't you realize that by acting like this, like a crazy woman, you're going to lose me forever? Why do you want to risk that?"

"What are you saying?" Judy asked, tears streaming down her cheeks.

Pam's heart was breaking. She didn't want to do this, but she knew she needed to. She knew she had to let this go, to let Judy go. She wiped away her own tears. "I'm saying that I can't be friends with you anymore, Judy."

"Pam…" Judy walked over to the kitchen wall, put her hand against it, and slid all the way down to the cold wood flooring.

"Judy," Pam whispered. She knew that Judy was dramatic, but she had never seen her this bad. "I can't lose Kathryn. I can't. And you won't *stop*. You keep trying. And you lied to me, Judy. You stood in your bathroom last week, and you *lied* to me! Right to my face. You're trying to make Kathryn look like a terrible person. And dammit, Judy, she is the best thing that has ever happened to me.

Why can't you just be happy for me? Why do you want me to be unhappy?"

"I'm sorry," was all Judy said. Sobbing, crying, unable to breathe properly.

Pam couldn't watch Judy any longer. She was rocking back and forth, inconsolable, and it was nauseating Pam to see her best friend like that and to know it was her fault. She wanted to kneel beside Judy and hold her, but she knew she couldn't. She didn't move. She kept her hands firmly planted on the countertop and her feet nailed to the floor. She knew she could not give in now. But looking at Judy, her entire world crumbling around her, Pam's resolve faltered. She started to take a step but was interrupted when her phone rang. She didn't want to talk to whoever it was. It couldn't be that important.

Just as that thought passed through her mind, the phone started to ring again. Pam finally reached over and picked it up, getting more and more fed up with the persistence of the person on the other end. "Hello?" she asked, the irritation in her voice showing through.

"Hi." Kathryn's voice was low, almost inaudible.

"*Kathryn.*" Pam's voice changed almost instantly. She felt her heart leap into her throat. "Where have you been?" She raked her fingers through her hair, frantic to find out where Kathryn was. She noticed that Judy had calmed down considerably and was now staring at the cabinet in front of her.

"I'm getting ready to leave work."

Pam saw Judy start to stand up. "Judy," she said as she covered the mouthpiece. "Wait."

"No, I'm fine. I'll talk to you tomorrow."

"Judy."

"No, Pam. I'm fine."

"You're not fine, Judy. Don't leave yet."

"Pam?" she heard Kathryn's voice on the other end. "You still there?"

Pam uncovered the mouthpiece. "Yes, I'm here. I'm sorry." She watched Judy put her shoes on and slide her arms into her coat. The sound of the zipper was deafening and seemed to echo throughout the house.

Judy looked back at Pam before she opened the door. "'Bye."

"Kathryn, hold on for a second." Pam placed the phone on the counter and rushed over to Judy. "Judy, seriously. Don't go just yet."

"No. We'll talk soon. I promise. Go, fix this with her." Judy's lips turned upward into a small smile. "I'll be okay."

"Are you sure?"

"Yeah, Pam," Judy said. She closed her eyes. "I'll be just fine."

"Kathryn, I'm so sorry," Pam said into the phone as she raised her hand and urged Judy to stay. "I know you don't want to hear this, but I have to call you back." Pam heard Kathryn's heavy sigh on the other end of the phone and then her quiet *okay* before the phone went dead. It was horrible timing, yes, but Pam couldn't let Judy leave without saying what she needed to say. "Judy, wait."

"Pam, please, stop trying to make this okay right now. I'll be all right. Just please let me leave. I can't pretend right now. I just need to go home."

"Is Tom there? Are the kids?"

Judy took a deep breath and then forced it out through pursed lips. "I'm going."

"Judy. Listen to me for one moment. You will find the one, *your* one someday. You are a good person, and all this unrequited longing for the thing that's missing in your life has not been good for you. Believe me, I understand. I also know life is painfully short. I've learned that in the last year." It was one good thing about grief. It had opened Pam to reevaluating her priorities. "Take some time to figure out what you really want." Pam realized she was talking as much to herself as Judy. Love was more important than she knew.

Judy looked into Pam's eyes. "Go fix this with her."

"I will. But I want you to know something."

"More words of wisdom?"

"Yes. Maybe it's a kooky Christmas blessing or something." Pam swallowed.

"Okay, my wise Santa," Judy said wiping her nose on her sleeve.

"Romance is like, well, it's like music. It makes our lives worth living." Pam couldn't believe her words; they flowed without thought. "But friendship, it's something different. More like sunlight. Without it, we can't survive. Not for long. I want you to know what you've meant to me." Judy had nourished her, and she would never forget that.

"Good-bye, Pam." Judy left the house, closing the door behind her.

Pam placed her hand on the doorknob. She wanted to go after her, but she knew she had to let go and let Judy figure things out for herself.

And Judy wasn't the only one who needed to get her act together.

"Shit," Pam said out loud. She checked the time on the clock. "Ten thirty. Dorothy, I'll be back soon." The dog's ears perked and then she rested her head again on the pile of blankets.

Pam grabbed her coat, threw her boots on, and rushed out the door. Her feet were flying as she trudged through the snow. She looked over at Judy's house, her bedroom light. She hoped that things would one day be okay between them, but for now, she needed to do exactly what Judy said. She needed to fix this.

❖

Kathryn readjusted her bag as she stepped out of the El train. She looked up and down the platform and noticed that she was one of the only people around. "Merry Christmas, Kathryn," she said to herself as she rolled her eyes. Her entire body felt frozen, and it wasn't even that cold out.

She knew that Pam couldn't handle this. She knew that her relationship with Judy was too deep and too intense. And the worst part of it was that she completely understood. Judy had never been just a fling for Kathryn. She was persistent and cute and insanely talented. Of course Pam would pick Judy. *Of course* she would.

Kathryn lifted the latch to the gate on the fence surrounding her small front yard.

Pam. She was sitting on Kathryn's steps, her arms wrapped around herself in her winter coat, her hat pulled down over her ears, the snow blowing like crazy. Kathryn wanted to pinch herself. The feelings, the way Pam's eyes sparkled, the look of determination and love. Everything was so perfect. And it was incredible. She couldn't believe all she had wanted this entire night was to see Pam, and here she was. It was almost too good to be true. Was this her Christmas gift or just more torture?

"Wow," Kathryn finally breathed as she let the gate swing closed behind her. Seeing Pam after such a long break was making it hard to think. It was as if Kathryn was seeing her for the first time all over again. And shockingly, she looked even more beautiful sitting on Kathryn's steps than she had in the boutique. "Hi," Kathryn said as she moved closer.

Pam stood and looked into Kathryn's eyes as she climbed up the steps. "I'm sorry. You have no idea what happened with Judy, and you have been overreacting this entire time. And I'll admit that I've been wrong, too."

"Babe, let's just go inside." Kathryn smiled as she put her hand on Pam's arm.

Pam let out a defeated sigh. "But..."

"Inside, please." Kathryn brushed past Pam to the front door, opened it, and then dropped her bag on the floor. She took her coat off and then took Pam's coat and hat. She hung them both in the closet and took a deep breath before she turned around and locked eyes with Pam. She was finding it extremely hard to not rush forward and throw her arms around Pam as she stood there in her wool socks, fidgeting with the sleeves of her cardigan sweater. Her blond hair was slightly damp from melted snow, and she looked just as unsure as Kathryn felt.

Kathryn motioned toward the kitchen. "Do you need something to drink?"

"Coffee."

"I'll have to make it."

"I know. That's why I asked for it."

Kathryn chuckled. She walked through the hallway and into

the kitchen, Pam trailing behind her. "You know, you're pretty mean when you want to be."

"Kath," Pam said, her expression determined. "You had no right to get so upset with me."

"Pam, let me relax for a few minutes before you get going. I can't deal with this right at this moment."

"Fine," Pam said reluctantly.

Kathryn pulled a box of Pecan Sandies cookies from the pantry and slid them across the center island toward Pam. "You like these, right?"

"You know me so well."

"I know. I really do." Kathryn moved closer to Pam and reached forward with her left hand to lightly place it on Pam's face. Her skin was so smooth, so soft, and so warm. "I missed you."

"God," Pam said with relief. "I know. I missed you, too."

"I'm sorry." She rested her forehead against Pam's.

"Kathryn," Pam said. "I can't handle you sometimes. You're almost too much for my heart."

"I know." Kathryn leaned her head back and sighed. "I'm a jealous person. I shouldn't have reacted like that."

"No, you shouldn't have, but Judy wasn't being trustworthy and neither was I. I never did anything with her, though. You have to believe me."

"I believe you." Kathryn paused. "And I trust you." She leaned forward and gently kissed Pam's lips and felt relieved when Pam returned the kiss. And in an instant, it was like falling in love with Pam all over again. Kathryn loved every second; the feeling of Pam's warm lips and the gentle nip of her teeth was all too perfect. And it had been entirely too long since their last kiss.

Pam pulled away and found her way to Kathryn's ear. "Take me upstairs and make love to me all night," she whispered, kissing her way back to Kathryn's lips.

Kathryn took Pam's hand in hers and pulled her up from the stool and up the stairs into her bedroom.

Standing beside the bed, she pulled Pam into her arms and said, "I don't want to ever lose you again."

"Then don't," Pam whispered. "Don't let go. Don't stop. Just don't."

"I'm so scared I'll fuck this up."

"Kathryn, baby." Pam pulled away and gazed into Kathryn's eyes. "You have to stop thinking. I want you and I want a life with you."

"I love you," Kathryn breathed. "So much."

"I love you, too," Pam said. "More than anything."

"Lie down," Kathryn instructed with a certain air of self-assuredness that she reserved for Pam. "I'm going to have my way with you."

Pam let out a sweet moan when she fell onto the bed. "By all means, your highness, you can have all of me, forever."

About the Author

Erin Zak hails from Colorado, where she grew up in a town of 2,500 people. She was a great athlete and even better student, maintaining a phenomenal grade point average while being involved with every club and activity she could. Zak started writing at a young age, letting her mind wander whenever she had a spare moment. It wasn't until high school that she really started to dig into writing full-length stories, only allowing her closest friends to read them.

Zak made her way to Indiana, where she studied communications at Purdue University. Eventually, she went back to get a master's degree in business administration. She put her passion aside while she started a career in higher education in the admissions office, helping students find their own passion.

Now living in Tampa, Florida, close to the Gulf of Mexico, Zak is hoping the warm weather and sun continue to feed her muse. Her wife and stepdaughter live with her, along with their family cocker spaniel. Zak enjoys films, especially science fiction and romance, and also loves cooking when time allows.

Books Available From Bold Strokes Books

A More Perfect Union by Carsen Taite. Major Zoey Granger and DC fixer Rook Daniels risk their reputations for a chance at true love while dealing with a scandal that threatens to rock the military. (978-1-62639-754-5)

Arrival by Gun Brooke. The spaceship *Pathfinder* reaches its passengers' new homeworld where danger lurks in the shadows while Pamas Seclan disembarks and finds unexpected love in young science genius Darmiya Do Voy. (978-1-62639-859-7)

Captain's Choice by VK Powell. Architect Kerstin Anthony's life is going to plan until Bennett Carlyle, the first girl she ever kissed, is assigned to her latest and most important project, a police district substation. (978-1-62639-997-6)

Falling Into Her by Erin Zak. Pam Phillips, widow at the age of forty, meets Kathryn Hawthorne, local Chicago celebrity, and it changes her life forever—in ways she hadn't even considered possible. (978-1-63555-092-4)

Hookin' Up by MJ Williamz. Will Leah get what she needs from casual hookups or will she see the love she desires right in front of her? (978-1-63555-051-1)

King of Thieves by Shea Godfrey. When art thief Casey Marinos meets bounty hunter Finnegan Starkweather, the crimes of the past just might set the stage for a payoff worth more than she ever dreamed possible. (978-1-63555-007-8)

Lucy's Chance by Jackie D. As a serial killer haunts the streets, Lucy tries to stitch up old wounds with her first love in the wake of a small town's rapid descent into chaos. (978-1-63555-027-6)

Right Here, Right Now by Georgia Beers. When Alicia Wright moves into the office next door to Lacey Chamberlain's accounting firm, Lacey is about to find out that sometimes the last person you want is exactly the person you need. (978-1-63555-154-9)

Strictly Need to Know by MB Austin. Covert operator Maji Rios will do whatever she must to complete her mission, but saving a gorgeous stranger from Russian mobsters was not in her plans. (978-1-63555-114-3)

Tailor-Made by Yolanda Wallace. Tailor Grace Henderson doesn't date clients, but when she meets gender-bending model Dakota Lane, she's tempted to throw all the rules out the window. (978-1-63555-081-8)

Time Will Tell by M. Ullrich. With the ability to time travel, Eva Caldwell will have to decide between having it all and erasing it all. (978-1-63555-088-7)

Change in Time by Robyn Nyx. Working in the past is hell on your future. The Extractor series: Book Two. (978-1-62639-880-1)

Love After Hours by Radclyffe. When Gina Antonelli agrees to renovate Carrie Longmire's new house, she doesn't welcome Carrie's overtures at friendship or her own unexpected attraction. A Rivers Community Novel. (978-1-63555-090-0)

Nantucket Rose by CF Frizzell. Maggie Jordan can't wait to convert a historic Nantucket home into a B&B, but doesn't expect to fall for mariner Ellis Chilton, who has more claim to the house than Maggie realizes. (978-1-63555-056-6)

Picture Perfect by Lisa Moreau. Falling in love wasn't supposed to be part of the stakes for Olive and Gabby, rival photographers in the competition of a lifetime. (978-1-62639-975-4)

Set the Stage by Karis Walsh. Actress Emilie Danvers takes the stage again in Ashland, Oregon, little realizing that landscaper Arden Philips is about to offer her a very personal romantic lead role. (978-1-63555-087-0)

Strike a Match by Fiona Riley. When their attempts at matchmaking fizzle out, firefighter Sasha and reluctant millionairess Abby find themselves turning to each other to strike a perfect match. (978-1-62639-999-0)

The Price of Cash by Ashley Bartlett. Cash Braddock is doing her best to keep her business afloat, stay out of jail, and avoid Detective Kallen. It's not working. (978-1-62639-708-8)

Under Her Wing by Ronica Black. At Angel's Wings Rescue, dogs are usually the ones saved, but when quiet Kassandra Haden meets outspoken owner Jayden Beaumont, the two stubborn women just might end up saving each other. (978-1-63555-077-1)

Underwater Vibes by Mickey Brent. When Hélène, a translator in Brussels, Belgium, meets Sylvie, a young Greek photographer and swim coach, unsettling feelings hijack Hélène's mind and body—even her poems. (978-1-63555-002-3)

A Date to Die by Anne Laughlin. Someone is killing people close to Detective Kay Adler, who must look to her own troubled past for a suspect. There she finds more than one person seeking revenge against her. (978-1-63555-023-8)

Captured Soul by Laydin Michaels. Can Kadence Munroe save the woman she loves from a twisted killer, or will she lose her to a collector of souls? (978-1-62639-915-0)

Dawn's New Day by TJ Thomas. Can Dawn Oliver and Cam Cooper, two women who have loved and lost, open their hearts to love again? (978-1-63555-072-6)

Definite Possibility by Maggie Cummings. Sam Miller is just out for good times, but Lucy Weston makes her realize happily ever after is a definite possibility. (978-1-62639-909-9)

Eyes Like Those by Melissa Brayden. Isabel Chase and Taylor Andrews struggle between love and ambition from the writers' room on one of Hollywood's hottest TV shows. (978-1-63555-012-2)

Heart's Orders by Jaycie Morrison. Helen Tucker and Tee Owens escape hardscrabble lives to careers in the Women's Army Corps, but more than their hearts are at risk as friendship blossoms into love. (978-1-63555-073-3)

Hiding Out by Kay Bigelow. Treat Dandridge is unaware that her life is in danger from the murderer who is hunting the woman she's falling in love with, Mickey Heiden. (978-1-62639-983-9)

Omnipotence Enough by Sophia Kell Hagin. Can the tiny tool that abducted war veteran Jamie Gwynmorgan accidentally acquires help her escape an unknown enemy to reclaim her stolen life and the woman she deeply loves? (978-1-63555-037-5)

Summer's Cove by Aurora Rey. Emerson Lange moved to Provincetown to live in the moment, but when she meets Darcy Belo and her son Liam, her quest for summer romance becomes a family affair. (978-1-62639-971-6)

The Road to Wings by Julie Tizard. Lieutenant Casey Tompkins, Air Force student pilot, has to fly with the toughest instructor, Captain Kathryn "Hard Ass" Hardesty, fly a supersonic jet, and deal with a growing forbidden attraction. (978-1-62639-988-4)

Beauty and the Boss by Ali Vali. Ellis Renois is at the top of the fashion world, but she never expects her summer assistant Charlotte Hamner to tear her heart and her business apart like sharp scissors through cheap material. (978-1-62639-919-8)

Fury's Choice by Brey Willows. When gods walk amongst humans, can two women find a balance between love and faith? (978-1-62639-869-6)

Lessons in Desire by MJ Williamz. Can a summer love stand a four-month hiatus and still burn hot? (978-1-63555-019-1)

Lightning Chasers by Cass Sellars. For Sydney and Parker, being a couple was never what they had planned. Now they have to fight corruption, murder, and enemies hiding in plain sight just to hold on to each other. Lightning Series, Book Two. (978-1-62639-965-5)

Summer Fling by Jean Copeland. Still jaded from a breakup years earlier, Kate struggles to trust falling in love again when a summer fling with sexy young singer Jordan rocks her off her feet. (978-1-62639-981-5)

Take Me There by Julie Cannon. Adrienne and Sloan know it would be career suicide to mix business with pleasure, however tempting it is. But what's the harm? They're both consenting adults. Who would know? (978-1-62639-917-4)

Unchained Memories by Dena Blake. Can a woman give herself completely when she's left a piece of herself behind? (978-1-62639-993-8)

Walking Through Shadows by Sheri Lewis Wohl. All Molly wanted to do was go backpacking…in her own century. (978-1-62639-968-6)

Freedom to Love by Ronica Black. What happens when the woman who spent her life worrying about caring for her family finally finds the freedom to love without borders? (978-1-63555-001-6)

A Lamentation of Swans by Valerie Bronwen. Ariel Montgomery returns to Sea Oats to try to save her broken marriage but soon finds herself also fighting to save her own life and catch a murderer. (978-1-62639-828-3)

House of Fate by Barbara Ann Wright. Two women must throw off the lives they've known as a guardian and an assassin and save two rival houses before their secrets tear the galaxy apart. (978-1-62639-780-4)

Planning for Love by Erin Dutton. Could true love be the one thing that wedding coordinator Faith McKenna didn't plan for? (978-1-62639-954-9)

Sidebar by Carsen Taite. Judge Camille Avery and her clerk, attorney West Fallon, agree on little except their mutual attraction, but can their relationship and their careers survive a headline-grabbing case? (978-1-62639-752-1)

Sweet Boy and Wild One by T. L. Hayes. When Rachel Cole meets soulful singer Bobby Layton at an open mic, she is immediately in thrall. What she soon discovers will rock her world in ways she never imagined. (978-1-62639-963-1)